THE BUTTERFLY EFFECT

PERNILLE RYGG was born in 1963. She has studied history and ethnology. For several years she worked as a set painter for film companies and for the Norwegian Broadcasting Company. This is her first novel.

JOAN TATE is the translator of Ingmar Bergman's fiction (published by Harvill) and his autobiography. She has also translated many books by leading Swedish writers, including the novel *Blackwater* by Kerstin Ekman. Her work has been recognized with an award from the Swedish Academy.

"We already have, in a corner of our hearts, two cult books from Scandinavia: *Vatanen's Hare* by Arto Paasilinna, and *Miss Smilla's Feeling for Snow*, by Peter Høeg. With its hip-hop melancholy, *The Butterfly Effect* makes of them a worthy trio"
MICHEL GRISOLIA, *L'Express*

"Terrific first novel" LUCRETIA STEWART, *Guardian*

"A thriller that moves along at a smart pace right from the start . . . gives promise of a bright future in crime fiction or general fiction for that matter" JOHN VILE, *Hobart Mercury*

"Impressive" LAMORNA KING, *Mail on Sunday*

"Wonderful . . . evocative description set in a culture that is both familiar and profoundly different" RUTH RYAN, *Siren Magazine*

Pernille Rygg

THE BUTTERFLY
EFFECT

*Translated from the Norwegian
by Joan Tate*

THE HARVILL PRESS
LONDON

First published in Norway with the title *Sommerfugleffekten*, by Gyldendal Norsk Forlag A/S in 1995

First published in Great Britain in 1997 by
The Harvill Press, 84 Thornhill Road, London N1 1RD

www.harvill-press.com

This paperback edition first published in 1998

1 3 5 7 9 8 6 4 2

Copyright © Gyldendal Norsk Forlag A/S, 1995

English translation copyright © Joan Tate, 1997

Pernille Rygg asserts the moral right to be identified as the author of this work

A CIP catalogue record for this book is available from the British Library

ISBN 1 86046 433 5

Map of Oslo by Reginald Piggott

Designed at Libanus Press, Marlborough, Wiltshire

Typeset in Bembo by Rowland Phototypesetting Ltd, Bury St Edmunds, Suffolk

Printed and bound in Great Britain by Mackays of Chatham

Half title illustration by Jody Hewgill

The Butterfly Effect

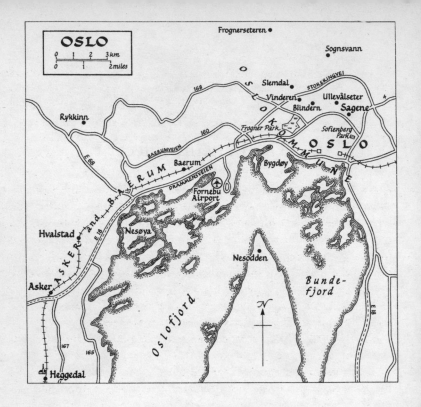

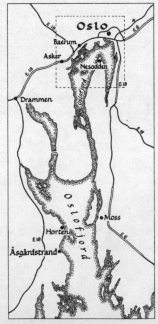

I

IT'S A REALLY shabby trick, the kind that makes me want to avert my eyes or give way to my most childish instincts and snivel. The little jerk when the machinery starts makes the flowers on the coffin tremble for a moment. It glides down infinitely slowly; the motion is so smooth, so discreet, that, without wanting to, I try to discern the hum of the engine through the music – without success. Presumably they use quiet hydraulics. Then I'm overwhelmed by a feeling that the coffin is on a conveyor belt taking it straight from the catafalque to the flames of the furnace.

The only tears I have are frozen inside me before the little disappearing act is over.

Then we move, those of us still alive, across the stone floor of the Vest Krematorium. The mechanism has made it impossible for me to believe anyone thinks he's resting in the room below; right now it feels as if he's burning, not resting. And, as always, I find myself wondering whether they burn the coffin as well.

There's nothing beautiful about it, no purifying fire, for we never see the flames.

Later canapés and sherry are served at Mother and Karsten's house in Charlotte Andersensvei.

I sit among Mother's emaciated relatives as they down roast beef and salmon with an almost lascivious appetite. The lady beside me has a huge aristocratic nose and an amused glint in her sunken eyes, presumably because she's enjoying the little triumph of seeing Mother's youthful error buried for good.

At the chapel all his shabby friends sat in the very back pews, and not one of them has dared come here.

I've done the rounds with the trays for the time being, but Benny is still attentively offering another glass of sherry here or a salmon

3

sandwich there. I know perfectly well why. He has no desire to sit down. He finds it far better to keep moving, with something to hold on to, even if it is only a plastic tray from Samson's bakery. But the sherry is no bad thing.

We walk back into town together, somewhat unsteadily, and he suddenly waves an arm at the passing cars.

"It could've been any of them."

"Yes," I say, "and we'll never know which one."

We part company at the lights on Blindernveien and I walk on alone towards the university. As I open the heavy door to the Department of Psychology, I see, just as I have seen hundreds of times since he was run down, that smashed and swollen face, and hope those bruised and livid features won't be all that I remember of my father.

The door to Astrid's office is ajar and when I look in, she is just putting on her smart grey overcoat.

"I thought you were in Trondheim," I say. There must have been more reproach in my voice than I intended; for a moment she seems thrown off balance.

"We got through it sooner than we thought," she says. "Igi, I wouldn't have made it to the funeral anyhow. How did it go?"

That hoarse voice of hers makes me want to cry. But I've told myself that I've done enough weeping on her shoulder. After all, she's my supervisor now, no longer my therapist.

"The funeral was OK, I suppose. Better than the ice show afterwards."

She smiles. Not even the narrow square glasses that go so well with her grey hair can make her face look stern when she smiles.

"And your mother?"

Psychologists always make "mother" sound so significant. It's the absolutely neutral way of pronouncing the word that does it.

"The Ice Queen. You know."

"Perfect pirouettes?"

"Christ, yes, unmoved by the cold. Have you decided about the conference?" I add in a transparent attempt to avoid the role of client.

"I don't think I'll go. Nor can I see any reason why you should

4

either. It'll be purely scientific, which is perhaps understandable. No offence meant, but you're dealing with slightly more unmanageable material."

As if I needed telling. As if I weren't aware that my attempt to link psychology with chaos theory verged on the dilettante. As if the essay in her hand didn't reek of my knowledge of the unmanageable material.

"I haven't read it yet," she says as she puts the papers into her bag, "but I'll start over the weekend."

She adjusts her silk scarf with those lovely hands that I've examined so carefully at times when I didn't want to answer her questions. A whiff of her scent reaches me, Giorgio as always.

"You must give yourself a little time, Igi," she says. "Research isn't supposed to be easy. If the answers appeared just like that, there would be no point in asking the questions, would there? You're not thinking of working now, are you?"

"Yes."

"I think that's pretty idiotic. You ought to take a few days off instead. I really don't want to see you here tomorrow, OK?"

"OK. But I'll stay for an hour or two now."

"As you like. But I doubt you'll find any solutions that way."

She puts her black velvet hat on at an angle and leaves me.

I hadn't thought of solving any problems. I'd thought of burying myself in them.

Benny's voice is as thin as a child's on the phone.

"Igi," he whispers. "I'm so bloody . . ."

The rest disappears into a hiccough. But I know what he is: so bloody depressed; betrayed; small.

And then Igi has to come, quickly.

Might as well. It's eleven o'clock and for the last few hours I've just been staring at the bizarre, colourful patterns on the screen in front of me, captivated, as so often before, by the incredible wealth of variation. But there's nothing very productive about it. I've stared and smoked and stared and smoked. The ashtray in my borrowed, officially no-smoking office is as full as my head is empty.

I let myself out of Helga Engs House with my plastic card. The icy cold of the last few days cools my forehead and temporarily clears my mind on my way to the Underground in Blindernveien. But only temporarily.

When I dive down the steep stairs to the nightclub, the smoke is thicker than at the office, as dense as the row of black leather jackets at the bar. And here the air is cut with a mix of expensive aftershave, so lavishly applied that even my poor sense of smell is afflicted. I always feel my femininity is inappropriate down here – I stand out like a sore thumb. It takes a while before I see Benny. He's sitting alone, as I expected, and, as expected, his mascara has begun to run.

This is no place to cry if you want to be one of the tough guys. But then that's never been Benny's aim.

I sit down opposite him on an uncomfortable stool. "Didn't he come?" I ask, somewhat unnecessarily.

He shakes his head.

I know that if he talks now, the tears will well up again, and it's so shaming for him that I'm the only one he can show. Me, and the other boys at the Black Widow.

I go and get myself a beer, not because I want one, but so as not to hurt him by being painfully sober. Benny bought himself one when his date didn't show up.

We've been here before, Benny and I – here and a few other clubs where my femininity makes me stand out from the crowd as much as Benny's does everywhere else. I have a whole world to wander about in wearing high heels, if I want to, but Benny has only the Black Widow and a couple of other places like it.

We hold hands across the table. It doesn't matter. It's not that unusual for boys like Benny to have best friends like me. And it's not as if either of us wears our wedding ring.

"Is that Revlon you've got under your eyes?" I say.

"Elizabeth Arden."

"The Revlon's better. Tear-proof."

"You hadn't any left."

That helps a little, so I go on.

"Cheer up, Mrs Heitmann," I say.

"You're Mrs Heitmann."

"Oh, so I am. Wrong again."

Old jokes that we pretend are new. Tonight they seem to be

having some effect – his eyes clear, he straightens up on the bench and rubs the worst of the mascara from his cheek.

Yes, it helps to have Igi around, especially when Benny's down in the dumps.

"Don't turn round, but there's a guy at the bar staring at me."

Oh, so it's not Igi, after all.

I take a trip to the ladies to keep out of the way of the electric charge between Benny and the bar. My face looks greenish and drawn in the mirror above the washbasin. No wonder boys prefer each other.

When I get back to the table, my stool is occupied.

"I'll be off, Benny."

"Aren't you going to finish your beer?"

Not convincing.

"You finish it."

Miraculously, the last trace of mascara on his cheek has vanished, or perhaps it is just eclipsed by his sparkling eyes.

When I turn round in the doorway, he has lit a cigarette and is gesticulating as only a genuine nutter can. As only the man I love can.

It's begun to snow and the last tram has gone. The snowflakes dance and the occupied cabs make Igi Heitmann, alone on her way home, feel blue.

Halfway up Markveien, I change my mind and fish out of my jacket pocket a loop of string with two solitary keys dangling from it. I don't want to go home tonight. I don't want to be the one who waits, huddled in one corner of the double bed, listening to the emptiness. Instead I decide to wallow in emptiness, in the loneliest and most wretched room I know: my father's office in Bernt Ankersgate.

The limp key-ring, my inheritance, is cold in my hand as I pass two speed freaks on Nybrua, not an effective talisman, to judge by the way it protected Father.

Outside the Café Sara, a girl is teetering on her platform shoes as she argues with the doorman. The rest of Torggata is silent. It's the empty hour between one and two, too late for those who have to go to work next morning, too early for those who either have

7

no work to go to or have a thousand other reasons not to give a damn.

Lina from the second floor is standing by the entrance in the rear courtyard, aiming a key with painstaking concentration at the keyhole. Before she misses yet again, I unlock it and together we go into the dark hallway.

"I'm really sorry about your father," she drawls, so spaced out it's as if language is a new and unknown medium.

"I hate cars," she adds, peering out through the curtains of her long sleek hair.

I stop on the first-floor landing in front of the door with the little notice that says that these are the premises of A. Heitmann, Private Investigator. I watch Lina's stick-thin body disappear up the stairs, and hope, as always, that she and her boyfriend don't feel like sharing a last roll-up sitting in bed. There's a shortage of smoke-alarms in Bernt Ankersgate.

Before I switch on the light in Father's little hallway, I shut my eyes for a moment to steel myself. Even so the bleakness hits me in the stomach like a clenched fist. I hope there's some brandy left in the bottle in the cupboard – I always understood why he needed it here.

His office was never an elevating sight, even when his slight frame did its best to fill the room with awkward bonhomie. When he started his own business it was meant to be a first step, a temporary base until he established himself. Then it became a permanent part of him, an accurate reflection of his professional life, but it was only when he had to give up his flat and moved his narrow bed into the little room next door that I realized he did indeed belong here.

I find the brandy. As when he was alive, the office is rather spartan – the hard swivel chair, the desk and the little filing cabinet could never give the impression that this was a flourishing business.

I sit down in his chair and wonder whether I look like him now, with the tumbler and the brandy bottle in a pool of light on the desk, while the room around me is filled with dead shadows.

When Mother finally understood that Father would remain a middle-ranking police officer for ever and divorced him, I was twelve. Old enough, she thought, to listen to her endless, bitter tirades about his failings, and old enough to believe her.

That was until Karsten appeared and it dawned on me that he had been around for quite a while. We'd been living in a house in Grefsen for barely six months when suddenly Karsten was standing in the drive one sunny Saturday morning directing the removal van. It was rather like being kidnapped. From then on I treated him like a prison warder, implacable in my opposition, despite his presents — clothes and toys I never ceased to regard as bribes. With the obstinacy of a child, I kept my loyalty for my father, hugged it to me and measured everything against it. I owed him that, I who had once wavered in my faith.

I suppose my need to pay back that debt was why, for two years after I'd finished my degree, I spent all my spare time at his office, sitting at this very desk for hour after hour, doing my best to sort out his papers, making all the telephone calls he didn't have the courage to make, driving him in his clapped-out Lada when he was too drunk to be behind the wheel himself.

Benny was furious, Mother complained, but that only made me more determined to get him to pull himself together, ignoring the fact that he had fallen apart long ago.

My attempt failed. I had already lost faith in my ability to reach the patients at Ullevål hospital; the therapy group I led together with a psychiatric nurse grew more and more boring, until the day when the great silence I had got used to in that oppressive room no longer upset me; it only made me tired, weary of spirit, and I fell asleep.

In the long period of recuperation that followed, when my sessions with Astrid were the only fixed point in my life, he did it: he pulled himself together, cut out the booze, worked hard for days on end, gradually regaining his lost confidence. It was too late, of course; too late to get the firm back on its feet, but he never gave up, and if he did sometimes resort to the brandy bottle, he made sure that it never prevented him from carrying out the occasional assignments that came his way.

There's a brown A5 envelope in the top drawer of his desk. He has written "Siv Underland, 1358 Solberg" in the scrawl I am probably the only person alive who can decipher, now that he himself has stopped solving mysteries. The telephone number below the address

9

is easier to read. Inside the envelope is a cheap brass pendant in the shape of a butterfly, with "12.5.60" engraved on the back.

If this was Father's last case, to recover a trashy necklace, it makes an appropriate ending.

It's six in the morning by the time I've ended my wake, downing the rest of the brandy in his honour. As I quietly close the door behind me, I have the envelope containing his last unsolved case in my pocket. He emptied his life so ruthlessly, it's right that nothing should be left behind, whether at the bottom of a bottle or in a desk drawer.

2

BENNY'S BACK IS warm against my stomach as I crawl in beside him, and in the hollow at the nape of his neck there is still a hint of someone else's aftershave. I turn away from the warmth and the scent and lie stretched out like a virgin beside him, tense in the space between sleep and wakefulness, that no man's land peopled by bad dreams.

He knows everything about grief and hangovers, so he lets me shower for a long time and brings me orange juice and fresh bread without a word.

I sit at the kitchen table in his towelling dressing-gown and crumble the bread into tiny pieces.

He puts two cups of espresso and hot milk between us on the table. They're two blue cups he bought for me a few years ago – quite why I've forgotten – but they're the loveliest coffee cups I know, just one indication of his unfailing good taste.

"Benny?"

"Yes?"

I pull more bread to pieces. He's put just enough milk in the espresso.

"Would you mind if I were away for a few days?"

He looks at me with his great unmade-up eyes.

"Where are you going?"

"I thought I'd stay overnight at Bernt Ankersgate. For a few days – a little while – I don't know."

He gets up and carefully fills the bowl under the pot of basil at the end of the table, by the window.

"Twice a day," he says.

"What?"

"It needs watering twice a day, that's the trick. Otherwise it'll die. It's as simple as that. Twice a day," he repeats.

My Benny. Both he and I know that such advice is wasted on me – I either water too much or too little, but never just enough.

"I'll miss you terribly," he says.

The telephone rings. It's Mother. Her voice is loud and shrill, as it always is when she phones me at home. She wants to know what I think about yesterday.

"Well, it was OK."

"Aren't you at work?"

"No. As you can tell."

Benny has turned the stereo up so that he doesn't have to listen to the conversation. Karin Krog.

"And where's . . . Benny?"

You have to be her daughter to hear the fractional pause before his name, as if she had forgotten it.

"He's here. He's making me breakfast."

"Oh. So were you out last night?"

"Benny was."

"Oh, I see."

Somehow Mother always manages to make me sound as if Benny and I are finding things bloody difficult. That's because, with some mysterious maternal instinct, she invariably phones when they are.

"*Spring can really hang you up*," sings Karin Krog as I put down the receiver. There's a long way to go before spring, although Benny's doing his best to pretend there isn't – I can see him through the doorway, carefully watering his beloved houseplants in the living-room.

"You do that," he says, still with his back to me. "Sure to do you good." His voice is soft and low, so as not to worry the plants.

"And what are you going to do about me?"

"Stop it. It'll only be for a short while, and in the meantime you can have a home-alone party with the boys."

"Never," says Benny, turning round, genuinely hurt. "Never here."

I know that. For all his transient and violent affairs, Benny is more faithful than I am, even though I never go out on the town to pick up boys.

12

He thinks I restrain myself because what I really want is a wife, and he fulfils that need. The idea is too complicated for me, like so much else.

Right now, there are too many pleasant reminders of our years together – the yellow-painted walls, the healthy greenery he has tended – too many claims on me for me to be able to say that I love him yet don't know how I can possibly go on living with him. Not that I've ever needed to explain that to him, I think, as I close the door quietly behind me, with my bag and my lap-top in my hand; he understood it better than I did.

The motes of dust floating idly in the long rectangle of light on the linoleum are the only things that move when I enter Father's office.

I stand my bag and lap-top in the middle of the floor in front of me; they look as isolated as Armstrong's flag on the moon or Columbus's cross planted on a Cuban shore – emblems of conquest, but, like the Sea of Tranquillity or the jungle ahead of the conquistadors, the room remains alien territory. My belongings are those of an intruder, and do nothing to make the room any more mine. "Father," they are saying, "here I am. *Where have you hidden your treasure?*" This childish question is met by nothing but deathly silence and I am filled with a sense of desolation and defeat. No secrets will be disclosed to me. Whatever hopes and dreams lived here have retreated into the shadows. Elvis has just left the stage.

I am about to dial the number written on the brown envelope, but I stand there with the receiver in my hand for a moment. The answerphone Benny and I bought Father, which I know he used in order to avoid having to pick up the phone on days when he couldn't trust his voice, is beside the telephone. His voice is still recorded on it.

I quickly dial the number. A young woman answers. I've clearly woken her up.

"Siv Underland?" I say.

"What? No, she doesn't live here any more."

"Do you have her telephone number?"

"I don't think she has a phone."

"But she must have an address?"

"Maybe. Wait a moment."

She gives me the address that is written on the envelope.
I thank her and ring off. I don't switch on the answerphone.

Karsten smiles warmly as he always does when he sees me. I have never understood why, because I never smile back.

It's regrettable that he's in charge of Father's papers, but he is a lawyer. He pushes the rent agreement for the two rooms in Bernt Ankersgate towards me across the mirror-bright surface of his desk. It's a wide desk, so he has to stretch forward and I can see his thinning patch.

"Here you are. In fact he has paid in advance, and the agreement is valid for two more months. That's what you wanted to know, isn't it?"

"Yes."

"You've got the keys, so it's up to you if you want to use the apartment."

His smile grows even broader and he looks at me with fatuous sympathy.

"I can promise you won't be thrown out. That is, if you want to stay there."

I almost change my mind. But not quite. He gives me the keys to the beat-up Lada before I leave. He's the one who collected the contents of Father's pockets from the police station.

The blustery blue afternoon is over and darkness is obscuring the anxious face of the city by the time I set off to accomplish what I want to do before the end of the day.

Having spoken nicely to the engine in Russian for a while, incredibly I manage to get some life out of the Lada.

"*Spaziba, tavarsj, spaziba,*" I say, and Gorbie growls contentedly. The car got its name because it looks like the Soviet ex-leader: it is reddish brown with several scratches. For some mysterious reason it is impossible to tune the radio in to a decent station: it offers me an invidious choice between inane young DJs trotting out jokes that are worse than those in a Christmas cracker, and youthful members of the God-squad, who sound remarkably similar. I go for the crappy jokes. The DJs have used the word "brill" three times before announcing gleefully that it's five o'clock.

It's only when I'm on the E18 to Asker that I remember I no longer need to respect my father's no-smoking rule, so I light up my tenth Prince Mild of the afternoon.

I head for the Dikemark psychiatric hospital because it's the only landmark I know in Asker. The central clock tower and massive wings of the old main building rise above the silhouettes of the tree tops clawing at the icy blue sky with their outstretched branches. A single spotlight illuminates the tower on which the clock marks the implacable march of time. For the inmates below, time has ceased to have any meaning, or is locked in a past which is as inescapable as it is incomprehensible. The shining clock measures out the time of Jesus Christ and all those who think three days in the kingdom of the dead are enough, but for the patients of Dikemark, their stay in limbo generally lasts much longer.

I have a feeling that Siv Underland's address lies a little way behind the hospital. That turns out not to be so, and I cruise around narrow deserted roads for a while before reaching the lake. If I had known the way, it wouldn't have taken me more than half an hour to get here from the centre of Oslo – in Norway that is all you ever need to leave the built-up areas behind and find yourself almost in the countryside.

Asker's local authority can afford to clear the roads even out here, and the snowbanks are so huge that I almost miss the turning. The light from a street lamp on the corner just reaches Siv Underland's mail box, which is within an inch of disappearing in the mass of snow. I peep into the box to see if she has come home and picked up her mail. She certainly hasn't.

Siv Underland has a lot of mail. The box is almost full – mostly iced-up newspapers several days old and a heap of junk mail.

I assume she's out, but nevertheless stump through the fir trees down towards the water. I can always leave the necklace on her doorstep, I think, as I make out a cabin surrounded by trees, staring at me with dark, sorrowful panes. Further along the bay is a little row of summerhouses; this one stands alone. In the summer no doubt it is a pleasant, secluded spot, but now, in winter, it can't be much to come home to – there isn't even an outside light shining a welcome. The path to the front door is narrow and almost snowed up. No one has been here for some time.

Naturally there's no answer when I knock, but the door swings open when I try the handle. I fumble round for a switch on the wall by the door. The darkness explodes into cold white light, and I find myself staring at a face criss-crossed with angry, blood-red streaks. My scream frightens me but they are my eyes staring at me from behind the brutal slashes.

Peculiar character, this Siv Underland. Maybe she makes a habit of scrawling messages to herself with lipstick on the mirror, an extravagance I myself would save for love-letters.

Or a farewell note.

The door to the other rooms is closed and that is where the stench comes from – a thick smell of something rotting, which makes my weak stomach heave before I've even opened the door. When I go in, it is like walking into a wall of foul air and tremendous heat.

There's no one in the small room. In the brief moment I manage to stay there before rushing out to throw up, I see a pan on the stove by the window; it is overgrown with something green and slimy that looks remarkably alive.

I take deep breaths of the cold evening air before daring to go back in, holding my nose.

She's left the little room with all the heaters full on, and a pan with something that was perhaps a fish dish on the hot plate. And she can't have left this morning.

I close the door hastily and look again at the mirror. Out in the hall, it's possible to breathe more or less normally as long as I do so through my mouth.

It's impossible to make out the words, even with my experience of deciphering Father's scrawl. Apart from a letter like a large P, it could easily be some foreign script. There's also something wrong with that P: it's back to front.

I look round and catch sight of the other mirror – an oval hand-mirror, the kind old ladies use to do their make-up. When I hold it at an angle, I can read the writing.

Mirror writing on a mirror. And I thought all the deranged minds round here were shut up in Dikemark hospital.

There are two names, over and over again, the letters intertwined, the names sometimes merging into one: "PetraSiv". "Petra is waiting," the message reads.

Petra may be, but Igi isn't going to hang about – not faced with this blood-red cryptogram, in this oven of a cabin, by the deserted, snow-covered fjord.

Igi runs, fast, filled with old-fashioned fear of the dark. It's not the sight of that disgusting mess in the pan, nor the strange words on the mirror that frighten me most. As I struggle up to the car I'm overcome by childish terror at the thought of the two black book-cases jutting out into the room in front of her kitchen recess. In the corner between them was a little table covered with some shiny black material. On it were two tall dark candles in slim candlesticks and between them a small icon which my nausea and fear prevented me from examining. It resembled a small altar, shimmering in the suffocating, stinking air.

3

THE SMELL OF stale smoke and old plastic seems wonderfully civilized as I slam the car door behind me and lock it with numb fingers. Nothing comes from Gorbie except a croak when I switch on the engine, and I have to try five times before he coughs into action. My comrade still, but only just. I have to rein in my impatience as he crawls along.

After a few minutes, I find a telephone box, a slim spaceship of light in the night.

There are only two Underlands in the phone book for Asker, and they have the same address.

The woman who answers is Siv's mother, and she doesn't think the writing on the mirror is a party game.

Something in her rigidly controlled unease makes me feel she's been expecting this call, just as you expect a long-overdue bill. You can persuade yourself you're in luck and it won't come, but deep down you know the debts that really count are always collected.

"Are you phoning from . . . Yngve's?" she asks.

"No, from a call box."

"Oh, really? Where is it?"

I give her the address, and she asks me to wait there until she's spoken to the police.

Some people's lives are like that: you don't know where your daughter lives, yet you expect a call like mine.

Øyvind Underland and his wife, Ellen, are the first to arrive at the phone box. Their faces are pale with a bluish tinge, as if they had frozen long ago.

The police car catches up with us at Siv's mail box. Underland leads the way down the path to the cabin, his hands thrust into his jacket pockets and his thick neck jutting forward. With long strides, he crosses the snow-covered patch in front of the steps without stepping in the existing tracks.

One of the policemen opens the front door and turns to me.

"Did you do this?" he says, shining his torch on the doorpost.

I shake my head, looking at the splintered wood. Only now do I see that the door's been forced.

Øyvind Underland pushes his way between the two policemen and switches on the light in the hall. Then he sees the mirror. As he stands there in front of the angry red streaks, his jaw works violently. He doesn't blink and his lips don't tremble; his hard profile is quite immobile, except for one large muscle that keeps twitching again and again.

Then he suddenly drops his folded arms, as if wanting to be rid of them, and goes out down the steps and stands with his back to us, his eyes gazing at the darkness.

The two policemen don't like the mirror writing, either. Nor the smell. Nor the heat.

One of them has a quiet word with Mrs Underland, who looks up at him through a pair of large, rather old-fashioned spectacles. She nods, and goes to stand beside her husband, without touching him. They make a mismatched pair, standing there in the cold. Øyvind Underland's back is heavy and broad. His wife looks painfully thin beside him, but her back is straighter than his. She didn't stop in front of the mirror in the cabin; it was the icon between the candlesticks that drove her out to her husband and perhaps accounts for why she can't hold his hand now.

The two policemen have to stoop inside the cabin. With their thick, padded jackets and their great boots, they have taken it over, as if it were now their property.

"We must call Hansson," one of them says.

We don't speak while we stand waiting in three separate groups – the policemen, the Underlands and me. In ancient Greece they killed the messenger who came with bad tidings. No one here has threatened me, yet I feel like a frostbitten leper. I light a cigarette to keep myself warm. I'm just as much of an intruder here as in my father's room, and here, too, there are ghosts that silence us.

* * *

A tall figure lumbers out from among the fir trees. As he comes into the light from the door to the cabin, he seems almost unnaturally large. He tugs at his coat collar and gives the Underlands and me a brief nod before tramping up the steps. He's inside for no more than a few minutes, then he reappears.

"Christ, it's cold out here," he says. "We might as well get going."

This is Inspector Samuel Hansson of the Asker and Bærum police. His bulk makes it hard for him to negotiate the snowdrifts. He's even fatter than I remembered, unless he just seems so big because he's holding a tiny dog under one arm.

"She's away," he says apologetically, as he squeezes himself in the back of the police car beside me. "That's why I've got Lola with me," he adds, nodding at the little dog.

Many years have passed since we last met. Samuel Hansson has reached that age when some men no longer talk about their wives by name, only their dogs.

"Funny place to meet again," he says. His voice is the same stout rumble. His huge hands, which I never tired of comparing with my own small ones as a girl, are stroking the dog's head.

Hansson and Heitmann. Laurel and Hardy, they called them at police headquarters. My slight father almost disappeared beside his portly colleague, and he always laughed in embarrassment at the jokes Samuel cracked with roars of merry laughter; I never understood them, but they made Mother's neck flush scarlet and her mouth blanch.

I remember him as a jovial uncle figure, but he doesn't seem like that any more. He looks fat and rather sad as he sits in the uncomfortably small seat.

"I saw the announcement too late," he said. "And I'm not that keen on funerals. We sort of lost contact after Andreas left."

"And you moved to Asker."

"Yes. Funny how far the distance into town seems sometimes. Do you know her? Siv, I mean?"

"No," I say, gazing straight ahead. "I found something of hers . . . in Father's office."

It takes me a while to dig the envelope out of my coat pocket, which is squashed against Samuel.

20

"Maybe the parents will recognize it," I say, as he tries to examine the pendant in the poor light.

"Did she go to see him because he was a private detective, do you think?"

"No idea. But it seems likely. I don't think he ran after young women much."

"No. That wouldn't be like Andreas, would it?"

"Of course, you never know."

He struggles a bit to get himself and the dog out of the car when we arrive at the police station. He carries Lola rather sheepishly, and I follow this policeman who doesn't like funerals.

We are installed in a meeting room on the first floor. At first Hansson sits poring over a map of the area around Siv Underland's cabin. Then he turns, crosses his plump legs and looks at us for a moment before settling Lola comfortably on his lap.

The Underlands are sitting opposite me in armchairs to the right of the conference table. Øyvind Underland is cradling his cup of coffee in both hands, his arms outstretched on the table. With his biceps visible beneath his shirt sleeves, his square torso and cropped hair, he reminds me of a wrestler. He has an aura of both physical and mental strength, which makes me think it must be hard to go to him with your problems. But he must have found a way to get people to do that, for he is a psychiatrist, the medical director of Dikemark psychiatric hospital.

Samuel Hansson opens the brown envelope and tips the contents out on to the table.

"Ms Heitmann here was going to deliver this to your daughter this evening," he says. "That's why she went to her house."

The pendant with its thin chain looks rather forlorn on the table in front of me.

Hansson dangles the pendant in front of the Underlands.

"Do you recognize it?"

Underland shakes his head.

"I've never seen it before," says his wife. "And Siv wasn't born in 1960."

"It seems you went to the wrong address," says Hansson, looking

21

at me with his mild eyes. "Have you any idea why your father wrote her name on the envelope?"

"No."

"But you worked with him, didn't you? Or else why did you come out here?"

"I did a few minor jobs for him, if you can call them that. But my real work is quite different – more up Dr Underland's street, actually."

Øyvind Underland nods when I mention my job, and I'm faintly flattered he remembers that I've used some research material from his hospital. But naturally that doesn't interest him much at the moment.

Hansson excuses himself politely, addressing the Underlands by their first names. There's a painful silence for a few minutes before I mumble something about the toilet and go after him.

I can see him through a glass wall at the end of the corridor, leaning heavily over one of his colleagues' desks. The dog is presumably on the floor, because I can't see it.

There are three or four other men in the room, and they all look so preoccupied that I choose to stay in the corridor, in the no-man's-land between private and professional mourning. I sit down on a chair beside the kind of office plant that is so highly polished it looks plastic, which is perhaps the intention.

After a while, Hansson comes out with a cup of coffee for me.

"You needn't stay any longer," he says. "We'll contact you when we know a bit more."

After drinking the stewed coffee, I button up my coat and walk past the door of the room where the Underlands are sitting stranded in their uncertainty. I am very conscious of my footsteps echoing down the long corridor leading to the exit.

Corridors to wait in. There's always a corridor like this, the worn linoleum stretching endlessly between us and those at the other end – those talking in subdued voices, with purposeful gestures, who know what has to be done, now and afterwards, when the waiting eventually comes to an end. A telephone rings somewhere. Someone is tapping at a keyboard. A woman dashes across the corridor to the photocopying room, holding a piece of paper which is undoubtedly important.

22

At the end of the passage, a fluorescent light is on the blink, flickering in a frenzy before extinction. It reminds me of the green light on the E C G machine beside Father's hospital bed, when his heart had stopped functioning predictably, and there was only a chaotic pattern of wild, arhythmic heartbeats, racing at tremendous speed and then stopping short. It was as if his body were a complex system that had to be in perfect equilibrium; once it had been disrupted, it could no longer survive.

Now I feel I have disrupted a chain of events I do not understand, and in so doing have changed things irretrievably.

I've just left the centre of Asker and crossed the first traffic lights signposted to Oslo when Gorbie gives up the ghost. He protests in Russian and lurches along for a short distance before expiring, or at least falling into a stupor.

I'm putting out the emergency triangle when a rust-spotted Toyota passes me and stops. It has a flashing heart in the rear window as if to advertise the disco version of the Good Samaritan.

The young Vietnamese who comes towards me is rather flash himself, with slicked-back hair.

"Problems?" he says, smiling, as if he liked them.

"Too right."

"I take a look? It'll be real cheap."

I look at him rather doubtfully. He looks far too young to have a licence, but on the other hand I'm Norwegian enough to get the ages of Asians all wrong, so maybe he has a doctorate and five children to boot.

"I do know what I'm doing. Been fixing cars since I was a boy."

I don't ask how long ago that was.

It takes him thirty minutes in the freezing cold to confirm that Gorbie will have to go to a garage. His father's garage.

"Can give you tow," he says.

"And then how long will it take?"

"Fix it quick. Now, if you like. If you nothing else to do."

I think about my bag sitting on the floor in Bernt Ankersgate. No, I have nothing else to do.

And he is quick. An hour later Gorbie sounds like a well-oiled neo-capitalist, his voice fat and ingratiating, as far as I can hear above the racket from the garage's wretched stereo.

The young man has poked about inside the filthy engine without getting a single black spot on his clean white shirt. But payment is strictly blackmarket. Maybe he's saving for a new stereo.

He points me in the right direction home: I need to cross the bridge beyond Heggedal church to get on to the E18.

The church is on a small rise, the front lit from below, a real Christmas-card picture. I glance up at it and as a result almost fail to notice a figure running on to the road in front of me. Gorbie's brakes shriek and we slide, with surprising decorum, right round in a neat circle. By the time I've got my breath back and dare loosen my grip on the wheel, the figure has vanished. The person who set me off on this ice ballet must have run down the hill from the church at a speed which implies it wasn't the Good Lord at his heels.

I am curious and getting home is the last thing on my mind. Gorbie groans, but he reluctantly makes his way up the steep slope to the church.

The entrance on this side faces away from the road, so it is not so brightly lit. Not that I have any problems seeing the church – the flames rising from the little chapel on the right give more than enough light.

I bang on the door of the nearest house I can find. A weary father of small children opens the door and phones for the fire brigade while I drive back up to the church.

By now the porch is on fire, tongues of flame licking towards the body of the church itself, which so far looks relatively undamaged. The small separate chapel is the worst affected: the flames engulfing its side walls meet across the roof in desperate fists of flame, fumbling, importunate, like the hands of an insane lover.

It's a beautiful, savage spectacle. I stand numbed, witnessing an ancient drama. There are no lunatics I understand so well as pyro-maniacs.

The sparks from the roof rise into the sky, a golden galaxy out-shining the pale stars. The flames have now devoured the roof, and the timber frame inside looks like a stark black skeleton in a sea of fire. One of the beams slowly gives way, slips into the burning space and vanishes. The roar of the flames almost drowns the sound of approaching sirens.

Another beam comes loose from the wall, hangs there like a scorched body, before crashing down into the waiting jaws of flame. Then, as a fire engine screeches to a halt behind me and the screaming sirens subside in a sob, the whole roof collapses. Sparks explode into the sky and a shudder runs through the front wall as the shock wave hits it; for a moment it seems to sway, then it cracks in two and half of it topples backwards.

Revealed in the gaping wound in the wall is the figure of a woman. Her torso rises and turns towards me before she too disappears into the flames.

4

M Y TEETH ARE making a horrible chattering noise. It's not because I'm cold, because I'm packed into one of the fire brigade's thermal suits. It's shock. At any moment now I may break into hysterical laughter, which is why I'm digging my nails into the palms of my hands.

Samuel Hansson is standing beside me, and he's still not convinced. My hair is presumably on end, and maybe I'm dribbling. Men find it difficult to believe hideous women.

"It's her," I say, teeth rattling. "I saw her."

He mumbles something I refuse to understand, and stares into the reeking remains of the chapel.

The firemen have stopped spraying the church with water, which is no longer necessary, and are concentrating on the chapel instead.

"So how many missing women are you looking for?" I say.

This time his mumbling is understandable.

"But what was she doing in the chapel – it's kept locked, and . . ."

"She wasn't in the chapel. She was in the wall. And she was dead. Don't go telling me that's an ordinary funeral rite in Asker. How often are churches burnt down here?"

"This is the first. And it's the wrong time of year: if the vandals are satanists, they prefer 6 June."

"And it wasn't exactly a professional job," I say, boldly. "The church itself is hardly burning."

"The foundations are higher. Perhaps that's why it didn't catch. And of course it was discovered quite soon after it started. Fortunately. You wouldn't recognize the chap you saw, would you?"

"I don't even know if it was a man. I just saw something black crossing the road. But it wasn't a black cat, that's for sure."

Even so, Samuel spits superstitiously into the snow.

* * *

One of the fire-fighters gets ready to go inside. Against the greyish-black smoke, he looks like a plastic figurine, a kid's Action Man, with exaggerated muscles. He moves with almost comic clumsiness in his protective suit, but that's because he's being careful. I have told them where she is, and he begins to pick his way around the area where the wall has fallen in. Cautiously, almost lovingly, he shifts rubble and brushes ash away. Now he's bending over something. He stands still for a long time. I can't see his hands, but his shoulders are moving as he uncovers something.

Then he stands up and comes out into the glare of the spotlights. He raises his visor and his face is a white mask in the night.

"It's not her," he says. "This one's been dead for a long time. If it's a woman, that is."

When the inspection team arrives, there's nothing but columns of smoke rising here and there inside what is left of the chapel. The fire has been completely subdued by the water, and the charred remains are beginning to don a layer of ice. It glitters like black lacquer.

The smell of smoke is still pungent, as if someone has been swinging a huge censer, in a grand funeral rite for the person lying there in the gutted chapel, who never received a decent burial.

The last of the inquisitive neighbours have gone back to the cosy warmth of their homes, and Samuel joins me again. He claps his hands as he watches the team making the area safe – not applauding, just because he is so damned cold.

"Are you fit to drive?" he asks.

I nod. I stopped trembling from shock some time ago and inside the fire brigade's thermal suit my hands are warmer than his.

"Could you drive me back to the station? The people here have more use for my car than I have. I must tackle a bit of the paperwork instead of hanging around."

In the car we are both silent, subdued by the heathen spectacle we've just witnessed. Fire and death in the midst of great cold.

Before I join the main road, I stop at a petrol station to buy some cigarettes, and when I get back to the car, I recognize where I am. On my right is a steep bank, and I remember sliding down it, holding Benny with one hand and a bag with booze in the other, one New

Year's Eve. It seems like a hundred years ago, but I don't want to go home to more death in a grey office; I want coffee and a pat on the shoulder, so I turn right and drive Gorbie slowly down the hill to see if I can find the place I'm looking for.

And there it is: Undelstadveien, with its charming family houses, and Christmas lights twinkling in the apple trees, could not be further removed from the scene of devastation I've just witnessed. The white house Tom shares with a couple of friends looks as idyllic as the rest. Tom's friends must have had children since I was last here, judging by the two bright toboggans propped up in the porch. The black cat curled up on the steps wants to go in to the warm, and so do I. There's a light on in the kitchen window.

Tom doesn't seem in the slightest surprised to see me. He just installs me and the cat on kitchen chairs and sets about making himself a slim roll-up.

His long hair is tied in a ponytail and there's a couple of days' stubble on his tired face. He's been on night duty at the hospital and is presumably too exhausted to react to anything. When I tell him about Siv, he looks askance at me and nods, then gets up to fetch a bottle from the kitchen cupboard.

"Red wine?" he says. Tom tends to put first things first.

"OK, if you'll warm it. And only one glass. I'm driving."

"You can borrow the sofa if you like. I'm not going to let you go that quickly, now you've managed to find your way out here."

"Do you know Siv?" I ask him as he starts making the mulled wine.

"I know who she is, of course. Asker's not that big a place. We bumped into each other at parties occasionally, that sort of thing."

There was a time when the same could be said of Tom and me.

"You know, I thought I was in love with you for a while," he says, grinning over his cup of coffee.

"And I thought you were in love with Benny."

"And Benny?"

"He thought I was in love with you."

He laughs his smoker's laugh.

"Simple, huh?"

"It was fun."

Tom had a little place in town at the time, then he dropped out of university and got himself a job back home in Asker. And disappeared from our lives. Benny and I stayed.

"Siv's a bit crazy," he says.

I ask him what his definition of crazy is, given that he's been working at Dikemark for years.

"Well, what happened to her was crazy. She was a good deal younger than me, but at fifteen she was one of those girls who hang out with older boys. It was as if she were on some kind of binge, despite being so young. Drank like an alcoholic, to get drunk. Maybe everyone's a bit wild at that age, but it was different with her. It seemed she was doing it deliberately, yet she wasn't really in control. In a couple of hours she'd be transformed from an ordinary giggling schoolgirl into . . . a bloody vamp, or whatever . . . throwing herself at anyone – a bunch of yobbos, mostly. Tragic. Then she stopped showing up – I didn't see any more of her . . . So she ended up living alone out in the forest. I didn't know that."

"Nor did her parents. But they weren't exactly surprised when I phoned, and it didn't sound as though they thought she'd just taken herself off on an extra long skiing trip."

"I can believe that," said Tom drily.

"Do you know her father?"

"Wonderland? No, you must be joking. He's in a different league. I'm just an ordinary mortal – I don't have any dealings with the upper echelons."

He grins and gets up to give the black cat some food from a tin. It reminds me of the contents of Siv Underland's pan and my stomach heaves.

"And you? Did you become a psychologist, or what?" he says.

"I did . . . until I found I couldn't get through to the patients because I wasn't in touch with myself."

"Tough?"

"Tougher for them than for me, probably."

"And now?"

"I'm doing something I call research. Do you know anything about chaos theory?"

"No."

"It's about patterns. In nature, order – systems – can arise

29

spontaneously, but only out of situations that are not in equilibrium – that are in chaos, in other words. A nice paradox, isn't it? It's important in chemistry and in biology, so it may also be significant in psychology. I'm trying to see whether similar patterns emerge in the psyche when it is at its most chaotic – in seriously ill people."

"Does that put you more in touch with yourself?"

"Oh, that's just my personal problem. Ideally it shouldn't have anything to do with my work."

"That's a bit thick, Igi!"

Tom laughs his throaty laugh again and gives a loud, expressive yawn, stretching so that his shirt glides up and I can see his hollow stomach. I assume he still lives mostly on cigarettes and coffee.

"I thought you were working for your father," he says. "Someone must have told me that."

I tell him Father is dead. Tom is familiar with grief of that kind – he met his father for the first time when he was nineteen and by then it was too late to have a relationship with him. Now I'm discovering that even when you've had all the time in the world to get close, you may be too late.

"But it's true I worked for him for a while," I say, to get us out of the parental pit. "Routine stuff, mostly. I had one reasonable success, but it was a rather shitty case."

"Oh?"

"It was some nasty old guy whose hobby was to phone up and order deliveries in his neighbours' names. Then he stood behind the curtain and got a kick out of watching gravel or soil or crates of frozen fish being dumped in their drive. The neighbours all knew who was behind it, but they couldn't get him to stop, until I told them to do the same to him. He stopped for good the day he had fifteen loads of chicken shit tipped into his garden. But the whole neighbourhood stank to high heaven for weeks afterwards, so I don't know how pleased they really were."

Tom chuckles and knocks back the last of his wine.

"Do you want to borrow the sofa? I don't want to be antisocial, but I've had so little sleep recently, and you look as if you could do with some yourself."

A glance at the sofa makes me realize he's right. I could do with a shoulder to cry on and a chest to sleep on, too, but there are limits to what you can ask of a friend you haven't seen for two or three years.

Tom fetches a quilt and bedclothes. Oedipus, the cat, jumps up on the sofa and looks daggers at me. I have company after all.

On his way upstairs, Tom sticks his head round the door.

"Are you still trying to convert that bugger of yours?"

I nod. If anyone else had put it like that, I'd have hit him, but to Tom the term "bugger" is as matter-of-fact as "left-handed" or "freckled".

"Heard about it. Wedding and all. Great."

I don't fall asleep straight away. My mind is racing, and Oedipus can't decide whether he wants to curl up at my feet or on my face. I persuade him to compromise and he settles under one arm. Another image appears in my mind's eye: the little altar at Siv's and the icon between the two candlesticks. It is black and smooth, a phallus, raised like a club for a blow.

"Mum, is the lady dead?"

"Yes," I reply before I realize the voice isn't part of a dream.

I start and open my eyes: a child is standing by the sofa. He might be four or five, and he's so well dressed under his snow-suit that his arms stick straight out from his sides. Someone ought to wipe the snot off his cheeks, but I gladly leave that to his mother – a woman standing in the doorway looking rather confused. She's beautiful, slim and athletic, with good features and a longish face. Her green sweater sets off her long dark hair.

"Oh, sorry," she says. "I thought . . . Is Tom in?"

"He's asleep," I say, hauling myself up into a sitting position.

"TO-OM!" yells the child.

"Yes?" comes the reply from upstairs. "Coming!"

The woman goes out into the hall again and I can hear her going upstairs.

The child stares at me.

"That's not your cat," he says, pointing at Oedipus.

"No."

"What's your name?"

"Igi," I say. "Igi Heitmann."

"You can't be called that," he says. "Is that your proper name?"

"No," I say. "My real name's Inger Birgitte."

"Why don't you say so, then?"

Because when we were playing handball it was impossible for the coach to yell Inger Birgitte in a way that made me score. Because Inger Birgitte makes me feel as if I have an invisible pearl necklace round my neck. Because you should have something to blow that snotty nose of yours with.

"Because it's so awkward and difficult," I say. "Especially for small children. What's your name?"

"Christian Magnus," the child says, and marches out.

One-nil, no question.

Once I have made my face look vaguely human again with the aid of cold water and rather drastic make-up, I join the others in the kitchen.

Tom is making coffee.

"Vilde Ventorp," says Tom. "Vilde lives next door, with Lars."

"And me," says Christian Magnus.

"And you, of course. Igi's an old friend," he adds, turning to Vilde. "Maybe she's got a story for you. She went to see Siv Underland yesterday, but she wasn't at home – and her parents don't think she sleeps around."

"Oh, really? What do they think, then?"

"Well, that something's happened to her," says Tom, looking at me. "Vilde works on the local paper, the *Budstikka*."

"She hasn't been reported missing, that I do know," she says.

"According to Igi, her parents seem to think she may have taken her own life," says Tom.

"We don't report suicides," Vilde replies stiffly.

I think about that altar, the forced door, the pendant in Father's drawer. The pan of fish. Maybe if you're going to commit suicide, you don't consider such details. Presumably you can't be bothered to turn off the heating, either. After all, it won't be you who has to pay the electricity bill.

"Do you know Siv Underland?" I ask Vilde.

"Not really. She's a bit of an oddball, living on her own in the forest. I don't think she has many friends. God knows what she lives on. I see her now and again, and she always seems really down . . .

the kind of person who'll end up as a bag lady before she's fifty."

"As I remember," says Tom, rescuing the glass of juice Christian Magnus has placed right on the edge of the table, "she wasn't like that before. Strange, but not a loner."

"People change, Tom. And she's not that much of a loner."

"What do you mean?"

"I don't know if it's true, but people say she goes to see that madman in Heggedal."

"The magician?" says Tom, looking suspiciously at Christian Magnus, who has got down from his chair and is having a conversation with Oedipus. "Well, in that case it's not surprising she's become a bit of a recluse."

"Who is this magician?" I ask.

"A real eccentric," says Tom. "Yngve Caspari. I find him rather amusing, but lots of people are quite scared of him – which pleases him, I think."

"He rents a derelict farm in Heggedal," says Vilde, "and holds séances, or masses, or whatever. Lots of peculiar people go there at weekends – members of his order."

"I don't quite understand," I say. "Is he a conjuror?"

"No, no." Vilde gives a short laugh. "Not that kind of magic. The real thing, he maintains – rituals, calling up spirits, and so on. I tried to interview him once, but it was quite hopeless."

"And the funny thing is," says Tom, "he comes from a really straight family. Property developers, I think . . . and there he is, just hanging out and meditating, or whatever."

Christian Magnus has caught hold of Oedipus's tail.

"As you work on the local paper, maybe you've heard about the corpse that was found yesterday," I say to Vilde. She nods.

"Corpse?" Tom rolls his eyes. I didn't tell him about the chapel last night. "If that's what it takes to bring you out to Asker, it's as well you haven't been here for a while." He still has that deep, good laugh.

I ask Vilde if the police have found out who it was.

She answers in rather a sharp voice, but that may be because her little monster is quietly trying to strangle the cat.

"What do you know about it?" she then asks, looking at me with interest.

33

"Well, I was the one who discovered it. If that's relevant."

"You mean you rang about the fire at the church?"

"Yes."

Tom chokes on his coffee.

"The police haven't given out any names yet, which isn't surprising. The list of missing persons for the last fifteen years or so is quite long. You didn't see anything unusual when you got to the church?"

I think back.

"Someone ran away from it just as I drove up."

"Can I quote you on that?"

"OK. Perhaps you can do me a favour in return. You wouldn't have that list of missing persons, would you?"

"It's at the paper."

"Can I take a look at it?"

"Why not?"

"Igi is the daughter of a detective, you see," says Tom. The contempt in Vilde's eyes becomes obvious, but she phones the paper and conscientiously writes down names, dates of birth and when they disappeared. Then she nods into the receiver and pushes the list across the table to me.

There are seven names on it. One of them I've seen before.

"Great," says Vilde, "I'll be there." She rings off and looks appealingly at Tom.

"You couldn't have Christian Magnus for a few hours, could you? I was supposed to be at home with him today as he's got such a cold, but . . . They may have found her – Siv Underland, I mean. Some kids playing at one of those huge tips for snow – the highways people have found something and alerted the police."

"I thought you didn't write about suicides," says Tom.

"How do we know it's suicide?" Vilde says defensively.

"I didn't mean it like that." Tom's voice is mild. "And of course I'd be glad to have Christian Magnus."

Vilde gets up without more ado. Christian Magnus bawls his head off as she picks him up for a quick hug and three farewell kisses.

"So where is the tip?" I ask.

"Maybe you'd like to come with me?"

She probably meant it ironically, for she is as surprised as I am when I say yes. I've learnt to act on impulses that surprise me, even if it isn't immediately obvious why.

Vilde goes out to start the car and Tom and I look at each other over our coffee.

"Things aren't too good between her and Lars these days," he says laconically.

"So does she come round to borrow your sofa?"

"Preferably my bed." Tom grins. "But it's too vulgar to sleep with your neighbour's wife."

Tom is getting old. He never had such scruples when I knew him.

"Do you think that magician guy set fire to the church?" I ask as I put on my coat.

"Yngve? No idea." He rubs the stubble on his chin. "But I imagine he wouldn't be upset if someone else did."

"No?" That little altar in Siv's cabin floats in front of my eyes.

"Don't wait until you find another corpse before coming again," says Tom, scratching my cheek with his stubble.

I'm not the only interested party at the tip. Bad news travels fast. Øyvind and Ellen Underland are standing by the red and white plastic tape used to cordon off the enormous snowdrift. Dirty grey heaps of snow have been tipped along the slope, which rises 50 or 60 feet above us. It's as if the monster of winter had stood at the top and vomited his excesses of recent months.

Snow has been dumped there only this morning, but it's easy to see where the two small boys were playing. A few yards up the slope where they were digging a black hole gapes open, the jagged pieces of snow around the edge like badly cleaned teeth.

Samuel Hansson's face is a dirty grey colour, like the snow. Presumably he hasn't been to bed at all. The little dog's nose protrudes from the crook of his arm.

"What are you doing here?" he asks, in a voice that is not avuncular.

"Do you want me to go?"

"No, no. The whole world and his wife are here already. Some idiot has even contacted the Underlands. Yet we don't really know if anyone's in there. Still, I'd probably have come too, if it were my daughter."

As we watch, the men clamber up to the hole and begin to dig. Ellen Underland's face is quite expressionless, her eyes hidden behind her large shiny spectacles; she is silent while more and more snow is thrown out of the hole.

She doesn't scream until it's obvious the spade has struck something that isn't snow. As the men bend and put their spades down, her face cracks. Her screams go on and on. The pain is almost tangible, shattering the glassy, frozen morning.

Øyvind Underland's great hands tremble as they hang impotently by his sides. He doesn't hold her, and nor can I, for when I try to put my arm round her, she strikes out wildly and pushes me away with unexpected strength.

Samuel manages to restrain her and in the end calms her down sufficiently so that she can walk to their car, parked on the forest track.

Underland and I stay to watch as the men kneel in the snow and begin to dig carefully with their hands. Slowly they uncover the frozen body, lift her on to a stretcher and wrap her in a green plastic sheet.

His eyes do not waver from what is happening in the hole in the snow. Then when they start carrying the stretcher down towards us, it's as if his backbone cracks. He turns round to leave, and he's a tired old man; he staggers, and for a moment I think he's going to fall.

5

IT'S BEEN THE kind of day owners of winter sports resorts long for. The sun slants through the car window and the snow-covered fields of Asker glitter and dance as in an ad for a chocolate bar. Unfortunately I've no desire for chocolate and the sharp light stings like acid in my eyes. It's all too much for me – too much light and too many houses with snowdrifts like milk moustaches along the eaves.

My eyes water and I can't blame it on the sun.

My bag and the lap-top look as abandoned as ever, sitting there on the linoleum when I get back to Bernt Ankersgate. Replaying my father's answerphone does nothing to cheer me up.

"This is Andreas Heitmann's office and I am not available at the moment. If you wish to leave a message, please do so after the tone and I will get back to you as soon as I can."

Not available at the moment. No. I play it back three times before deciding that's enough. Then I wipe his voice off. There. Mute for ever. The ghosts in the room have grown quieter, but they seem to be looking at me.

I wonder whether Siv Underland ever left a message on the machine, whether she came here. Perhaps she sat in the chair I'm sitting in, with Father behind the desk. A young woman and an older man, both to die so close together. That thought was what was hammering behind my eyes on my way into Oslo. By looking through the frozen newspapers in Siv Underland's mail box, I realized she disappeared the day my father was run over.

Lina and her boyfriend have woken up on the floor above. They're feeling perkier than I am. They're playing the Stones over breakfast so loudly that the ashtray in front of me is vibrating. As I phone the officer at Oslo police headquarters dealing with Father's case, I wonder what kind of wake he thinks I'm celebrating.

37

No, he tells me, still no witnesses – nor the driver himself, of course.

Upstairs they have moved on to Tom Waits by the time I put down the receiver – night music, music for dark streets where you walk alone until two yellow eyes appear and the monster behind the headlights makes the song end in the rattle of a throat full of blood.

I've tried to avoid thinking about the driver up to now, except with token sympathy, as if he or she were the victim of an accident too, someone who was in the wrong place at the wrong time, just like my father. But now I need to know who it was – a drunken businessman or a teenager stealing his father's car. I'm willing to forgive them, provided I can escape this awful coincidence.

Synchronicity is what Jung calls meaningful coincidence, and even if the parallel events he was referring to are disturbing for different reasons, I would prefer this coincidence not to have any meaning. I know the best way I can avoid the idea of synchronicity is to believe that Siv Underland did commit suicide; then I can also believe that my father died a natural death. I need someone to convince me of it, and I think about the magician in Heggedal. He at least knew Siv's address, unlike her parents.

My clothes smell of smoke, and if I'm not to give in to the yearning for whisky in Waits's voice, I need a wash.

In the shower, I feel overwhelmed by the unpalatable inheritance of a century of psychoanalysis: an intense distrust of our own motives, the relentless search for filth in the mental dustbin Freud made of the subconscious.

I know it well. We indulged in that kind of thing as students. Night after night we drank red wine and produced patterns as burdened with fate as Greek tragedies. We never achieved catharsis, of course, but that didn't stop us going on. Nor did it prevent my patients – those not too doped by their own or the hospital's drugs – from brooding on their own trivial, ghastly motives, turning over the stones of the psyche and finding masses of revolting creepy-crawlies underneath them.

Then the busybody who lives inside my head sticks her oar in, as she does whenever I'm exhausted, or when I can't make up my mind about something. It's not for me to poke my nose into other people's business, she says. I'm just running away from what really ought to concern me: my work, my sex life, my mother. There are one or two unpaid bills at home, remember? And what about the dirty washing, not to mention the extra few pounds on my hips?

I turn off the shower before she gets carried away with the inevitable sermon about my appearance. Given that I'm female, it's hard to escape when the busybody sticks her spade into the mire.

"Oh, shut up," I say to her, trying to think of something to stop the stream of criticism.

The shower carries on dripping, and the dismal sound gives me the answer I'm looking for. Regardless of how regular a drip seems, one which is out of sync always appears, altering the rhythm. The point at which it happens is unpredictable, but the break may well be the beginning of a new pattern, a new rhythm.

"Bifurcation point," I say with satisfaction. The busybody in my head is not particularly intellectual, so I explain: it is the point at which a developing system appears to be able to choose between two equal routes, and no one can tell beforehand which of the two will be chosen. Chaos theorists love the concept, because it is where creative chance appears to play a part in rigorous sciences such as mathematics and physics − a dot of free will in a sea of determinism.

I grab hold of the fact that chance may have led me to Siv's cabin, and, to drown out the busybody's objections, I slam the door behind me and go out to start the car.

Strangely enough, Gorbie manages to cough up a bit of national radio for me: sport on one wavelength, a Lapp station on the other, broadcasting a quiz in a Sami dialect. I get hooked, and by the time I reach Heggedal, I think I have learnt the south Sami word for "brill".

It doesn't look as if any snow has been cleared out here and the narrow track that leads to the farm buildings is treacherous.

One of the upstairs windows is broken and someone has mended it with a piece of plywood to stop the draught. The door to the shed next to the dilapidated farmhouse is open and reveals a privy in which snow has drifted up against the wall.

Two chairs and an old cardboard box obstruct my way to the front door; the person who lives here certainly isn't concerned with welcoming visitors.

No one answers my knock, but there are a few lights on downstairs and on a landing.

I try the door. Whatever awaits me inside, it can't be as bad as the last time I made my way into a strange house, and I also sense signs of a new ruthlessness in myself, as if I've cast off some fear or inhibition.

The double doors are stiff, but not locked.

They open on to a dark hall, but in the ebbing twilight I can make out a row of empty pegs and a door by the stairs.

"Hello! Anyone home?"

No reply.

There's light coming from the room beyond the hall. I open the door and stop for a moment to take in the room.

The soft light from a table lamp makes the windows look black and the furniture casts deep shadows. The room is a chaos of books and papers, jammed on shelves, stacked on every inch of the floor, and in heaps on all the surfaces. Between the piles of books are abandoned glasses and bottles, some covered in dust.

I pick up a sheet of paper from the low table by the stove. Both sides are covered in dense, crabbed handwriting in black ink, and it's only one of many. Whoever lives here writes a great deal, with no fear of anyone else reading it, to judge by the sheets strewn all over the room. They are so closely written that presumably the content would remain private anyway – I can certainly make nothing of it.

The books don't tell me much more; most are in languages I can't read – Greek and Latin are not required by the social sciences faculty, and quite a lot are in what I assume is Arabic. A few in English and French are in a special little recess: Aleister Crowley and his occult companions. Definitely not book club material, but food for thought, perhaps, for arsonists of the more academic kind. If they exist.

Concealed behind a dusty tapestry is a door. What I have seen so far is all elegant camouflage, like a series of Chinese boxes. The derelict exterior and the insanely untidy room with its collection of books are designed to hide the impressive occult library that meets my eyes. Here spartan order prevails.

The room is icy cold, without a stove or even an electric radiator. I assume that in here nights are not spent sleeping. There are no lamps, only two candlesticks in one corner. Heavy curtains cover the only window; I can't make out whether they are black or just some dark material, which must shut out all light whether it's day or night. Even if it had been pitch dark, I would have recognized the atmosphere in here: it's dense and full of a presence alien to me, but I've seen this before, albeit on a reduced scale. The similarities are unmistakable. There are two or three chairs along the walls, no pictures, except for one with a large circular motif in the middle. And there, in one corner, is the little table covered with a dark cloth. The only difference between this altar and the one in Siv's cabin is what has been placed between the candlesticks. The shadow from my body just reaches the table, and where my head should be, a skull is grinning at me, as if someone had stripped the skin from my face as I stepped into the room.

The sounds from above are faint, yet I jump as if I'd fallen asleep in the heavy air. I'm thankful to be woken, so I quickly close the door behind me and go out into the hallway and stop in front of the dark staircase.

The sound comes again: a rustle like someone walking in dead leaves.

I'm a thief in the blackness, treading softly on each stair and breathing cautiously.

A window above me shows a faint square of dark blue twilight. A door is half open. It's bitterly cold and I try to reassure myself that the sound must have been made by a window that has been left open. Then I see a figure in bed beyond the door.

Someone is lying there, quite still. My childish fear of yesterday engulfs me for ten long seconds, until I realize that the breathing I can hear is not just mine. I slip down the stairs again.

I find I have a book in my hand, so instead of leaving the house immediately, I go back into the room off the hall.

The light has been turned off.

Two hard hands grasp mine and force them behind my back. Securing them with one arm, he puts the other round my neck, and it's no affectionate gesture. The bang as the book I was holding hits the floor is deafening after that long silence.

The car, I think. Of course, they've seen the car, that's how they knew I was here.

The light is switched on again, directed straight at my face, dazzling me so that I can't see the man talking to me.

"Sanskrit," says the voice. "*Bhagavad Gita*. The book you dropped, I mean. You can let her go now. Thanks."

My hands are freed, and the light is lowered slightly. After a moment I can see again; the man in front of me is taking off his black coat and then hands it to the small guy who restrained me. He takes the coat out into the hall. The other man lowers his long body into one of the dusty chairs by the stove and only then does he look at me.

He's dressed entirely in black. What is more surprising is the quality and cut of his clothes. His room gave me no reason to expect such an elegant and distinguished figure. Brown hair swept back above a pale forehead, deep-set eyes and a mouth Benny would like.

"An unusual entrance," he says, resting his hands on the arms of the chair. "I've nothing against that so long as the visit is also interesting."

"I phoned yesterday," I begin. "A young woman answered. My name's Igi Heitmann. You're Yngve Caspari, I presume."

"Correct. And why did you ring yesterday?"

"I was looking for Siv Underland."

"Ah. And did you find her?"

"In a sense. It turns out that she's . . . dead."

He doesn't move. His long body remains stylishly draped in the chair, his hands still; only one foot twitches in an involuntary reaction.

"Dead?"

His pale forehead glistens, the colour and texture suddenly resembling the skull in the other room. He puts a hand on his mutinous knee.

"An accident?"

"You could call it that. She was found . . . in a snowdrift. Shot through the head."

"What?"

"The gun was in her hand when she was found."

Neither of us says anything when the small guy returns and sits down in the darkness by the window. I can't see his face, but he leans back with his arms folded across his chest, a waiting statue.

"Suicide, then?" says Caspari, his eyes still on me. For a moment his narrow face looks as vulnerable as a child's, and his eyes widen, as if in surprise. But it's not grief he betrays when he speaks again, it's anger.

"I suppose that's also a choice. Respectable, you could say. If you've reason to – great pain or . . ." He falls silent before the tremble in his voice becomes obvious. "I just wouldn't have believed . . . Not now, I mean. But of course there's a kind of freedom in that choice too."

"Did you know her well?"

"Naturally. She was one of my . . . disciples." He gives a brief, cold laugh, full of self-mockery or self-pity.

"What do you mean – disciples?"

"Pupils. Not hangers-on, as people make out. There's no dependency in relations between master and pupil."

He makes an effort to pull himself together, sits up straight, props his elbows on the arms of the chair and rests his chin on his long white fingers. He looks as if I'd asked him to give his opinion of the state of the world and am now awaiting his answer with breathless anticipation.

"If this had happened two years ago, I might not have been surprised. No, probably not. But now . . ."

"What happened between then and now?"

He raises one eyebrow as if irritated by the interruption.

"A great deal. First and foremost, she met me. No doubt the confused fool who came here two years ago could have done such a thing. I've no sympathy with suicide. She'd totally misunderstood me on less important matters, when . . . The point is that after two years here she should have learnt that there are other and much better ways of dealing with . . . difficulties. Methods which are both more exciting and more effective."

"You mean . . . that?" I say, nodding towards the hidden door. "What do you call it? A . . . temple?"

43

I can't help making the word sound as alien as it feels. A wry smile shows that he is amused.

"My private temple, yes. For modern ritual magic. Incidentally, unauthorized persons are prohibited entry."

"Your front door is terribly easy to open."

"I know. Unfortunately that's the kind of practical problem I find it difficult to take an interest in."

"Siv had something like it. In her cabin."

"Did she?"

"But a different icon, or whatever it's called. A phallus."

He laughs. "And that shook you, I imagine? It's not as vulgar as you may think. The lingam has a venerable tradition as a religious object. It represents Siva. Rather crudely, you could say that Siva stands for the masculine, creative force – the equivalent of the Judaeo-Christian Jehovah. The lingam is simply its direct representation."

"So it's an Indian religion you practise?"

"No. I prefer to call it modern ritual magic, as I said."

"And what does that involve?"

"Do you mean do I practise black magic? Do I worship the devil and eat my neighbours' small children? Not often, not often."

He smiles to show he hasn't got blood on his teeth.

"I'm afraid I'm quite ignorant of the subject," I say.

"I'm aware of that. It's not uncommon. Most people who take an interest in esoteric knowledge think that it means going about with a crystal ball round your neck. But that's not the case." He waves one hand impatiently.

"So what is it about?"

"The fact that through my activities, through being a pupil of mine, Siv Underland learnt that you do not have to be a victim – a victim of circumstances, of today, of your own subconscious forces. *That* is what magic is about. It's really quite simple. You can live without consciousness, guided by chaotic forces you are unaware of, or you can make use of those forces. It's a choice you make."

"You make it sound like a form of therapy."

Again he gives a reluctant, embarrassed laugh, as if laughter were rather painful, a little too ordinary for him.

"Therapy is definitely not what it is. It's work. Hard work. If Siv

44

had wanted therapy, she could have gone to her father. I'm not a father to anyone. A lot of people misunderstand this, and come here with their miserable lives wanting me to help them. That's not how it works, they're not the kind of people I can use. And then I have to . . . get rid of them."

"But Siv didn't misunderstand? She didn't need therapy?"

"I think she was probably sick of it. After all, her father is the head of Dikemark psychiatric hospital – but perhaps you know that?"

"Yes, I do. And you mean that Siv was in a state to make use of her . . . subconscious forces. How was she supposed to use them?"

"They're there to steer your own life. To control it. To avoid precisely the kind of situation which leads to . . . to suicide. I thought she was up to it. But I must have been wrong. I thought it would be good for her to stand on her own feet."

"And you told her so?"

"Yes."

"Was that why she moved out?"

He looks at me in some surprise.

"You seem to be well informed – about Siv, at least."

"Not really. But it's true she lived here until quite recently?"

"Yes, it is. I . . . encouraged her to move, you might say. Where did you get all this information about Siv?"

"She contacted my father, who ran a private detective agency. I want to know why."

"Can't you ask him?"

"He's dead."

He looks thoughtfully at me.

"Not suicide, too, surely?"

"He was knocked down by a car."

On the same day as Siv died, it seems, but I've no desire to tell him that.

He straightens the lamp a little in order to see me better. His eye sockets fill with dark shadows as he leans across the low table between us, increasing his resemblance to the skull next door.

"And you? Are you . . . a detective, too?"

"No, I'm just a researcher."

Into a different kind of chaos from the forces he's interested in.

45

Yngve Caspari sinks back into his chair and purses his handsome lips as if in a kiss. It makes him look like an angel, one of those who will herald the Day of Judgement, maybe.

"I think that's enough. I've got something to consider, so I suggest you go now. And next time you want anything of me, please could you knock first?"

I get up and begin to do up my coat,

"Heggedal church, do you know it?" I ask.

His face is averted as he lights a cigar from the box on the table. He doesn't reply until it's lit.

"Yes."

"Someone set fire to it last night."

He blows a cloud of smoke up at the ceiling.

"And you're wondering whether I did it? I don't go in for childish pranks."

At the door I turn with my hand on the handle.

"When did you last see her? Did she come here?"

For the first time, there's a trace of uncertainty in his voice as he answers.

"I don't think I've seen her since she left."

I open the door to the dark hall. A face confronts me – a blue oval, looking straight at me below heavy eyelids. It must be the person who was in bed upstairs. I wonder how long she's been standing there.

"I'm going now," she says hurriedly.

Caspari conceals his rage with a smile.

"Elisabeth, dear, haven't you learnt that it's naughty to listen at doors?"

"What makes you think I was listening? I just wanted to say goodbye. I must go."

"You can come with me, if you like," I say.

"I think Elisabeth will stay a little longer," says Caspari, opening the front door for me.

"Haven't time," says Elisabeth, pushing her slim body past me.

We look back and only the little red dot of his cigar shows that Yngve Caspari is still standing in the doorway watching her go.

6

GORBIE IS RECALCITRANT in the cold, and Elisabeth sits shivering beside me while I try to get the engine going. She tucks her hands inside her long sweater. She's far too thinly clad, but she's at the age when girls think they look fat if they dress well. I guess she's nineteen, but she could be younger.

"Can I cadge a fag off you?" she says, without turning to look at me.

While I'm lighting it for her, I see she's pretty in a classic, young way – blue eyes, fair hair and a soft, rather childish, kissable mouth. She's bitten her nails much too far down to use nail varnish.

"I'm Igi Heitmann," I say, once I've finished threatening the car with another overhaul at the Vietnamese garage.

"Elisabeth Falk," she says. "Great car."

"Really great, if you like surprises. Perhaps it was you I spoke to yesterday?"

"Did you?"

"Yes, on the phone."

"Oh, that."

"Where are you heading?"

"I suppose I'll have to go home," she says, letting a cloud of smoke out together with a sigh. "To Hvalstad. Only if you can be bothered, I mean, otherwise you could drop me off in Asker."

"Of course I'll drive you home. But you'll have to show me the way. I don't know my way around here very well."

"Do you live in Oslo?"

"Mm."

"I'd like to live in the city."

She makes the city, half an hour's drive away, sound like a great adventure, the answer to her dreams.

"Most of the people who go to Yngve live in the city."

"Do you know many of them?"

"A few. They're a strange lot."

"Did you know Siv Underland?"

"The screwed-up lady who used to hang out at Yngve's? I've met her, but it's a while ago."

"Before Yngve asked her to move out?"

"Oh, he didn't ask her to move out."

"Didn't he?"

"I know he says that he threw her out because he was tired of sleeping with her. But I don't believe it."

"So what do you think happened?"

"She left him. But I don't understand it. She should have been pleased Yngve even looked at her. There are better-looking women." She laughs.

"Yet she was the one who decided to leave?"

"Mm. Yngve was dead upset about it. Even though he denies it."

She thinks for a bit.

"Are you a friend of hers, or something?"

"Oh, no."

"I mean, I'm sure she's OK, she's just a bit odd. Sort of lonely, you know. Frustrated."

"She's dead."

"Jesus."

It's quiet for a moment. The headlights bore a tunnel of light through the darkness ahead of us, and a few snowflakes dance innocently in the air.

"I didn't really know her. I haven't seen her for ages."

She has no more to say for the rest of the journey, apart from giving me directions. Death is nothing to young girls, except as a part of the adventure, an exciting secret whispered by a dark lover, not something you meet one evening when you're going home to your mother and father.

The home Elisabeth is reluctantly going back to is palatial, a dream villa from an American TV series. The whole façade is floodlit, so that every bay window and pillar stands out. I drop her off at the front door. The drive is completely clear – it must have so many heaters under the asphalt that she could walk on it barefoot. The Falk family are certainly high-flyers.

I drive back to the centre of Asker, stop outside the shopping centre and walk through the dreary pedestrian precinct to the police station.

Samuel Hansson is still at work. His face is grey and his tight shirt has two large sweaty patches under the arms. Even if the suicide rate here in Asker, Norway's wealthiest area, has doubled over the last year, I doubt if he often has to deal with two cases at once. Lola looks considerably more awake than her master.

"You've come at just the right moment," says Samuel, yawning hugely. "To sign your statement. How's the shock?"

"I feel it most when I cry," I reply, a girlie joke that passes him by.

The statement seems OK, and even lacks the famous police spelling mistakes.

"Have you got five minutes?" I say after signing it.

His office is a no-smoking zone, and the small smoking room is full.

"Let's go to the Polo," suggests Samuel.

I'm surprised at his choice, for anyone over forty looks out of place in the rather trendy café he takes me to. Samuel's fat thighs spread over the spindly wooden chair as he sits down. He looks like an overgrown potato stuck on a couple of matchsticks. No one seems to mind that he's smuggled in Lola – dogs are almost certainly banned.

"Not much chance here of meeting people I've put inside," he says, nodding at the open, yellow-painted room. "Which isn't true of the other places around here. They also do bloody good hot chocolate."

We order one each, with a generous dollop of cream on top. Uncle pays.

"It was quite a night, eh, Igi? I'm beginning to be too old for this game – burnt-down churches and that kind of thing."

"Do you think someone from around here did it?"

"We've got our fair share of oddballs – religious freaks or whatever."

"Siv Underland did have that . . . altar in her cabin."

49

"Was that what it was supposed to be? It didn't look religious to me. That figure . . ."

Uncle turns scarlet, even though (or perhaps because) Igi is no longer a little girl.

"It's called a lingam. A religious object from India."

"Goodness. Who told you that?"

"Yngve Caspari. A religious freak if ever there was one. But he doesn't go in for burning down churches, he says."

"Have you talked to him?"

"Yes. Siv lived there, until recently."

"We know that. But . . ."

"But it's nothing to do with me, you mean. It did have something to do with my father, though. Before he was killed."

Samuel fidgets and the chair protests. He doesn't like me mentioning my father, or perhaps he's thinking about the funeral.

"What do you think about Siv?" I say, to break the painful silence.

"Me? I'm not supposed to think anything at all."

"Yes, but?"

"But it doesn't seem totally improbable that it should end like that – to her parents. She wasn't exactly . . . happy."

"With them?"

"With her life."

"With Yngve Caspari?"

"Well, unlike you, I haven't had time to talk to him, so I don't know. Her parents didn't know much about her relations with him."

"Or that she'd moved out?"

"No."

"Not a close family, then?"

"She appears to have been a bit . . . well, you saw that altar. But they did know about the cabin. They rented it when Siv was a child. Maybe she was going back to her childhood?"

"And you reckon she did it herself – shot herself?"

"The gun was in her hand when we found her, and she had gunpowder marks both on her hand and on what was left of her face. The only thing that's a bit odd is that she'd fired it twice."

I light a cigarette to give me time to think about what he's just said. Then I smile at him sweetly.

"That could mean she fired only one of the shots herself, couldn't it? The one that caused the marks on her hand. And therefore . . ."

"It could do, but it doesn't necessarily follow."

"And no one heard the shots?"

"The gun had a silencer, but in any case the place is pretty remote."

"And the writing on the mirror?"

"It's her handwriting, if that's what you mean."

"Mirror-writing."

"Strange, of course. But who knows what goes on in a troubled mind."

"And do you know who the other corpse might be?"

"It's a woman, that's all the forensic people can say so far. They're comparing her teeth with the missing persons' dental records this evening. But she'd been there a long time. And there's no reason why she should be from around here, so it'll take longer to identify her."

I shove the list of names across the table.

"From the archives of the local paper, the *Budstikka*. Number three is Petra Holmgren. 'Petra is waiting', it said on the mirror, didn't it?"

He nods. Lola licks his hand.

"I wasn't working here then, so I don't know the case. Siv must have been . . . seven when she disappeared. It may have made an impression, of course."

Too right. After all, she happened to have a pendant with Petra's date of birth, 12.5.60, engraved on it.

He looks kindly at me as we part company.

"Listen," he says, "you know Andreas thought the police were the best people to deal with this kind of case. Even if he did leave the force."

"Yes."

"You'll come to me, won't you, if there's a problem? I don't think you should be . . . ferreting around on your own."

"No," I say, crossing my fingers behind my back. If he wants to play the kind uncle, I still know a few little-girl tricks. "Just one more question. The gun. Was it hers?"

"No. It was reported stolen, actually, after a break-in a few months ago."

"Where?"

"The Holmgren family residence, if you must know."

Lola barks enthusiastically, as if she's just heard a good cat joke.

I stay on at the café after Samuel leaves. He's right, of course, about my father. On the other hand, I have inherited nothing except his little office; that and, as Benny says, a tendency to think too much. Sombre thoughts, usually, and this particular train of thought leads me into darker realms than most. Neither Yngve Caspari nor Samuel has convinced me that Siv took her own life, so I still have to follow my father down the dark street he trod the night he was killed.

Benny is more for deeds than thoughts, when it comes to boys and other things. As I stand by the public telephone leafing through the Asker directory to the letter H, I suppress an intense desire to phone him. Not that I need him to tell me what to do. When I find the address, I've already decided: it won't hurt to take a look at the house where Siv may have obtained a gun.

The house seems quiet, almost dead.

I sit in the car smoking a cigarette to help me decide whether to take a step further along this route and ring the bell. The modest house in Borgenveien is painted grey, and the low roof makes it look as if it is crouched in the snow, wary of danger. A lamp is shining in one of the rooms, spreading a cautious light over the cleared drive up to the front door. No skis or toboggan lean against the railings, and the steps look vulnerable and bare, covered with a thin layer of new snow.

I might as well try the bell. I doubt that anyone will answer. But after pressing the shrill, angry thing twice, an elderly woman opens the door a crack and looks at me with sharp, anxious eyes.

"Mrs Holmgren?" I say, quietly, realizing that caution is essential in this house.

"Yes?"

Siv Underland's name acts as a kind of password. The small grey-haired lady lets me in and switches on another lamp in the living-room. Even so, the room remains dim, the shadows enveloping us like soft quilts.

Petra Holmgren's mother has a narrow face etched with deep lines. It is not just age that has scored the leathery skin until it resembles an aerial view of a sun-scorched, rocky landscape: empty, barren, majestic in its loneliness.

She sits on the edge of her chair, with her knees pressed neatly together. She doesn't want to make things comfortable for herself, even if she does surround herself with numbing darkness.

"Siv came here, didn't she?" I ask her.

"Yes. She remembered Petra so well, although she was only a little girl at the time. When Petra . . . disappeared." She falls silent, as if the word still contains something too great, too incomprehensible for her. The gentleness of her voice contrasts sharply with that hard face.

"We were neighbours, before the Underlands built their new house. It's very grand, I think. I've never seen it."

Her hands, hard and sinewy, keep smoothing an invisible crease in her skirt.

"Leonard was so fond of Siv. She was almost like an extra daughter, another little girl. She came and went as she pleased. She used to play with Leonard in the garden. He'd been given a camera and we've almost more photographs of Siv than of Petra. I look at them sometimes, despite myself. It's as if I need to see that my daughter really existed. They all look so happy – Petra, too, usually . . . It was Siv who saw her that day, you know," she adds.

"Saw her?"

"She saw her getting into the car. His car. The man they said was her lover. The one who took her away. The only person who saw her go was a little girl of seven."

I wait. Laila Holmgren is back there sixteen years ago, reliving that interminable day which ended everything for her.

"Do you remember what his name was?"

"Jan something or other. Jan Johansson, like that Swedish jazz musician. I never met him. I didn't even know she had a boyfriend before she disappeared. There was a note in our mail box. That was all. A note. I showed it to Siv when she came to see me a few months ago. Do you want to see it?"

She moves slowly among the shadows of her living-room, and fumbles in a bureau drawer. The piece of paper she shows me is yellowed and brittle, ragged at the edges as if someone has taken it out again and again to try to make sense of it.

"I can't stand it any longer. Don't try to contact me," it says in round, schoolgirlish handwriting.

Brief, harsh words, but the photograph she hands me must have dealt an even crueller blow. A young woman smiles at the camera, a breeze gently ruffles her hair. She looks happy beneath the blue sky, and she's screwing up her eyes, as if the sun were low. "Forgive me," it says in the same handwriting under the photograph. No signature.

"Posted in Copenhagen, many months after she left here. Leonard took it to the police." Laila Holmgren's voice is a toneless whisper, as if her feelings could no longer reach the words.

"We thought perhaps they might find her then, in Denmark. But the police could discover no trace of her. I've tried to tell myself that she meant well with that photograph, that she wanted to say that all was well with her, she just couldn't bring herself to write. But we heard nothing more."

Her busy hands have left her skirt and are clasped together as she massages one palm with her thumb.

"I still think I see her sometimes – in the street, or in a shop, and I try to imagine what she looks like now. After all these years, she must have changed a lot."

I think about the woman in the wall. Even if it wasn't Petra, she's no longer the young woman in the photograph smiling sweetly into the sun. The girl is wearing a chain round her neck, with a pendant shaped like a butterfly.

"Leonard isn't at home," says Laila Holmgren as she lets me out, perhaps to justify the two safety chains on the door. "He works so hard. Although he doesn't have to any longer."

I don't ask her about the gun; the word itself seems too brutal. But if Siv did use it on herself, she at least had a reason to take it from here.

Outside it is snowing again, and the footprints I made when I arrived are fast disappearing.

7

THE COURTYARD BEHIND Bernt Ankersgate is a black abyss as I walk under the arch. The light above the entrance has gone again, and there's never been a doorman. As I fumble about, unlocking the door, a black shadow rushes past my legs with a wail of protest. Inside Oswald, Lina's cat, looks at me with such reproach in its eyes, I consider taking it in. But there's every indication they haven't yet gone to bed up above – the stairway is vibrating with the bass in the music they've chosen tonight.

I knock loud and long on their door. The decibels hit me straight in the face when Lina's boyfriend opens the door, as does the smell of dope and incense. The guy – whose name I can never remember, only that it's something rather inappropriate like Fredrik or Prebe – is too spaced out to notice the cat slipping inside. He thinks I've come to join in the fun, and, his eyes half-closed, he jerks his head towards the small group sitting cosily in silence round a candle. Benny's recipe for surviving noisy neighbours' parties is to join them, but I shake my head and, as it's impossible to explain anything as complicated as the cat, I leave him to his confusion and totter back down the rickety stairs.

Unpacking my quilt and bedlinen from my bag, I almost regret not staying up there. It's not because the music is going to keep me awake, but because I've decided to sleep on the sofa in the office, instead of investigating Father's bedroom, where the sound may be less overwhelming. To me, that room is taboo: I've never set foot in it, and I don't wish to now. It would be much simpler to change his bed and go to sleep on his mattress, under his quilt, but I don't want to know whether he has a single bed in there, or a hopeful one-and-a-halfer; I don't want to know what he has in the drawer of his bedside table.

I remember spending the weekend with a friend when I was about twelve. Giggling, she found in her father's wardrobe a bundle of pornographic magazines which today probably wouldn't make me blink, but which were pretty powerful stuff for us at the time. It left me with a horrible taste in my mouth, but I don't know if it was the content, or the fact that we suddenly knew something about her father. I don't think my father kept a similar bundle, and if there are stains on his sheets, I ought to be adult enough to tolerate them. But I don't feel all that adult here. The music upstairs changes to Tom Waits again, and I can sense my ghosts watching me from the shadows. They have the company of a third tonight – the ghost from the chapel in Heggedal, who may have been called Petra Holmgren.

If Siv Underland came here with Petra's necklace and told him about the photograph of her wearing it, maybe she and Father put two and two together?

When had she been given the pendant, and by whom? By Petra . . . or someone else? Siv and my father must have realized that the photograph does not tell the story it was meant to tell: instead of confirming that Petra was alive when the photograph was sent, it implies the opposite. No matter where Petra went after she disappeared, she couldn't have been wearing the pendant when the photograph was supposed to have been taken.

"PetraSiv" was what Siv had scrawled over and over again on the mirror in the cabin, the names entangled as she gazed at the multiple reflections of her own face in the two mirrors. Distorted, overlapping letters, touching each other.

And now Siv is reaching out to touch me, too – through my father.

I give up any attempt to sleep – I'm past that stage now. My body is aching with lack of it, but my mind is speeding. I light a cigarette and dial Benny's number. No one at home. What a surprise. Perhaps he's not keen on coming back to an empty double bed, either, so I have to be content that he hasn't filled it. Though that isn't really my business any more.

It's very late when I phone Samuel Hansson. What he rather reluctantly tells me conjures up pictures I'm familiar with. In my teens, I looked inquisitively at my father's forensic medicine books. I know that it takes time for a person to disappear, and death is only the first phase, the beginning of a new process: decomposition, decay.

The degrading enzymes are already active when the body is alive. When death occurs, the process accelerates and spreads to the internal organs – kidneys, liver, lungs, heart. In this phase, the external layer of skin remains untouched, and, apart from its bluish-white colour, the body mostly resembles the living human being. Then the decomposing organs produce more gas and the volume of the body increases dramatically for a while, particularly the stomach and intestines, where the skin is drawn tight across the swelling entrails. Gradually fat and muscle tissue are also attacked, and the decay spreads to the outer layer of the body.

Slowly, slowly, the dead body is stripped. Flesh, fat and entrails loosen from the skeleton, dissolve or are eaten away, until it is laid bare and all resemblance to the human being it once was has gone.

I picture her remains on a zinc slab beneath a cold light. With the thoroughness of an archaeologist, the forensic scientist has marked and sorted the parts of what was the skeleton of a young woman. The joints would have come apart as the chapel wall collapsed. They have been pieced together again, so the skeleton appears whole, functional, like timber framing, as if awaiting the human shape that clothed it.

Samuel's exhausted voice fills my imagination. A hair or two escaped decomposition, he tells me – she was blonde. When she died she was wearing a blue blouse – they found some fibres between the stones she was lying on and one of her ribs. The remains of a nylon stocking were stuck to the inside of an almost rotted leather shoe. She had a good, regular set of teeth, with fillings in four molars. She was about twenty. She had never given birth or suffered any serious illness before someone administered the blow that left a gaping hole in her skull.

They have compared her teeth with her dental records and, yes, when she was alive she was Petra Holmgren.

It's half past four by the time Lina and her guy conclude their concert and I slide beneath the thin layer of a dream.

I wake up unrested, and am glad dreams are easy to forget. I wash them down the plughole as I shower, and after a coffee I am under the impression that I'm ready for a new day. I go to the university to reinforce that illusion with another: that I am in a fit state to take an interest in what is my real job.

With the help of a few cigarettes I can normally rely on my powers of concentration, but today they desert me. Sitting in my office on the sixth floor, I look out over Oslo, buried in white. The snow has even settled on the streets of the inner city and I can see almost the whole of Bundefjord is covered with ice.

I have a transcript of a tape in front of me but I can't summon up any interest in it. So what if there is a mathematical formula for the intervals between each time a lady of ninety suffering from senile dementia repeats the name of her son? At the moment that tells me nothing but that she is missing him, and there's no comforting mathematical beauty in that.

I have a mass of similar material, on computer, on audio tape, on video – a collection of physiological disturbances: twitches, grimaces, shaking heads, slavering mouths, blinking eyes. Usually I find them fascinating, but today they remind me of a chamber of horrors, a collection of perversions betrayed and displayed for public gratification. Today the symptoms cannot be separated from what exists beneath the surface, and I can find no pattern, no higher creative mathematics.

They used to fill me with awe, these pure formulae that express the world of these strange lives, and I was excited by the search for them. But that now seems infinitely far away, as if the last few days have put a wall of death between me and the knowledge I found so purifying.

My conviction about the universality of chaos theory and the wonderful creative spontaneity of open systems was such that my highly sceptical faculty head supported my application for a post-graduate grant; yet today I feel caught in the triviality of everyday research and can't do a thing to counteract it.

I'm bad at pursuing more than one thought at a time, at spreading my interest thinly over several subjects; my unsuccessful attempt to rescue my father by taking on two jobs taught me that. My one-track mind now makes me turn my back on my desk and I don't hear the phone until it has rung three times.

It's Ellen Underland. She would very much like to meet me. Does that suit you, she says. It does. It suits me right now.

The taste of playing truant from school comes to me as I leave the office – tart like apples.

The great house on Otto Blehrsvei in Nesøya looks as if the architect has taken a series of greenhouses and put them together in the most unlikely fashion. It consists almost entirely of planes of glass juxtaposed at confusing angles. The glass gives the impression that you can see in everywhere, as if those living inside have nothing to hide, but as I approach the entrance, this sense of openness disappears. The surfaces have been designed to reflect each other, so that in fact all I can see is a distorted image of the cold windows, the icy garden and my own splintered figure.

Ellen Underland is not dressed in black. Here, at home, she is wearing a burgundy velour dressing-gown. It makes her look as if she has only just got up, but I suspect she hasn't even been to bed. Her eyes are blank and staring, the rims red and swollen, behind her spectacles; she looks as if she's been crying for quite a while. She must be about forty-five and this morning she looks her age. There's a kind of defiance in her lack of any attempt to hide her grief. She looks me straight in the eye and there is a challenge in her tearful gaze.

We're sitting in a room that is almost all glass. The great cold panes reflect the rays of winter sunlight off the thick layer of snow covering the terrace and the lawn. There is nowhere to hide here. In low tubular steel chairs with neutral cushions, we are exposed to the merciless flood of light.

"Perhaps you know why I've asked you to come?" she says.

"Because of my father?"

"Yes, I . . . I wondered why she'd contacted him. It seems so odd. I mean, I know no one who's had anything to do with a . . . with anything like that."

"Well, unfortunately I can't tell you much. I don't know what, if anything, she wanted him to do. Apart from the fact that he had that pendant."

"Oh, well. I had hoped that . . . I didn't expect her to have any use for . . . someone like that."

"So what did you expect? When I phoned you from her cabin, you didn't seem surprised."

"I've always been afraid for her. Frightened of something happening to her. Only now do I really see how afraid I was. As if there was always some threat, something she should be protected from. It's ironic, isn't it? That I needn't be afraid for her any longer."

I ask if I may smoke, and she looks rather confused, as if it were a remarkable question. But she produces an ashtray and, with a smile, asks me first for one then for a second cigarette. Maybe there are several things she needn't be afraid of any longer.

"Siv never felt at home here," she says, making an expansive gesture that includes more than just the room and the garden outside. "She always longed to be back in Borgenveien, where we used to live. That made me angry, I remember. Perhaps because I did too. I was angry with her for a lot of unnecessary things like that. It was better when she moved out – lonelier but better. Do you think that's harsh?" The challenge in her eyes is there again. "Of course, you don't have any children, do you?"

"No."

"She was an only child, you know. I've always thought it would have been much simpler if she'd had a brother – or a sister. But perhaps that's because I had a brother when I was small, and we tended to stick together against the world. Maybe it wouldn't have made a difference to her, I don't know. There's so much I don't know. We fought so. In adolescence. When she was a teenager, I mean. I should have been less childish, but I wasn't . . . She hurt me. I let myself be so hurt by her, by her rejection."

I have no children, but I do have a mother. I know what Ellen Underland is talking about.

"It's as if there are two different people when I think about her. One young and innocent . . . a beautiful child. And then someone quite different, suddenly. Not innocent. Not particularly beautiful. We never faced it."

She laughs, an unpleasant laugh, a whip she cracks against herself.

"We should have been such perfect parents, shouldn't we? Mother a teacher and father a psychiatrist. We should have known everything there is to know about children and the young. And in fact we never got to grips with it at all."

She blows a thin, deliberate stream of smoke out into the high-ceilinged room as if wanting to pollute it, to cover the clean, clear surfaces with filth and ash.

"She argued with you, did she? Not with her father?"

"He wasn't around – not very often, anyhow. I was the one who had to impose all the restrictions, ask all the stupid questions. 'Why are you back so late?' 'Have you been smoking dope?' I was the one who spied on her, smelt her clothes, eavesdropped on her telephone calls. Not surprising that she hated me. Øyvind escaped all that because he wasn't here."

She's no longer looking at me as she talks. Her eyes are turned towards the frozen garden, where the rose bushes are covered with sacking and a thick layer of snow, protected from the cold by the cold itself.

"It happens so quickly. One day she's a slender, careful young girl and the next . . . a crude, vulgar woman. She suddenly started using make-up in a way I've never done, laid on thick, like a tart. Where did she learn that? Not from me, that's for sure, but she had that awful friend – Tone Indrelid, her name was. They were always together, an inseparable pair."

She stubs out her cigarette so clumsily that it continues to smoke in the ashtray, then she wraps her arms round herself and rocks slowly back and forth in her chair.

"And we were ashamed. I was ashamed. We never talked about it, Øyvind and I, but I could see that he, too, was ashamed of his daughter. No parents are prepared for things to go so hellishly wrong with their child. That their child should be so . . . difficult."

"Did things go hellishly wrong?"

"Well, what do you think?"

"Sorry, I didn't mean now. Before. Earlier."

"She never settled to anything. Heavens, I've written so many applications for her, to schools she never started at, for courses she only bothered to attend once or twice. She just left jobs. In the end I refused. Said she'd have to cope by herself. Perhaps things would have been better if she'd had to do that from the start. Do you think so? That I ruined her with all that protection? Nothing's supposed to do as much harm as an over-protective mother, is it?"

"No. I don't think you ruined her," I say – not that I can console her: it makes no difference what a stranger thinks, and I doubt she's even listening to me.

"I don't know. Things looked better for a while, after she moved out. She stopped taking things. Worked in a kindergarten. I think she liked that. I could see she was lonely, but maybe that was better than carrying on with those former friends of hers. Then she made contact with that . . . magician. At first she told me a bit about it. Not Øyvind. He loathed it all, but she confided in me a little. Then she stopped, grew distant . . . talked so rarely to us about anything, as if she didn't want to have anything more to do with us. As if she looked down on us. I longed for her to break with him and leave. But we never talked about him, really. I just thought it was so unpleasant that they had a relationship."

"So she never told you she'd left him?"

"No. But she said something that pleased me a little while ago. She wanted to begin again, she said, whatever that meant. I didn't dare ask if it had anything to do with him. I probably didn't want to know. But I thought she seemed so much better, as if she'd abandoned something bleak and unhealthy. Now I think perhaps it wasn't so good after all, and it might have been better if she'd stuck to that mystic. I mean, she wouldn't have used that gun until she'd finished with him."

"You think she took it, do you?"

"It must have been her."

"Do you remember Petra Holmgren?"

"The girl who disappeared. Of course. We were neighbours. Siv loved her. Admired her. Petra was so beautiful, you see. She was much older than Siv. She used to babysit for us and was almost like a big sister to her. Siv imitated her – her movements, her way of talking. Siv went in and out of their house as she pleased. Virtually lived there. When Petra disappeared, it was almost like losing a member of the family. Siv grieved for her. But she didn't want to talk about her. That must have been the first time she retreated from me, as if it were my fault Petra had left. After a while we moved. We thought it would be better for her not to stay there, missing Petra. But that was wrong, too."

She falls silent.

"But I thought . . . It was nothing, really, just a feeling."

She stops.

"Yes?"

"It was never anything concrete. And they seemed so nice, both of them. Just rather different to us, that's all."

"Are you talking about the neighbours?"

"Yes. No. I never thought about it at the time, but later, when Siv . . . changed so, then I wondered whether she . . . could have experienced something. It was only talk, nothing to take much notice of. As a mother you're so hypersensitive . . . when it comes to that sort of thing. You know, it was his firm that built the chapel."

I leave her sitting by the cold windowpane, her eyes on the buried garden, her hands folded as if in prayer. But who is there to listen to her prayers?

As I walk towards the car, a woman across the road watches me. I come from a marked house. In the old days they painted a cross on doors where the plague had struck. These days, it's done with a photograph in the newspaper.

8

OUTSIDE LIGHTS LINE the drive leading to the Falks' residence in Hvalstad like an old-fashioned avenue of elms. In daylight you can see they are made of plastic and they merely reinforce the impression of nouveau riche bad taste. I know it's my mother's upbringing that makes me smile inwardly when I see them: we love having our prejudices confirmed.

Elisabeth doesn't look wholly awake when she opens the door, although the dulcet tones of the bell can hardly have woken her.

"Oh, it's you," she says. "Come on in."

She looks even younger than when I last saw her. She leads me into a living-room where the furniture looks as if it is being pressed against the walls by the vast area of parquet flooring. We pass through three equally large rooms before we come to the stairs down to her basement domain.

The smell of incense and the Palestinian scarf she uses as a tablecloth are an attempt to distance this room from the furniture showroom above, but the poster of a horse and the pink all-over wallpaper mean that it does not quite succeed.

She doesn't look surprised to see me in the least. It takes me a while to realize this is because she's used to things happening without ever having to wonder how. I try not to think of it as typical of "the younger generation" – nothing makes me feel older and more sedate.

Elisabeth cadges a cigarette off me and waves her hands rather vaguely, as if to disperse the smoke. I recognize the movement and I feel for her: she'll lie about the smell this evening, saying that I made it.

She appears not to remember Siv Underland's death, nor is she interested in the corpse in the chapel wall, but she does remember the fire.

"Oh, yes, Yngve talked about it. He's against that kind of thing."

"Is he?"

"Yes. I guess he thinks it was really childish. So he doesn't like everyone assuming he did it."

"Who's everyone?"

"The police, the newspapers, the lot. Don't they? Anyhow, they've all asked him about it. He gets quite stressed out by it. He hates that sort of phone call, and he doesn't want anyone to visit right now, not even me."

"Do you think it was him?"

"Me? No, I don't. I was there that night. But you mustn't tell my mother, OK? She thinks I was staying overnight with a friend, and she'd go spare if she knew I was with Yngve. She's dumb," she adds drily, as if it's a fact she's resigned to, which doesn't upset her particularly.

"But if you were there, that's good. It means he couldn't have done it."

"No, but you see, I shouldn't have been there. He tends to carry on with his rituals and things at night. I don't think he sleeps much. I watched videos mostly the night of the fire. I'm not that interested in those sessions of his. It's exciting a couple of times, but then it gets boring. Or I start laughing. He looks so distant, doesn't he? I once had such a fit of giggles while a whole lot of them were at it, and since then he doesn't like me being there."

"Were there several people there?"

"When?"

"The night the chapel burnt down."

"Oh, then. No, only Yngve. Well, and Charles, of course."

I realize Yngve need not let Mrs Falk discover where her daughter spends her nights, because Elisabeth wouldn't make a very good witness, should he need one. Still, I suggest that perhaps she ought to tell the police where she was that night.

"Maybe," she says, helping herself to another cigarette.

"You don't know whether Yngve knew Petra Holmgren, do you? They must have been roughly the same age."

"Who's that?"

"The woman they found in the chapel. The dead woman."

65

"Oh, yes. That bastard's daughter."

"You mean Leonard Holmgren?"

"Yes. The guy who owns Yngve's house."

"Why is he a bastard?"

"Don't know. Just what I heard. Yngve used to be in the same class as his daughter. She ran away from home."

"That's the one. She was killed."

"Oh. Is that who it was?"

I begin to wonder whether Elisabeth takes after her mother more than she imagines – she seems pretty dumb herself.

"I thought it was Holmgren's sister or someone. Anyhow, Yngve doesn't much like him. Don't know why exactly. It's not as if he has to pay him anything."

"Does he live there free?"

"He says so, but I think his father pays the rent. I mean, he's got pots of money."

"Yngve?"

She laughs.

"He hasn't got a bean. Only enough for clothes and books . . . but books are awfully expensive." Her forehead furrows, as if the price of books worries her. "It's his father who's got pots of money. I think he would have found Yngve somewhere else to live, but Yngve didn't want that. He's not really on speaking terms with his father. Anyhow, I think he pays the rent, even if Yngve denies it. He says his father has something on Holmgren."

"What might that be?"

"Don't know. Something to do with the daughter, perhaps. Everyone knows Holmgren's a bastard."

She stretches.

"I've been bored all day. Can you give me a lift into town?"

In the car she says she can't be bothered to talk about Yngve any more, it bores her. She stares straight ahead unless she's twisting the knob on the radio with her chewed fingers.

I'm far from bored by the subject. I wonder why Caspari's father agrees to pay the rent for his son who isn't talking to him.

I drop Elisabeth off at the Oslo City shopping complex. For a moment, she looks slightly bewildered, then she turns round and heads for the huge swing doors with the languid, almost hypnotized gait typical of the young people on the pavement.

Bernt Ankersgate is strangely silent. Lina and her man can't have got up yet. I'm buzzing after meeting Elisabeth Falk, as if her ennui has produced its own antidote in my bloodstream. I make a big pot of strong coffee and then sit doodling on one of the pieces of paper headed A. Heitmann, Private Investigator. In the left-hand corner the doodles begin to join up, making overlapping shapes, a bit like the writing on the mirror.

Holmgren and Underland were neighbours when Petra disappeared. Holmgren's firm built the chapel where Petra was found. Yngve Caspari used to be in the same class at school as Petra, and until a few months ago Siv Underland lived in his house – the house where, according to Elisabeth Falk, Yngve lives for free, because his father has something on Holmgren. Siv was killed by a gun that came from the Holmgrens' house. Ellen Underland wonders whether Siv had some traumatic experience as a child, exactly what she's too afraid to tell me, for fear of being thought a scandal-monger. Or that's what she wants me to think. And Yngve Caspari wants people to think it was he who finished with Siv, not the other way round.

I remember the jigsaw puzzles of my childhood – we spent long wet summer days doing one of my father's thousand-piece jigsaws on the dining-room table. I built up the sky in one corner while he methodically worked on fitting together the tiny figures outside the cathedral in Reims or in front of a Chinese pagoda. I was never any good at puzzles. It was the smell of my father's cigar that kept me at the table, that and the calm with which he worked, as painstaking as a cat washing itself.

My little Asker puzzle is far from complete. I focus on a bit of snow-covered landscape with the corner of a house on it – Leonard Holmgren's farm, where Yngve Caspari lives. I phone Caspari senior's firm and get a depressing digital version of "Imagine" while I wait to be put through. The 1970s meet the 1990s, like on the pavement outside Oslo City.

I haven't eaten anything all day. With the telephone receiver clamped between my cheek and my shoulder, I tear open the bag containing a filled baguette.

My reflection in the windowpane: a grey face, crumbs on the desk, cigarette smoke rising in a slim coil from the ashtray. How different from the eight-year-old doer of jigsaw puzzles. I turn away from the window and its picture of my bad bachelor habits – the only thing missing is a splash of brandy in my coffee.

I put aside the baguette. It's full of cheap margarine, as I expected. I reach for another cigarette, knowing it's another bad habit to deaden hunger by smoking like this. Fortunately, the travesty of "Imagine" is interrupted at that moment and replaced by a voice brimming with the kind of enthusiasm you learn to acquire on a sales and marketing course. She seems to think it such fun that I should be phoning her, and can she help me in any way?

"I'm ringing from Holmgren's office," I say. "Accounts."

"Yes?"

"There's something I'd like to check on our last invoice. Can you find it?"

Of course she can! It's nothing short of wonderful that I should be asking her to do so. She taps happily on some keyboard.

"Here we are! Payment went from us on the eighth. It must have gone into your account long ago."

"Of course. We've had some absence due to sickness, you see, so I'm going through the books now. It's just that the copy from the bank is rather poor. I can't see what the sum is. It's rent, is it?"

"Rent?" She titters in amusement. "That would have been steep – 150,000 kroner!"

I titter a little myself.

"It's just down as a withdrawal," she says.

"That's it, yes. Is it a one-off payment, or what?"

"Just a moment."

She taps for a while again. Then there's a rustle of paper and she's talking to someone, but the voices are too low for me to catch the words.

"You say you're phoning from Holmgren's?"

She now sounds slightly dejected.

"That's right."

"But this payment should have gone to Holmgren personally, not to his firm. What's the number of the account you have?"

"What number did you pay it into?"

68

"You must be able to read that on what you have there. Are you sure you're phoning from Holmgren's? What was your name again?"

There's not much enthusiasm left in her voice and I feel I ought to beat a retreat.

"Ah, now I understand. Of course the money's gone into his personal account. It says so here. I just hadn't noticed it. He must have mislaid his copy and it's come to me. So that's all in order. Many thanks indeed."

I ring off in a bit of a sweat, but I turn round and grin with satisfaction at my reflection. The bachelor has almost earned herself a small brandy. Anyhow, there's no reason to stub out my cigarette.

9

IT'S TOO EARLY for brandy, and it's too late for a decent walk, so I decide to go skiing on the lighted trails.

Benny isn't at home when I stop off in Markveien to pick up my gear. I decide to start from Sognsvann instead of taking the leisurely downhill trail from Frognerseteren, which is better for contemplation than giving myself a really good thrashing.

I don't get into my stride until Åklungen, but on the climb up from Ullevålseter I can feel the twenty-packs being thumped out of my body. It's a way of combating my junk lifestyle, a trick I've practised ever since I started taking out my rage against Karsten on my opponents on the handball pitch. In recent years I've had to make do with self-inflicted torture, but it serves the same purpose.

The men in skin-tight racing suits ski faster than I do, and I clench my teeth as I choose to stick behind one of them. I manage to keep up with him for just over a mile, then I have to let him go, but it has left my mind empty and clear.

On the last climb up to the station I am alone, and there is plenty of time before the next tram, so I slow down – not because of the taste of blood in my mouth, I tell myself, but because I want to admire the snowy trees. Slowcoaches always try to convince themselves that the racers might just as well have worked out in the gym.

I hear him before I see him, and I know perfectly well who is lurking beyond the next bend. I've seen him many times before, but thought it was too cold for him today. He's an old flasher who walks along the ski trails, howling out his loneliness and tugging at the poor shred of flesh between his legs as if trying to pull it off. I know he's harmless, but it's dark and I don't want anyone to spoil my peace of mind right now.

Of course that's what he manages to do. As I pass him, I catch a glimpse of his blue frozen member in his hands, and he goes on yelling at me long after I've left him standing alone in the track. "I've no one!" he shouts. "No one loves me!"

I feel no pity for him; I'm just tired and angry, because he's intruded on me, because he's ruined the reward that lies at the top of the last slope: the sight of the city sparkling below me. This evening it doesn't look like a cluster of glittering jewels set off by black velvet; tonight it looks like trashy, cheap bijouterie, and I know perfectly well that only the darkness conceals the lid of carbon dioxide that threatens to smother Oslo.

I even miss my tram and am frozen stiff by the time the next one comes. Of course the flasher gets into my carriage just as it is leaving and I have to put up with his racist monologue behind me all the way to Slemdal.

Benny is stupid enough to phone when I'm in the shower, and he gets the whole works about lonely men and their bloody intrusive loins.

"Hello," he says when I've finished. "Did that help a bit? To get it off your chest, I mean?"

"Not much. If you'd just left your beloved, would you then put a kind of erect prick on your bedside table?"

"Have you done that?"

"No. But perhaps you're not the right person to ask."

"Oh, come on."

"It wasn't on the bedside table, in fact. It was a kind of altar." I tell him about Siv.

"She left her dinner, you see. To shoot herself."

"Well, not everyone likes food as much as I do. I would've thought dinner was a good enough reason not to do myself in. You don't feel like roast aubergines, do you?"

"No."

"Mushrooms marinated in garlic?"

"No."

"Don't you think you're concerning yourself rather too much with death at the moment?"

Yes. Basically I do.

"Part of me just wants to lie here wearing a black armband and think about my father. Yet I can't do that because there's something

71

I can't get out of my head – something that's nothing to do with him. Benny, I'm not very good at this mourning stuff."

"Do you have to think about those girls?"

"No."

"But you do all the same."

"Yes. Otherwise I'll begin to think about you and me. More mourning."

That was gratuitous, but I've only a towel round me and I'm cold.

"Oh, I see."

I hate it when the misery in his voice is my fault. It's much easier when the reason is one of his boyfriends.

"I shouldn't have phoned," he says.

"Why did you, in fact?"

"I just wanted to remind you that I love you."

In the silence after I've rung off I wish Lina and her man were at home – then I could have pretended it was their hi-fi keeping me awake.

As so many times before, I wonder whether I suddenly fell in love with Benny because I felt flattered. I was high as a kite on the fact that he wanted me, even though I was a girl. I and everyone else knew that he only had to wiggle his backside to make the boys at the old Metropol squint-eyed with delight – yet he wanted me. Not as camouflage, not as an ornament, but in all seriousness.

I could have no greater proof of genuine love, I told myself, and, with my eyes wide open, I entered into what we proudly proclaimed would be "a hell of a turbulent marriage".

The turbulence models I can call up on the computer create beautiful, intricate, constantly shifting patterns, but they tell you nothing about what it is like to be caught up in the turbulence – whirled around by forces you can't control, simply having to give yourself up to love.

We almost laughed ourselves silly planning the wedding, in full cross-dressing: me in white tie and tails and Benny in a full white wedding dress. I didn't even end up leading the wedding waltz – he was too good a dancer – but Mother came over all breathless when I tried to do so, which gave us a good laugh.

I have loved Benny for what will soon be ten years and I still fall for him. I wasn't prepared for him to be such a bad husband and such a good friend. It's the mixture that's difficult.

It's always been the problem: the absences, the waiting; equivocations and approximations – almost but not quite all.

"Either/or" is no big deal; it's "as well as" that hurts.

In the morning I ring Leonard Holmgren's office and they tell me I'll find him on the building site in Teatergata. It's not hard to find. The main shell is complete, but some of the external walls are missing, and the thick concrete floors rest on iron supports that look too flimsy to take their weight.

Inside two young guys in blue overalls are having a coffee break on the ground floor. The huge space heater is making such a racket I have to go right over to them before they can hear me.

"Are you the interior designer?" one of them asks, with a hint of a lopsided grin.

"No, why?"

"I just thought . . . she's turning up a bit later."

I give him a thin smile back. I suppose interior designers are still the only women who set foot on building sites. No-woman's-land.

"He's through there," he says, nodding towards a wide doorway. "But I wouldn't go in if I were you."

"Why not? Isn't it safe?"

He laughs and unscrews his thermos with masculine ease.

"The roof won't come down on your head, if that's what you mean. You try."

They watch me cross the floor and I wish I were wearing a boiler suit too, instead of a tight coat which makes my steps short and girlish as I pick my way over planks and pipes.

The corridor leading to the middle of the building is ill-lit and the floor is strewn with cables. I hear a voice roar: "That's no bloody excuse. You should've finished two days ago, and now my lads are having to sit around twiddling their thumbs. I can't bloody well afford this kind of delay."

I stand in the doorway of a great open room. A man in a sheepskin jacket has his back to me and his helmet looks ridiculously small on the top of his head. The chap he's yelling at is bright red in the face and the cigarette between his lips has burnt dangerously low. I wait for them to finish their row, but there doesn't seem to be any more.

"Leonard Holmgren?" I say.

"Yes?" barks the man in the sheepskin jacket, turning towards me.

He has great bags under his eyes and a stiff moustache below a handsome Roman nose. It must be his thick mane of hair that makes the helmet look so small – brushed back off his forehead, it is grey at the temples and falls in a handsome wave over his ears. I should think Leonard Holmgren is quite proud of his hair. On the other hand, he's quite short.

"My name's Igi Heitmann," I say. "I'd very much like to talk to you for a moment, if you've got a minute or two. It's about . . . a private matter."

Leonard Holmgren turns back to the man with the cigarette.

"Then you'll be finished by three," he says, his voice calmer now. "And I don't mean five past. I mean three. OK?"

"I've said so," the other mumbles, but Leonard Holmgren is already on his way out.

In the dark corridor, he turns to me, his teeth flashing white in a broad smile.

"You have to scare them a bit, you know. They needn't have finished for a day or two more. Nothing like a rocket up the arse to get the buggers moving."

The two young guys by the heater get up when we come in.

"They'll be ready by three," says Holmgren brusquely. "In the meantime, you can bloody well clear up a bit. It looks like a bombed-out brothel in here!"

"I've got exactly five minutes," he says, when we're out of the building. "Did you say Heitmann? Any relation of that detective, what was his name . . . Anders . . . Andreas?"

"My father."

"Really? You don't look much like him. Did a job for me once. Looking for . . . Petra. I could've saved my money."

"When was that?"

"Ten or twelve years ago. I was earning a lot at the time, so I thought it worth a try. Didn't tell the wife about it – I didn't want to raise her hopes if nothing came of it. But it would've been a great surprise, eh – if he'd found her? He went to Sweden and

74

Denmark, but couldn't find any trace of her. And now we know why."

He looks down at the ground and spits just in front of his heavy shoes.

"I've spent nearly twenty years of my life cursing my daughter. It doesn't feel good. Do you know what people think when someone disappears like that? They think there's a bloody good reason, don't they? That Petra must have had a bad childhood, that it's the parents' fault, mine and Laila's. They all think they know something about it. In the end you start to believe it yourself; Laila, my wife, did, anyhow. She turned over everything between heaven and earth – what we'd done, what we hadn't done. Wore herself out completely, wore me out, too . . . For what? People hardly think you've a right to look them in the eye afterwards. Not that I cared. If someone stares at me, I stare back – it's the only way to get them to cut it out. But Laila couldn't do that. She just bowed her head. And that made me so angry, I wanted to scream every time I saw it. But I couldn't go around telling people they were wrong, that Petra was everything to us, that I'd made bloody sure she lacked for nothing and didn't have to endure the grinding poverty of my childhood. Crazy, eh? There I was, working my arse off all those years to be able to buy her things . . . and then she was suddenly gone. It was so empty at home, I couldn't bear it. All I could do was to go on working. Never been much good at sitting twiddling my thumbs. You have to take risks. If you want something done, you have to do it yourself, that's what I think. Can't rely on some authority or other to fix things for you. Employing your father didn't help much, but I tried, didn't I?"

He's talked too much now. His shoulders are heaving and he needs someone's arms around him or a secretary to comfort him.

"What do you actually want of me?"

"I'm the person who found your daughter. In the church wall."

"Really. Finishing off your father's job?"

"Your firm built the chapel, didn't it?"

"Oh, yes. But any sod could get in there at night. And it must have been some bloody sod. The old bitches will have something else to talk about now, I imagine. The way the police go on and on about that fucking wall, you'd think they were nothing but a bunch of old bitches too. Excuse the expression. Anything else you want to know?"

"Was it at the time my father worked for you that you bought the farm? As you were earning so much, I mean?"

"What farm?"

"Where Yngve Caspari lives."

"What about it?"

"I just wondered how he manages for money. He hasn't got a job, has he?"

"I've no idea what he does. And I don't give a damn. That place is worth nothing, it's only got water and an outdoor privy. No one wants to live like that any more. It's not as if I'd get any money for it."

"So he lives there for free, does he? Are you just doing him a good turn?"

"For God's sake, I can do what I damn well like with my own property! Any more of your bloody nosy questions?"

"Yes. What did you use that gun for?"

"I've never used it for anything. It was my father's. From the war. I didn't even have any bullets for it. If you're thinking of taking over your father's snooping, then you'll have to go and harass someone else. I've bloody well had enough of it from the tax people and the police. OK? I don't give a fuck who lives in that shack or what they get up to there. And now you've damn well held me up quite long enough."

He turns on his heel and marches back into the building, then remembers where he's supposed to be going and hurries over to his car. He sits drumming his fingers on the wheel, then flings the door open and comes over to me again.

"Sorry. I didn't mean to get so het up. I've got a hell of a temper, you see. OK?"

He obviously thinks he's now smoothed things over.

"Just one more question," I say, knowing his outburst means he'll have to listen.

"That photograph sent from Copenhagen. Did you save the envelope it came in?"

"No. I didn't. What I wanted to do was burn the whole thing."

He strides back to the car and makes the rear wheels spin before swinging out into the street with the kind of macho roar teenagers make when they've seen Schwarzenegger in a film. It almost looks as if I'd stuck a rocket up his arse.

So my father's empty office does contain a message for me, after all – not filed under F for father, or under I for Igi, but under H.

Holmgren, Petra. Disappeared from her home, 18, Borgenveien, on 28 August 1979.

A few yellowed, typed sheets. Perhaps he was afraid of not being able to read his own writing, or perhaps he sent a copy of his report to his client, Leonard Holmgren.

A copy of the photograph is there, too, the one I've seen, in which she's peering at the camera and is wearing a brass butterfly round her neck.

He went to Copenhagen with the photograph – with no result, of course. And, as Leonard said, he went to Sweden, to Tunö, a windy island in the archipelago outside Göteborg. That was where he talked to Jan Johansson, not the Swedish jazz musician, but the last person to see Petra Holmgren alive – unless someone else killed her.

The conversation with Johansson takes up a lot of space in the report, and I find myself underlining the key points. He came to Asker only a few months before Petra went missing and got minor jobs with Holmgren's firm. He remembered the last one well – they were building a chapel by some church. It was through working for Holmgren that he met Petra. Nice girl, according to Johansson, but he occasionally doubted whether she really cared for him, and wondered whether she only went out with him because he had such a snazzy car. (I put a query in the margin: how angry might he have been because of that?)

On the fatal day, he had decided that he couldn't bear to stay in Asker any longer and got into his car to leave.

He picked up Petra outside her house, drove her to the old Østfanestasjon, was given a hug and never saw her again. He bumped into a mate of his, had a good look round town, then went to Trondheim to stay with a friend. He didn't give another thought to Petra until one day the police raided his friend's house and caught them making hooch. He was sentenced to a few months inside for illegal brewing and after that he'd had enough of good old Norway.

Dad noted that Johansson's account of picking up Petra agreed with the statement made by a seven-year-old neighbour, who saw his car stop outside the Holmgrens' house and Petra getting into it. That information was provided by Leonard Holmgren. The girl was the young Siv Underland.

Did my father remember her name when she turned up at his office all those years later? Or did she have to mention Petra's name first, given his consumption of alcohol in the intervening period?

My father had typed Johansson's address and telephone number in brackets after his name. They're underlined – in ink that hasn't faded. Although I'm no expert, the underlining looks pretty recent to me.

No one answers when I dial the number, nor did I really expect anyone to.

Astrid phones a little later to remind me that we have tickets for a concert in Oslo cathedral that evening. I know what she's paid for them, so I have to go, albeit with reluctance.

It's one of our weepy favourites, Fauré's *Requiem*. Astrid thinks we ought to have an official weepy evening about once a month, but the tickets were bought before my father died, and I feel I've already done my fair share of weeping.

The cathedral is full, apart from the seat next to me.

"Is Benny going to be late?" Astrid asks.

"He's not coming."

I give her a brief explanation.

She looks disapproving. I know what she's thinking. Astrid has a standard answer when I'm a bit down about Benny and his boys: "Find yourself a lover."

I manage to get through the "Sanctus", but in the "Pie Jesu" I crack. *Dona eis requiem, sempiternam requiem*, "Grant them rest, eternal rest." Astrid's hand in mine is poor compensation for Benny's.

Back in Bernt Ankersgate either Lina or her partner must be intent on renewing their relationship; they save me from drowning in mawkishness by playing nothing but hip-hop.

IO

THERE ARE DAYS when the centre of Oslo seems steeped in filth. Dirty brown slush spurts up from car wheels, bin-bags overflow with disgusting, rotting food; trembling glue-sniffers in their usual places beg with absurd modesty for "two kroner", old women with wild eyes yell at passers-by, threatening gangs of young Moroccans roam the streets. The rest of the population is either drunk or dreaming of having enough money to get plastered.

They are hate-days, racist-days, when I learn more about what makes us tick than any study of sociology or psychology can teach me; days when I can sense the sour pensioner I may become, the bitterness of being unemployed; days that nourish the murderer within.

Fortunately, they don't occur very often, for usually I can't imagine living anywhere but here, in the rather seedy part of Olso dubbed Little Pakistan or Little New York or Homo Fields, in honour of the marvellous mixture of people who live here.

I dislike those days, but I benefit from them.

It's one of those days when I go in search of Tone Indrelid.

According to the telephone book she lives in Sagene, in Bjølsen-veien. But her name isn't on the entry phone, where the original cards have long been replaced by scrappy pieces of paper in varying states of disintegration.

Only one of the apartments answers when I buzz – an anxious-sounding woman who doesn't know of a Tone Indrelid. She doesn't let me in.

Just as I'm leaving, a weedy little guy comes up pushing his bike and pulls out a key-ring.

"You going in?" he says in a friendly voice.

"No, yes . . . I'm looking for a woman called Tone Indrelid. But she doesn't seem to live here."

"They've moved," says the weed and opens the door.

"Do you know where?"

"No. Downtown somewhere. But Rolf works on a site in Maridalsveien, I think. On an enterprise scheme, for the council. He did, anyhow. He's her lover." He laughs quietly. "They messed around and drank a lot, you see. The old girls around here didn't like it."

"Can you remember his surname?"

"Now, what was it? It just said Tone and Rolf on their door. I'm afraid I can't remember."

Before I go, I have to ask him one more thing.

"Isn't it a bit early in the year to be cycling?"

"I always bike. Got studded tyres."

That's all it takes to make me forget that half an hour ago I thought Oslo was the pits.

Maridalsveien is too long for me to cruise up and down looking for a building being restored, so I phone the council and am passed from office to office until someone eventually tells me that it's number 74b.

"Do you know if someone called Rolf works there?"

She laughs.

"No idea."

Number 74b does indeed look in need of restoration. Downstairs a plump young mother with small children directs me to the top floor.

There are four guys up there, aged between twenty and forty, busy insulating the roof. None of them is called Rolf.

"He's off sick today," says the forty-year-old, making the most of the opportunity to have a fag.

"Have you got his telephone number?"

"No. But they're sure to have it in the office."

I lend him a pen and a piece of paper and he writes down the number.

"Ask for Øystein."

Øystein is out. By the time he rings back, I've almost lost interest in tracking down Rolf.

"Tell him things'll be fucking bad for him if he doesn't turn up tomorrow," he says.

80

I reckon Øystein can do that himself, but I thank him nicely for his help.

I let the number ring for a while, and then, to be sure, I dial again. I know from experience that I'm bad at numbers, telephone numbers included.

This time a man's voice grunts.

"Is that Tone Indrelid?" I say, rather foolishly.

"Not in."

"Do you know where I can get hold of her? At work, or somewhere?"

The grunts must be drunken laughter of sorts.

"At work, did you say? That's good. Christ knows where she is, but you could always try Schou's."

The laughter turns into a hacking cough before he rings off.

The pub reeks of stale beer, and the haze of thick blue smoke is keeping the early morning light at bay. A few of the city's less fortunate souls have gathered here, perhaps to escape the cold outside.

The woman behind the bar points Tone out to me. As I make my way over to her table, I realize that the soft drink I'm clutching may be seen as a reproof by the other customers, and it's commented on by the little group of shabby guys who, had they ever had a job, would be approaching pensionable age.

Tone's not alone at the table, but her companion, a chap of about forty staring fixedly at his half-empty glass, is well out of it – getting the glass to his mouth is more than enough for him.

"Is it all right if I sit here?" I say.

"Can't stop you, can I?"

She's younger than me, but she looks older. If it weren't for the puffy complexion, the burst blood-vessels on her cheeks, the failed attempt to hide the decay with make-up, her face would be beautiful. The bright turquoise sweater must once have suited her, before her body had swelled to make room for all the pints of beer. Her eyes are glazed with alcohol, but she's not drunk. Not yet.

"I'm interested in a girl you once knew," I say.

81

"Jesus, interested in a girl! Sorry, I think you've come to the wrong place. I don't know no lesbians."

Her laughter is as coarse as the guy's on the telephone. So they have more in common than just alcohol.

"Siv Underland. You knew her, didn't you?"

"You a cop, or what?"

Angry eyes, no more laughter in her voice.

"No. I just got to know her before she died, and I'd like to find out more about her – talk to someone who really knew her."

The lie comes easily, as if the soft drink in my hand gives me some kind of advantage I allow myself to exploit. To punish me, it tastes flat and unpleasant, but I resist the urge to join them in a morning beer.

"Christ, I was really sorry to hear that she'd killed herself. I don't have much to do with people out in Asker any more, but someone phoned me. I did think of sitting down with some old diaries and scrapbooks and so on – live well, roses are red, and all that – but I couldn't bring myself to. How did you find out I knew her?"

"Her mother mentioned that you were friends."

"Her mother. That bitch. Panicked when Siv stopped being the girl of her dreams. God, we had some fun, but it was a long time ago – or it seems it, anyhow."

Like all alcoholics, she has the ability to change mood in a second. She leans across the table and we're best buddies now.

"What about a beer, eh?"

Why not? The boys at the pensioners' table mumble their approval as I walk past.

"We were at school together. You know, terrible twins, two peas in a pod, all the way – she was two years younger than me, but there weren't that many kids on our road. We stuck together after she moved, too. Though I never felt at home at her parents' place. Intellectual snobs, they were. Piled a whole lot on to Siv – the done thing, what nice girls are supposed to do – music, gym. Awful for her, because she was so nervous. And when she at last came out of her shell a bit and wanted to join in, live it up a bit, then all hell broke loose."

"Why do you think she was so nervous?"

"Hardly surprising with parents like that. They have to have

82

perfect kids, don't they? Successful kids. Kids they can tell their friends about."

I didn't grow up in Vinderen, one of the smartest parts of Oslo, for nothing. I know what she means: the syndrome where the children have every moment of free time channelled into meaningful activities. And I've come across both mothers and daughters so screwed up by that syndrome that they sat, rigid with anxiety, at the counselling sessions at Ullevål hospital.

"I suppose I didn't really fit in ... not the right sort, am I? I didn't understand it at the time, when we were young, but I realized they didn't like me, hated Siv and me being friends. We never spent time at her place, always at mine. Siv really liked it. At our house she could eat bread and butter with sugar on it." She laughs. "That was because it was bloody cheap, of course, but we weren't aware of that. Once she sneaked over to see us, one day when she'd been off school because she was sick. That was about the bravest thing she'd ever done. Then she started trying stuff out – you know, drink and all that. Who doesn't when they're fifteen? But her mother got quite hysterical. As if the world had come to an end because her daughter came home plastered on a Saturday night. She gave us hell. And then suddenly it all stopped. Siv disappeared from the scene, retreated, turned so cold and negative, I gave up phoning her."

"When was this?"

"I must have been nineteen, I guess. I'd just met Rolf. He was taking up most of my time, so it was a while before I noticed she was saying no to absolutely everything."

Siv would have been seventeen. She didn't get to know Yngve until she was twenty-one, so there were a few lonely years in between – the years when her mother applied to all those courses and jobs for her.

Tone concentrates on her glass for a while.

"Does the name Leonard Holmgren mean anything to you?" I ask.

"That dirty old bastard. What about him?"

"Why such a bastard?"

"Maybe I should feel sorry for him, his daughter running away and all that, but if she knew what her father did to girls, then perhaps it wasn't so strange."

The sound of cars in the street reaches us through the window and I can feel the muscles tightening in my jaw. Tone Indrelid can't be someone who reads the tabloids very often, something I normally prize quite highly. A few moments go by before I speak again.

"How do you know that?"

"Just what I heard. Someone once sprayed 'kerb-crawler' on his car, you know. Probably someone who'd seen him picking up a prostitute. Funny, isn't it?"

"Was it Siv?"

"No, that I can't believe. Why should it be her? Holmgren gambles a lot, too. Rolf has seen him at the races. He almost went right down the drain. Kept losing."

I take note.

"So you and Siv lost contact completely?"

"Yeah. I didn't see her for ages. Isn't it odd? We lived quite near each other, but we never met. Not until last autumn."

"You met her in the autumn?"

"Yes. She came in here, just like you. Suddenly wanted to talk. She seemed a bit weird, as if she'd seen the light, become a born-again Christian or something . . . I was rather irritated by her, but it was OK seeing her again. She asked lots of questions, about how things were for Rolf and me and so on. At the time things were pretty rough, so I probably moaned a bit – I'd just had an abortion . . . And she gave me that card."

"A card?"

"Yes, of a woman she went to. A healer. Some alternative stuff. She said this woman was fantastic and had helped her a whole lot, and she wanted me to go to her, too. But nothing came of it. Can't have helped Siv all that much, either, since she's gone and shot herself."

"Do you remember what the woman was called?"

"No, but I think I still have the card somewhere. Wait a mo."

The flimsy yellowish card is somewhat crumpled after being in Tone's purse, but the wording is still perfectly legible: "The Rainbow. Siri Ekelund, Therapist."

Her childhood friend may not have wanted to, but I'm going to follow Siv to the Rainbow.

* * *

Tom phones me from the Café Sara and wants company. He's in town buying LPs, and my heart softens at the thought; Tom is a CD-objector. He accepts my offer of an Irish coffee, the speciality of the house, when I arrive, although he has to go to work in an hour or two's time.

"Of course it has to be vinyl," he says, smiling with satisfaction at his coffee. "Did you find Yngve?"

"God, yes. Very odd meeting."

Tom roars with laughter when I tell him about my break-in.

"Yngve doesn't believe she killed herself."

"Doesn't he? What does he think?"

"I'm not quite sure. But it's a bit odd that she should steal Holmgren's gun three months ago, and then suddenly decide to use it, having got hold of a silencer and bullets for it herself, according to Hansson. Did you know they'd been lovers – Yngve and Siv?"

"No. Somehow I've never imagined him having a normal sex life. Not a very pleasant thought. He doesn't seem exactly affectionate."

"Her mother doesn't like to think about it, either. It looks as if Siv didn't have an easy relationship with her parents."

"Sure. That much was obvious from the petition in the newspaper. You know Siv got deeply involved in the controversy about the development of Dikemark? Not what people expected of her, I guess. Especially not her father."

He notices I'm looking blank, so he updates me a bit.

"You know Dikemark's being shut down? There are only about half the patients left, compared to when I started working there. Once it's closed, the buildings and the site will be up for grabs. A bunch of developers were planning to turn it into a conference centre with offices for big firms and so on. If you ask me, it's too far away from the centre of Oslo for that, but you never know. Energy Valley is coming our way."

Energy Valley is the local name for the E18 out of Oslo, which goes past Fornebu Airport. It's a parody of America's Silicon Valley, because a lot of successful, hi-tech businesses have built their head-quarters there in recent years.

"What did Siv have to do with that?"

"Nothing, really. Except that she lived in Asker, and I don't suppose she wanted more of it bought up by that kind of firm. And that was a bit difficult for her darling daddy."

"Why?"

"As medical director of Dikemark, he has a say in the future of the hospital, and supported the development plans. If you're interested, you should talk to Vilde – she knows all about it."

Tom has to go.

"Do you have any idea where a girl like Siv might obtain a silencer?" I ask him. "I wouldn't have a clue about how to get hold of such a thing."

"I know someone who might," he says.

I stay in the café for a while, making patterns in the ashtray with the tip of my cigarette.

I try to think of at least five alternatives, none of them any good, before I resort to dialling Karsten's number.

He sounds as jubilant as if he'd won the lottery when he hears my voice. I know he'll want something in return when he promises to try to find out what he can. He doesn't know Caspari by name, but he has always given me the impression that he knows everything worth knowing in the world of finance.

"Then you can come to dinner tomorrow to hear the result. That'll please your mother no end."

So that's the trade-off.

I spend the evening with two fried eggs, missing Benny.

I can't get to sleep on Father's sofa, even though not a sound comes from the floor above. Perhaps they're dead, too.

I would probably be more comfortable in his bed in the tiny bedroom, but I still can't bring myself to sleep in there – and it's not because of the smell of frying from the restaurant next door.

I lie awake in the dark thinking about butterflies.

A butterfly flutters its wings somewhere and starts up an irreversible and unpredictable process. Something is changed for ever.

Its every movement is the result of a huge number of tiny parts working together. All relatively complicated processes consist of single events that influence each other. In mathematics, models of such processes, in which the parts are interdependent, are called non-linear equations. They have no exact solution, but many possible solutions. Mathematicians used to solve them by finding a similar equation that had already been solved and modifying the answer to come up with the most likely solution. They assumed that the difference between the most likely solution and the exact solution must be minimal.

In reality it's enormous, because non-linear equations are models of dynamic systems – of processes in which the question, the problem, is changed by the answer; and so the tiny gap between the mathematician's probable answer and the real answer is amplified as the system develops.

In meteorology this phenomenon is called the butterfly effect.

To be able to forecast the weather with absolute accuracy is part of the dream of explaining the present, and foreseeing the future, through an understanding of the past.

It's an impossibility. Not just because of the sheer quantity of information you would need, but because of those damned non-linear equations – or rather the processes of which they are models: dynamic systems, systems in movement.

The weather is that kind of complex system, consisting of an infinity of minor and major influences: wind; currents; high and low pressure; the rotation of the earth; the topography of the landmass; the temperature of the seas. The flight of a butterfly.

The movement of its wings will influence its surroundings, and potentially lead to a chain of events of enormous proportions.

The little butterfly soaring up from a leaf may, some time in the future, on another continent, create a storm.

Sometimes it's enough to flutter your wings to set off a chain of events whose outcome is equally irreversible, equally unpredictable. Like the butterfly, we are ignorant of what we are doing.

II

THE SNOWPLOUGH HAS done such a poor job on the back-streets of Vinderen that I'm not sure if it's been there at all. The deep tracks made by cars in the snow have frozen and become sheets of rough ice, making parallel parking a nightmare.

Fortunately for the inhabitants of Charlotte Andersensvei, they don't have to leave their cars on the street: they all have garages.

One of the things I loathe Karsten for is that he has one of the most hideous garage doors in Oslo. It's of solid varnished oak and has more panels embossed with copper nails than the most elaborate church door. I try to avert my eyes as I walk up to the house – one glance is enough to ruin my mood. And I've decided to be a good girl tonight.

Karsten serves the ladies cocktails, but fortunately doesn't insist we drink them in the bar in the basement. Instead we sit uncomfortably on the hard Chesterfield chairs in the room I know he thinks of as the library – even though I have never seen him with a book in his hand. I spent several years of my life in this house but no part of my soul has been left behind here.

Mother is looking attractive in her burgundy wool suit. I'm aware that she is busy negotiating a minefield: if she loses her concentration even for a moment, the conversation may suddenly slip into danger-ous areas. So she tells me, at length, and with the right touch of humour, how she came to buy the suit, the new pewter decorative plates and the huge painting by the fireplace.

She knows I think that in Karsten's company she makes herself seem more stupid than she is, and that makes her nervous. My only way of indicating I have no intention of being obnoxious is to listen attentively and with a semblance of enthusiasm.

If she's still taking the tablets I once discovered in her cupboard, she's certainly popped one today.

That was the only occasion I've hurled something at a wall and felt sweet joy as it smashed. And the naked despair in her eyes brought us closer than we've ever been. I stood watching her sweep up the broken glass, then, instead of giving her a hug, I left. We've never mentioned it since, either of us.

She serves us fresh asparagus with crème fraîche, then monkfish with oyster mushrooms in white wine sauce. It tastes marvellous and empty.

Karsten still seems to think it tremendously amusing that I don't eat meat. As he jokes about it, I see Mother's knuckles whitening on her fish knife. I once ruined a Sunday dinner by describing in detail the rearing of chickens, the tapeworms you can catch from pork and industrial slaughtering methods. But that was back in the days when I considered furs a provocation.

They've been to the theatre. They've been to Rome. They've been to exhibitions and have had visitors. They've even arranged a funeral, but we don't talk about that.

Mother rests for half an hour while I clear up. Karsten comes out into the kitchen with a glass of cognac, the correct accompaniment, I presume, to a business conversation. He's unbuttoned his waistcoat.

"A funny little company you're interested in."

"Really?"

A "little company" can mean anything from a giant corporation downwards. Karsten only deals with the big boys.

"Yes. Caspari built up a property empire of cheap, rented accommodation – there have been worse examples of Rachmanism, but he's bought up a lot of blocks of flats and turned them into bed and breakfasts for the homeless and asylum-seekers. It's much more profitable than having ordinary tenants, obviously. The council pays well, and there's no danger of tenants defaulting on the rent, and so on. He buys up council flats, too – he's made that a speciality."

He takes a sip of his cognac and leans against the sink unit. I know that posture. Now he's going to explain the realities of life to young Igi.

"The state demands that the council acquire some liquidity, you see, to balance the budget better. And selling council property is about the only way the local authority can do it."

"So Caspari turns flats into b. & b.s, then rents them back to the council?"

"Exactly. And the rent is paid by the state. After all, the council has to put all those layabouts somewhere, and it can't keep pace with the increasing demand."

I've promised myself I'm going to behave tonight, but he's not exactly making it easy for me.

"But it sounds horribly uneconomic. Not for Caspari, but . . ."

"It isn't for the council, either, really. Private enterprise can run those places much more cheaply than the council can."

"Because they provide a poorer service."

"Because the employment conditions are different. The main thing is that the council gets money to pay their debts. And saves money for the taxpayers."

"So everyone's happy. Caspari, too, one hopes. Not to mention all those layabouts."

We're heading for the kind of argument Karsten and I have had a thousand times before. They give Mother a longing for her pills, and red patches on her face from anxiety, so I stick to my promise and close the conversation in typical style here in Charlotte Andersensvei − by taking a big gulp of cognac.

The *Asker og Bærum Budstikka* is a strange hybrid − a mixture of a provincial paper interested in the most trivial local events, and a serious newspaper with ambitions and responsibilities like the quality press. It succeeds in pleasing both advertisers and readers; for a local paper it has one of the largest circulations in the country, and the income level of the readership makes it an attractive place to advertise.

The newspaper office is in the middle of nowhere, past the turning to IKEA. Vilde is waiting for me in the glassed-in canteen on the ground floor. In the offices surrounding the atrium in the middle of the building I sense the relaxed but intense atmosphere of hard work which makes me miss teamwork.

I am formulating a theory of mine, but it's not definitive yet, so I don't want to expose it to Vilde's journalist's eyes, and am therefore rather vague with her. As Siv Underland is the only thing we have in common, that's where I begin.

90

"Criminal cases are not really my line," says Vilde. "And when it comes to Siv Underland . . ."

". . . it's not even certain that it's a criminal matter," I say. Maybe I'm paranoid, but I still think there's a trace of contempt in her eyes. Perhaps it's not directed at me. She may just be worn out; maybe Christian Magnus has measles or spotted typhus or some other kindergarten lurgy.

"It's not her death I've come about," I say. "Tom mentioned that Siv had an article published by your paper. I wondered what it was about."

She tosses her head and her eyes are a fraction more friendly when she looks at me again.

"Oh, that. It was probably only to do with falling out with her family. It's crazy," she adds wryly, "but as soon as you have children, you start worrying about what they are going to criticize you for when they're teenagers – whether you were too strict or too easygoing or . . . But Siv Underland only put her name to a letter. It was about Dikemark, so it probably annoyed her father."

"What did it say?"

"Well, it's quite a while ago, but if you're really interested . . ."

"I am," I assure her. "But am I disturbing you?"

Now we've both been equally polite – the politeness of people who aren't sure whether they like each other.

"I've got about fifteen minutes," she says. "Do you remember the scandal when the Reitgarten hospital was shut down?"

We're on the right track, so I nod, not too eagerly, I hope.

"That was when they discovered that the patients didn't get any better when they were kept in large, centralized psychiatric institutions," she says. "They stayed there too long and had no contact with their local environment."

"Yes – you get sicker inside than you do outside."

"Exactly." She allows me the interruption, so perhaps this is a subject she's interested in. "Dikemark was one of the really large hospitals at the time, with nine hundred patients, and about two thousand employees. Now there are no more than half that, and it's still being run down. And Dikemark is an Oslo hospital, even though it's sited here in Asker, so the patients who are discharged are transferred to Oslo's health authorities – you may well wonder what kind of care they provide, but that's another matter. What's really interesting is that nothing's been decided about the future of the property."

"No?"

"On the one hand, Oslo city council owns it, but on the other, it is in Asker. The employees mostly live locally, and they don't necessarily move with the patients into the city. So a few years ago an inter-council committee was set up to work out what should happen to the site and all the buildings. A number of business people joined the committee, and that may be why the plans ended up having very little to do with psychiatry. They proposed a kind of grandiose industrial park, to bring in even more hi-tech firms, with a conference centre and so on. They argued that the area is close enough to attract interest from Drammen, too."

"But I thought you said there weren't any plans for what to do with the area?"

"There aren't any more, no," says Vilde. "You see, some of the committee members were tarnished by all those revelations about corruption in Oslo, both on the commercial side and on Oslo council. The whole Dikemark project was discredited and shelved. It was also a typical product of the 1980s boom, and it caused quite a stink. There was an outcry, people signed petitions – including Siv Underland."

"And Øyvind Underland?" I say.

"He was in with the businessmen with the grandiose plans. I'm sure he wasn't pleased to see his daughter's name on the list of signatures."

"And were there suspicions of corruption in connection with the plans?"

"No," says Vilde. "The project didn't last long enough to be investigated. The council became so cautious that the project was dropped. And now apparently no one has any ideas for the place. The buildings are being emptied of patients, departments are being moved into Oslo, and jobs are disappearing, but there's an almost palpable silence about the future of the site."

A guy with thinning hair comes over to our table. It's Vilde's photographer and she has to go. She's rather reluctant now, but I'm quite happy to be left on my own. I get myself another subsidized cup of coffee and consider what she's told me. It has fleshed out my little theory, but it's not yet fully formed.

Dikemark hospital would be like a dream come true for Ingve Caspari's father, the man who likes buying up council property. The site is presumably too large to house only those whom Karsten so charmingly refers to as layabouts, but with a little imagination Caspari ought to be able to put it to good use. Assuming he gets his claws into it.

The problem with my hypothesis is that it doesn't explain why Caspari should be interested in paying off gambling debts for Leonard Holmgren. Of course it's possible that is to do with something quite different, like Yngve Caspari being in the same class as Petra Holmgren and perhaps knowing her better than Caspari senior likes to think.

I can't very well ask Caspari about it. But I can use a method I learnt as part of my research: I can set out to disprove my hypothesis. And the best way to do that is to confirm that there is no connection between Caspari's payments to Holmgren and his possible interest in Dikemark hospital.

I ask if I can use the telephone at reception and I ring Tom. He's doing a shift at the hospital. He agrees to help me without much hesitation.

"OK," he says. "I'll give you today's quotes on the rumour exchange. But it'll cost you a dinner, at my place. I'll do the wine and you bring the food."

"You remind me of my stepfather."

"Oh, no. How come?"

"He also makes deals like that. Trading rumours for dinner. Go ahead with the gossip, and I'll decide whether it's worth more than a cup of instant soup."

He laughs.

"Holmgren's firm used to do masses of work here at the hospital – some years ago," he says in a conspiratorial whisper.

"But not now?"

"No, I don't think so. I don't pay attention to that kind of thing, but according to the gossip, there used to be vehicles with the Holmgren logo on them here, before all that fuss about corruption. A whole lot of things were tightened up then – contracts with suppliers and so on. Nothing fishy came to light, unlike elsewhere, but everyone became extremely cautious. And they say that a lot of new firms suddenly won contracts for equipment, repairs, and so on."

"And Holmgren was one that was squeezed out?"

"Yep."

He clears his throat.

"Igi, you know what it's like. A lot of rumours have started flying around since those two girls were found — things I've never heard about until now. People are saying Underland got that glasshouse of his built on the cheap."

"By whom?"

"You can guess that yourself. Holmgren, of course."

"Ah, so Holmgren is said to have built a house for Underland in exchange for getting the work at Dikemark, is that it?"

"That's what's implied."

"And it seems even more likely, given that Holmgren hasn't had any work there since everyone became so cautious."

"That's right. Well, what's it to be? Packet soup, or what?"

If I had an expense account I'd offer to take Tom to a posh restaurant, but I don't say so. I'm no great cook and have no desire to raise his expectations.

Something is still niggling me. I'd like to know whether Øyvind Underland knows Caspari senior, and, if so, what he thinks of the reuse of council property he's involved in. As I dial the number of his office, I wonder whether Siv ever asked him the same question.

12

HE DOESN'T WANT to talk to me. I phone four or five times and am given the same answer – that he is in a meeting. My calls are not returned, so I decide to beard him in his den.

I give him time to have his dinner, then swing the car into Otto Blehrsvei. The great house with its odd angles and broken gables again reminds me of a grotesque greenhouse that has been taken apart and reassembled all wrong.

Underland is just getting into his Pontiac. Instead of sounding the horn or winding down the window and calling out to him, I drive past the house and turn into the next side road.

He sets off in the direction I've come from and I follow at what I consider a discreet distance.

The evening rush hour on the E18 has abated, but the lanes of traffic snake along in unbroken streams heading for the city, entwined in a slow, sensuous dance with the serpent coming in the opposite direction.

The gunmetal-grey Pontiac is up ahead. It's a TransSport, the latest streamlined model, an upmarket version of the more popular Space Wagon – my favourite name for a car, which encapsulates a whole range of boyhood dreams. Psychiatrist Underland is riding towards the city in an expensive toy which is both prairie wagon and spaceship. I try to come up with similar dream combinations for girls, but draw a blank.

My car radio is still stuck; to pass the time, I count the number of times the inane young presenters say "brill". Perhaps there's a pattern in it?

Underland parks in the multistorey below the concert hall and I give him plenty of time before leaving Gorbie on the floor below.

I spot his camel-coloured coat as I come out. At the Klingenberg cinema, I'm only fifty yards behind him; he turns the corner into

Stortingsgata and I follow him on the other side of the street. Then I cross over and greet him as he stands waiting for the green light.

He's not pleased to see me, but he can't hide behind his secretary this time.

"Oh, it's you?" he says, shamefacedly, as if we shared an unpleasant secret.

"I tried to phone you several times," I say.

"Yes, I know. I've been frightfully busy, I'm afraid. And I've also had other things to . . . think about."

"Of course. That's understandable . . ." I don't want to let him get away with making me feel guilty, so I press on: "There was something I wanted to ask you."

"About your thesis? Unfortunately I can't remember what it's about . . . Can I phone you tomorrow? Or next week? I'm due at a meeting right now, and haven't much time, so . . ."

He attempts a faint smile.

"It's not about my thesis. It's about Leonard Holmgren."

That wipes all trace of the smile off his face.

"What about him?"

"I wanted to know a bit more about his firm. And what you think of it."

He doesn't remind me of a wrestler now. His body shrinks inside the expensive coat – it's no longer an impervious suit of armour.

"I can't stand here in the street and . . ."

He glances at his watch, but I know he's just giving himself a moment to think.

"Maybe we could pop in somewhere?" I suggest. "Just for a minute or so?"

He nods.

"A few minutes should be all right."

I can see he's steeling himself again as he walks ahead of me into Peppe's Pizza, stiffening his neck, straightening his shoulders, lowering his visor.

It's the nearest place, but it's not ideal. The subdued lighting supposed to give it a rustic atmosphere embarrasses both of us, as if we'd chosen to meet here to avoid being recognized.

"Basically I don't know Holmgren all that well," he says. "We were neighbours. That was all."

He tugs at his shirt collar with one hand, as men who keep themselves fit like to do when they want to show their neck muscles are too big for the collar.

"But you know that Yngve Caspari lives on his property?"

"Yes, but so what?"

"And that Holmgren had major financial problems at one time?"

"I know nothing about that."

"No? He gambled on the horses, and lost. Anyhow, he's managed to pay his debts somehow or other."

"Now, listen. I haven't time to sit here talking about things that have nothing to do with me. I . . ."

"Just a moment. There's some indication that Yngve Caspari's father paid those gambling debts for Holmgren."

"Is that so?"

"Do you know him, Caspari senior?"

"I've heard the name, I think."

"Caspari has rather special kinds of business interests. He buys up council property and rents it back to the council. Which makes me wonder why he should be willing to pay Holmgren's debts."

"I have no idea!"

"No? You are in an influential position at Dikemark – a place I imagine Caspari would be very keen to get his hands on."

"I don't understand what you're getting at. I can't see any connection, even if this . . . Caspari had plans in that direction, which I doubt."

"That's exactly my problem, too. I can't see any connection between Caspari's business and his helping Holmgren out of a fix. Unless . . ."

"Unless what?"

"Unless there's a link between Holmgren and Dikemark hospital. He did a lot of work there at one time, didn't he?"

"Maybe he did. He runs a big local firm."

"But then it suddenly came to an end."

"We have standard tendering procedures, like everyone else."

"I've heard that those procedures were tightened up considerably a few years ago."

"All public bodies are expected to be more cost-effective. That's not exactly a secret."

"So Holmgren became too expensive?"

"I've no idea. Nor does it interest me in the slightest."

"What did you pay him to build that house for you?"

The visor snaps shut almost audibly. From behind the iron mask, two steely eyes stare at me, filled with hatred.

"I don't think this is particularly clever of you. I wouldn't take it a step further, if I were you."

"What do you mean by that?"

"Just what I say. I'm no fool. I can hear what you're implying. They're wild guesses and fantasies. Unhealthy fantasies. And I order you to drop them. At once."

"Is that what you said to Siv, too?"

He leans across the table. The candle lights up two small red flames inside those iron-needle pupils of his.

"Siv has nothing to do with this. Do you hear? Nothing."

"She was involved enough to sign a petition in the paper about it, wasn't she?"

"She was . . . mentally disturbed. Isn't that enough, for Christ's sake?"

He gets up abruptly and shoves aside the waiter, who has only just appeared.

I don't know if I've made much of a dent in his armour. But "mentally disturbed" should never be enough for a psychiatrist.

We hadn't got as far as ordering anything so I dismiss the waiter rather more politely and follow Underland outside.

He's nowhere to be seen, but I run up to the corner and just catch sight of his camel-hair coat disappearing through heavy doors. I can't follow him: women are not allowed into the Freemasons' lodge.

The next day I keep my promise to follow Siv to the Rainbow.

Siri Ekelund's telephone number is printed on the card. The voice that answers is calmer and deeper than any woman's voice I've heard before. She deliberates for some time before agreeing to offer me an hour's consultation, reluctantly squeezing me in between two clients.

"I really need the time to prepare myself," she says. "But as you're an acquaintance of Siv's, I'll make an exception."

On the way up to see her I wonder whether I should disabuse her of her little misunderstanding. It turns out I have no choice – it's not simple to lie to Siri Ekelund.

A small woman dressed entirely in purple, right down to her thick woollen socks, sits in the lotus position on the sofa, and she makes it look comfortable, natural, as if we were designed to sit like that, instead of finding it so unpleasant to keep our backs straight.

I don't feel I can imitate her, but I feel stiff and limited sitting cross-legged. To my annoyance, I find I've also folded my arms across my stomach, and hastily undo them. She has made it very clear that her time is money – three hundred kroner an hour, to be precise, which I have to fork out to be allowed to talk to her – but she's not going to read my body language quite that easily.

She's gazing at me in a way that makes me feel anxious and want to cry. For Siv, perhaps – or for myself. That friendly therapist's gaze reminds me of Astrid, even though she never brought me so close to tears.

The attic room is bare: a sofa, a work table, white walls, blinds of white rice-paper that filter the bright sunlight and give the air an ash-grey hue. The only homely touch is a series of objects on small tables and shelves: stones, images, figurines, icons. And candles. There is a strong smell of incense.

Surroundings for a modern witch perhaps, or a good fairy. Her eyes are sharp enough for the former, her voice gentle enough for the latter. Healer, she calls herself, and what's left of my education at the Department of Psychology makes me ready to apply the brakes.

Then she fixes me with those clear eyes of hers. Her voice is exquisitely calm and could be irritating, mannered, if it weren't for its vibrant undertone of intensity.

"What do you want of me?"

"Siv Underland was a client of yours, wasn't she?"

"Was?"

The question in her eyes is naïve, almost childlike. She doesn't know Siv is dead.

"Don't you read the papers?"

"Not if I can avoid it."

"She died about ten days ago."

The woman in front of me bows her head and takes several deep breaths. The sound of her breathing is like long gentle waves breaking on a flat beach.

"The police think she committed suicide."

Her face is paler when she raises her head and two great shining tears roll down her cheeks. She gets up and puts one of the candles on the low table between us. She says nothing. They are the first tears I've seen shed for Siv Underland.

"I found she was missing. So I'd like to know a little more about her, who she was."

"You must realize I'm under an oath of confidentiality."

"Yes, of course. But it so happens that I . . . I've had a bit to do with therapy myself."

"What kind of therapy?"

"I'm a qualified psychologist."

No reaction. If her brakes function as quickly as mine, she shows no sign of it.

"I know that every therapist, regardless of their field, suffers when something like this happens."

Suffering is a word I tend to avoid. It usually becomes empty in my mouth, large and unmanageable, and it surprises me that it sounds so natural here, just as "pain" would . . . and "love" – such words are so often homeless.

"And, unlike the police, I'm not convinced that she took her own life. You're perhaps the person who knows most about her state of mind, her feelings."

A meditative hum emerges from her lips. She looks at me with that disquieting gaze again.

"Siv was going through a tough process, of course. Therapy is always tough."

This time we both say nothing for a moment. I don't want to interrupt her. She has perhaps given me a kind of opening, but it doesn't feel like a victory, the result of playing my cards right. I don't think Siri Ekelund is influenced in that way. Something in those clear eyes implies that she has seen a need in me, and has made it visible to me. Other people's eyes are the mirror of the soul.

"She worked hard. And she was brave."

Again she hesitates for a moment.

"You see, we worked in rather a different way from what you may be used to. I'm not that keen on talking. We're so clever with words, most of us. And so clever at interpreting. I don't think we get very far with words. Talking makes it easy to run away from emotions. And they are what's important."

"So you work with . . ."

"Images. Fairy tales, maybe. Sounds, movements. My clients also keep a diary at home."

"Did Siv, too?"

"Yes, they all do. It's useful in many ways. It describes a development."

She looks slightly uncomfortable and changes position.

"This doesn't feel quite right."

"Talking about her?"

"Talking. We are distancing ourselves from her, aren't we, if we turn this into a discussion of methods. Siv is dead. I had a relationship with her when she was alive. You clearly have one now."

She gets up abruptly, goes into a side room and comes back with a file.

"My case notes on her. I write down a little occasionally, and keep the images she creates. Created."

So we sit side by side and leaf through a report on Siv Underland's soul. The notes on the sheets of paper do not tell me much, sometimes there's only a word, occasionally a short poem, one longer story. It is the drawings that make a deep impression – Siv has rubbed the crude, clashing colours into them with a hand that must have been clenched tight around the greasy crayons: black, red, orange; poisonous, poisonous yellow.

Some of the drawings are abstract, the paper covered with brutal lines crossing each other again and again, like a Jackson Pollock, except that Siv's use of colour is much more explosive. Some of the sheets are blank except for a single, striving shape – a violent red semicircle, or a strident turquoise diagonal.

But there are figurative pictures as well.

One depicts a girl in a white skirt with what must be flowers round it. But both the flowers and the girl are smeared with brown and black, cancelling out the idyllic motif beneath. Several of the pictures contain two figures: a little girl and a grown man. And one is of a man on his own. It has been coloured in so hard that the pen has left marks in the paper, as if she wanted to tear it, to obliterate this huge male figure. He's naked, but instead of a penis, his lower body is obliterated by a brutal blood-red.

While I'm looking at it, I have to take some deep breaths, and Siri Ekelund puts her hand on my stomach, having asked my permission first. I can certainly feel the dark, hard lump of grief and rage better under her dry, warm hand.

"Do you think she was the victim of incest?" I ask.

"What do you think?"

I have this painful, fierce gut reaction, but my head refuses to think; it is just full of the endless discussions we had about child abuse in the university canteen.

"Perhaps what we believe is not important," she says. "We're both capable of subjecting these pictures to a barrage of interpretation, aren't we?"

Indeed we are. Phallic force, vagina-like tunnels and brutal rage, soft, feminine forms cut and wounded – it is easy enough to identify it all.

"Perhaps you realize what can happen if we start imposing our interpretations here?"

Yes, I do. The ambiguity disappears: a line is a penis, a hole is a vagina, a figure is a portrait and every situation is a description of a concrete event. An emotion is a sentence.

"The pictures only work when they are allowed to be open. They say nothing when we put our stamp on them. That's a kind of murder, too. But if they're allowed to . . . just be, they can always surprise you. Sometimes very much so."

"Things aren't always what they seem."

"No. You know frogs are princes. And sometimes so are dragons."

"And where does this get us in Siv's case?"

"What do you think?"

I'm beginning to get fed up with her technique of bouncing my questions back at me, but I have to fall in with it. I've used it myself.

"Something happened at some time. Something bad. But she wasn't sure what?" I suggest.

"Something like that."

"Didn't you get any further than that?"

"I don't think it's always so important to know exactly, do you? This isn't research, it's about healing wounds. For some, it's important to know. Some ask about hypnosis, for instance."

"Did Siv?"

"She asked, but I'm very reluctant to do that. Not with her."

Of course not. Not if what might appear under hypnosis is too devastating.

"But she felt something was radically wrong in her upbringing, and she very much wanted to know what it was?"

"Yes."

"And you?"

"I had no reason to believe anyone but her. It was she who had lived that life. She knew best. You see, if I indulge in too many of my own thoughts and interpretations, then that is what I bring to the session, and there is a danger she may internalize my interpretation."

"But it concerned her sexually?"

"Yes. But we lock ourselves so quickly into that, at once thinking of sex. Energy is more important. The feeling of it."

"And what did she think about . . . whoever it might be who had that energy?"

"She mentioned men in the family, around her, of course. There are always so many possibilities. Fathers, grandfathers, uncles, brothers, neighbours, teachers . . ."

"Only men?"

"No, no. Not necessarily. But with Siv it was probably about a . . . a type of masculine power. Not that women can't have it."

My session was over. Siri Ekelund is decisive about time, like all therapists.

I notice the little madonna figure on the small table by the door as I put on my outdoor clothes. She is looking down, as if she deplored the evil in the world or was brooding on a secret. Not much masculine power there, but power of a different kind. I don't know whether I begrudge Siri Ekelund the ease with which she can surround herself with such figures.

13

OUTSIDE SIRI EKELUND'S room perfumed with incense, it is the hour of harsh winter twilight – light that is neither soft nor melancholy, as in spring. At the end of the street is a blue underworld sky, the horizon stained red by the dying sun. Wailing kids are being hauled home from kindergarten, the tail lights of cars in the traffic jam stretching down into town glow an angry red, and inside the trams people are staring straight ahead, their faces green in the unnatural light, as if under water, drowning on their way between work and the television.

It's an evil hour this, the midpoint betwixt and between, and I find it difficult to sustain the temple peace induced by my visit. There's something insistent in the way we move along pavements at this hour. No one thinks of giving way to anyone on the narrow strip between parked cars and posters warning us of possible snowfalls from roofs. If the way home were longer and the shopping bags more numerous, the small children wouldn't be the only ones shoving each other into the gutter.

There's no space for Siri Ekelund's careful distinctions here. Every-thing appears in lurid colour, in tabloid-style headlines, as in the evening papers we carry home. We are too exhausted to think in any other terms.

Siv Underland was an incest victim, the flashing traffic lights warn me. And so was Petra Holmgren, the exhaust pipes hiss suspiciously. Leonard Holmgren is a dirty old bastard, the trams screech on the corners.

And by the time I've got back to Bernt Ankersgate all that is left of Siri Ekelund's calm voice is that litany of male figures: *Fathers, grandfathers, uncles, brothers, neighbours, teachers.*

I look at Father's bedroom door, the one I am so careful to keep shut. Pull yourself together, I say to myself. But I'm pervaded by my distrust of the hour before the winter night falls, and I want someone, anyone, to give me a clear answer, to heed St James's words: "Let your yea be yea; and your nay, nay."

I try Samuel Hansson. I can hear short barks in the background as he picks up the phone. The nameless wife is still away.

"Do you think Siv was the victim of incest?" I ask.

"Igi, you must leave this to us."

"Her life points to that, doesn't it?"

"As far as I can make out, Siv Underland was involved in a lot of peculiar stuff. It doesn't alter the fact that, in all likelihood, she committed suicide. Indeed, the opposite may be true."

Quite. His logic is absolutely sound, and Igi is a silly fusspot.

"What about Jan Johansson? Not the jazz musician, but Petra's lover. Have you found him?"

"What do you know about him?"

"As good as nothing. I suppose you know a bit more."

"Igi, this isn't a game. You've nothing to . . ."

"I know. Have you found him?"

He sighs.

"It wasn't that difficult. He's inside for assault and rape. He's got a snowball's chance in hell with his wafer-thin alibi."

Jan Johansson need not suffer from feeling an insignificant nobody ever again. When you blow up a passport photograph, the result always looks like our collective idea of a criminal, and even if that isn't the tabloids' explicit intention, I don't suppose it does their sales any harm. He squints at me from the front page with deep-set, staring eyes, his cheeks sunken and unshaven. He's no longer an ordinary rapist, of no interest to anyone but the victim, and, possibly, his mother. Today Jan Johansson has become the main suspect and national villain.

His prospects don't look too good. One of the newspapers even mentions that he was out on parole the week Siv died. That information is not reported in the others; the Oslo police must be leaking like a sieve, but at least they are doing it selectively.

It's no longer Samuel Hansson's case. "Special Branch taking over" reads the headline above a photograph of three men carrying folders under their arms. I recognize one of them, Hans Ivar Søreid. He's the only person I ever heard my father talk about with bitterness.

On a grey morning like this, reading the tabloids always fills me with a sense of inertia. I let self-pity wash over me as I remember the only time my father took me into his confidence, to tell me about the big set-back in his career.

He was slightly drunk. We were celebrating my getting a place at university by going out for a meal. We were sitting opposite each other, rather awkwardly, in a restaurant I knew was too expensive for him: father and daughter on their own, without the safety net of being in familiar surroundings.

"So why did you leave the police?" I asked, abruptly and for no particular reason. At first his words were slow and hesitant, but then he spoke with a vehemence I had never seen before. My idealized father disappeared and in front of me sat a little man who had hoarded all his bitterness over the years.

If growing up means losing your illusions, I grew up then.

"We had him, you see. But we couldn't prove anything. We'd known for months it was him, known for sure. And then you get fed up – it's a kind of compulsion: you've damn well got to clear things up. It's not as if confrontation is an untried method – it's worked lots of times. So we confronted him. Told him we knew what he'd done. We didn't press him, just put it to him."

At this stage, he polished off his third brandy.

"Then the guy went and killed himself. I dare say it's happened before – I don't know. But of course we were called to account. The case was my responsibility. None of my colleagues reproached me. Not directly, not to my face. But they avoided me, as if I were contagious. I knew what it was all about. Hansson and I were due for promotion, but I realized that I'd ruined my chances – I reckoned they'd give him his due. But then that creep came . . ."

His voice broke, and he ordered another brandy he didn't need.

"That jerk Søreid. Far too young, far too inexperienced. But clean. And he was well in with the powers that be. And it was my fault that Samuel didn't . . . didn't get the chance. Because we'd always worked together. I stuck it for the months I had to. Then I left."

I try to escape the memory of how in the cab he went on mumbling about Freemasons. He was swaying on the pavement as the cab drove off.

I light a Prince Mild and decide to go and see Samuel all the same. At his office they say he's taken some leave, so I go on up to his house in Rykkinn.

He's in the middle of a solitary, early dinner when I get there and he looks unashamedly relieved when I politely refuse the fish pie full of bones and additives. Lola has finished her helping and is sitting expectantly by his chair.

The pie in its tinfoil container and a bottle of beer are on the table in front of him.

"I don't go to much trouble when she's not at home," he says, looking like a kid who's been caught taking money from his mother's purse.

The tell-tale signs that his wife is away are easy to spot. Samuel's guilty face makes it clear that she's the one who puts photographs of children and grandchildren on little crocheted mats on every available surface and so would probably not tolerate either his jacket hanging on the back of a chair in the living room or the heap of newspapers on the sofa. Not to mention a towel drying over the top of the bathroom door.

I feel like telling him I won't give the game away, but he removes both the jacket and the towel, then stops, at a loss, by the heap of newspapers.

"Your food's getting cold," I say, and he settles for straightening the heap instead of moving it. I recognize the manoeuvre. I also think a squared-up heap looks almost tidy.

"Well," I say, "how does it feel having the case taken away and given to Søreid?"

It hurts, I hope. Søreid was brought in over Samuel's head before, even though I know Samuel may think it was my father's fault. So I go on.

"That was the worst thing for my father, you see – feeling that he wrecked your chances."

"Really? Is that what Andreas felt? We never talked about it afterwards. Anyway, it's not clear that he wrecked all that much. I mean, Søreid had . . . the gift of the gab, didn't he? He was up-and-coming . . . It wasn't my decision, you know, to bring in Special Branch. But it's fairly routine."

"So that isn't why you're taking leave?"

"How do you know that?"

"I rang your office, of course."

He concentrates on the food for a moment, and finishes it off in a few minutes. How sad it is to eat alone, always rushing to get it over and done with. Lola is allowed to lick the tinfoil.

"Coffee?" he says.

I nod.

"Given that it's no longer your case," I say, "does it bother you that I'm still interested? Think of it in terms of a daughter's curiosity. After all, it may well have been the last case he was dealing with."

I know I'm resorting to blackmail. Samuel probably feels that, too – and is reluctant to go along with it. So he stands by the kitchen cupboards with his back to me, gaining time to think by hunting out coffee and cups.

"Can we try out the reasoning behind the suspicions against Johansson?"

He raises his shoulders. Very busy with the coffee. I can almost hear his mind whirring. He's still not sure whether this is unethical.

"If you like," he finally says with a sigh.

He doesn't sound exactly enthusiastic, but I pretend I'm deaf to such subtleties.

"OK," I say quickly. "Let's suppose that Johansson did it. He was Petra's lover. He wanted to get out of Asker that day, and according to Siv Underland's statement she saw Petra get into his car at three o'clock. After they'd left, a note Petra had written was found in her parents' mail box. If Petra put it there, it's probable that they'd planned to go off together. But the words in the note were rather vague: 'I can't stand it any longer. Don't try to contact me.' That sounds more like a farewell note to a lover than to parents. So she may have written it to Johansson, and he put it in the mail box, presumably after he'd killed her, to make her parents think she'd run away. That would have been quite enterprising of him, and rather brave."

Samuel brings the coffee and a tin of custard-creams. After I've tasted the coffee, which is far too strong, I ask if I can have a little milk. Samuel looks rather worried. His wife probably makes it just right. I suppress a grimace and go on.

"He had a good opportunity to get rid of the body in the chapel. He was building that wall and the guy who came to work the next morning couldn't know how much Johansson had concreted the day before. But he couldn't have risked doing it immediately after killing her. He must have waited until nightfall. After he'd been to town with his mate. When did he get there, by the way?"

"About half past four," says Samuel, deciding to have milk in his coffee too. "They had a drink or two at home before going into town. Johansson spent the night at the friend's flat, then left the next morning. Went to some friends in Trøndelag. He was arrested there for moonshining in November, and questioned about Petra's disappearance. He said he'd driven her to Østfanestasjon and never saw her again."

"Then he must have gone to Copenhagen and sent that photograph before he was arrested – the one Holmgren forgot to keep the envelope of," I say. "That was also rather cunning, don't you think?"

Lola has jumped up on to Samuel's lap and is licking his great hands with her pink tongue.

"Of course. But why shouldn't he be a bit cunning? They've got a reasonable case, but it consists purely of circumstantial evidence. The only thing that connects Johansson directly with Petra is Siv Underland's testimony. And she can no longer be questioned."

"What about her death, then?"

"He was on parole that week. But I don't really think they'll pay much attention to that. It's much more likely she committed suicide."

But if she didn't, I think, then the simplest way for Johansson to get hold of her was through my father. After all, they had met each other, and if Johansson had felt threatened by Siv, she must somehow have been in contact with him.

"Don't you think it rather strange that he mentioned the chapel to my father? That he'd worked there, I mean. He needn't have done that."

"Maybe he thought it wouldn't matter," says Samuel, his mouth full of biscuit. "He'd been moonlighting for Holmgren, and that may have been why he said nothing about it when they questioned him in Trondheim. But at the time Andreas spoke to him, he was beyond the reach of the Norwegian tax authorities."

I still think it shows a perverse kind of humour, but then I know nothing about Johansson's sense of humour.

"This coffee's not up to much, is it?" says Samuel.

"No."

"That's what I thought. Almost undrinkable?"

"Almost."

He sighs and gives Lola the last biscuit.

I must pay back a debt I owe to Tom, so I have to go. As I leave, I have a strong feeling I've overlooked something important – not because I've deliberately closed my eyes to it, but because I haven't paid enough attention.

14

THE E18 IS not the only multi-million-kroner construction project to cross the local authority boundary between Oslo and Asker. Driving along the main road, I am following a small, invisible stream of firms that moved into Asker to avoid the increases in property tax imposed by Oslo city council once its political complexion developed the barest hint of pink. As a result, of course, the neighbouring councils of Asker and Bærum received a few extra million in taxes, which they could then spend on even more attractive amenities, which, combined with pleasant surroundings and nice neighbours, drew in more businesses, thus feeding the whole process.

A number of left-wing people do live in Asker and Bærum, and they are quick to point out that their councils also have some problem areas. They have the same apologetic tone in their voice as I remember having when I used to say I lived "just north of Majorstua", because that was a relatively mixed residential area – not something you could say about Charlotte Andersensvei.

I try to imagine where the problem areas of Asker and Bærum are – somewhere between the television stars' villas and the royal estate, perhaps?

Tom laughs loudly when I suggest that the problem consists of an over-consumption of sherry in the mornings.

"I'm hungry," he says, sitting up in bed. "And what's more, I don't like being naked in front of other men – at least, not in my own bedroom."

Tom smiles and runs his hand through my hair.

"It's OK, Igi," he says. "Was Benny here as well?"

"No," I reply, knowing that's only partly true.

"But he is now?"

"I suppose so."

Of course he is. It's only now that I've got rid of the restlessness in my body that I understand why I made love with Tom, and why it has left such a nasty taste in my mouth.

I feel I have abused Tom, deceived him. Not because I want revenge on Benny, nothing so crude, but because he was the one I wanted to understand; it was his satisfaction I wanted to feel, not mine or Tom's. And I haven't achieved that. My body's relaxed now, but not my head, for I don't understand him any better.

I can understand the excitement, the joy of discovering myself in a stranger, in a body I don't know. It's the way Benny escapes from the thin veil of sadness that covers our bodies like a moist film afterwards: that's what I don't understand. Perhaps he forgets it, or perhaps he simply doesn't experience it.

Tom sings noisily out of tune in the bathroom as he pees, and that helps.

I open the carton of coconut milk and pour it over the shiny slices of onion that have sizzled for a while with a generous amount of garlic.

"Dear God," says Tom, looking sceptically at the coconut milk.

"You can use grated coconut, too," I say. "It's cheaper but not half so good."

He takes a gulp of red wine and goes on chopping fresh coriander.

He's done so many night shifts at the hospital that he needs something with a bit of a kick to it. We decided on Indian, because he said he's tired of Mexican, and, as he's paying, I don't mind buying ingredients that cost twice the price they would be where I live.

He puts on Bowie while we do the cooking, and seems rather grumpy because I've bought only vegetables. While I rinse the limp okra, which you can only buy in a tin, I miss Benny. Suddenly it feels obscene to be cooking dinner with another man – it's more intimate than when we were making love.

Tomatoes, cauliflower, okra. Coriander. Curry paste dissolved in water. I draw the pan to the side while the rice is cooking.

Tom opens another bottle of red wine.

I taste the curry and wonder what's missing.

A little ginger, Benny would have said. *And you've used too much garlic, as usual.*

I love you, I would have answered.

Tom hasn't any ginger and nor will he notice the difference.

You're getting rather bourgeois, I say to myself, and sit down at the kitchen table opposite Tom.

"You used to like Bowie," he says. "As far as I remember."

"Mm, yes."

"But no longer. So what's the latest thing?"

"Tango."

"How fashionable."

There's a trace of a wry smile on his face. He likes winding me up and I am competitive enough to go along with it. No one beat me at staring competitions at school, when the aim was to hold your opponent's gaze as long as possible without looking away.

The rice is ready. I give Tom a decent helping and he digs in with the enthusiasm only stick-thin people can allow themselves.

"Pretty good," he says between mouthfuls. "Reminds me a bit of chicken curry. Minus the chicken."

Oh, Benny.

"Igi," says Tom, scraping his plate. "After this, we need some beer. How about going into Asker? There's a guy there I'd like you to meet, who knows more than most about being on the fiddle. He used to hang out in a place where ladies like you shouldn't go alone. Not if they're interested in guns and so on."

The stairs to the Cellar go straight down into an eternal twilight. The clientele perhaps has no great interest in daylight, and doesn't want to be reminded that it exists. But there's nothing gloomy about the atmosphere: the club is decked out like the tackiest kind of ferry, and drunken revels are in full swing on the dance floor. In front of the bar stand several men who appear to have had more than a couple.

Tom greets people at every other table as he comes back with two beers.

"I'm impressed," I say. "Is this your local, or what?"

"Not exactly, but I pop in occasionally."

"Are they mates of yours?"

"Acquaintances, mostly, from Blakstad psychiatric hospital. I worked there for a few years, as a change from Dikemark. But it's the same old story. It gets a bit of a pain always bumping into ex-patients, like here. At least at Dikemark the nutters come from Oslo, instead of being locals."

He takes a cautious sip of his beer.

"Well, Igi, this is the biggest supermarket in Asker. You can buy absolutely everything here. Cheese from Smør-Pettersen's. Fillet steak from Rimi's. Cigarettes and booze from here and there. Clothes. More or less the entire assortment of pills. Heroin, if you like. Gossip is free. Other types of info cost anything from a couple of beers upwards."

"This must have been one of the places Hansson was keen to avoid, so that he didn't have to talk to people he's put away," I say.

"Yeah. Bjørn'll be around sooner or later. If there's anyone who knows about fixing things in Asker, he does. And he usually likes talking to me. We've talked a lot together over a cigarette."

"At Blakstad?"

"That's right. Nice guy, really. Gets a bit paranoid sometimes, from all the shit he's taken. And then he gets hung up about being locked away. And he has been quite a bit, there and elsewhere."

We're into beer number two when a small guy with long fair hair like an angel comes over to our table. His denim jacket is a trifle too short at the waist and his trousers have slid down his backside, as they do when people sit around a lot.

"Got yourself a new girlfriend, Tom?" he says.

"Oh, no," say Tom and I in unison.

"Sorry," says the angel, holding out a hand yellow with nicotine. "At least you're both agreed. The name's Bjørn. Do you work at Dikemark, too, or what?"

"Oh, no," I say again.

"Igi is studying chaos," says Tom with a grin.

"Well, you've come to just the right place. Or maybe you should have come over to my place. Not that my girlfriend would've been that pleased. Got a kid now, y'know, Tom. If anyone can make chaos, then it's a woman and a kid. Nappies and all that. D'you know how much a little'un shits?"

He laughs and sits down.

"Listen to me. If there's one thing I think stinks, it's women talking about nappies, and here I am doing it myself!"

The angelic Bjørn has a good laugh and he makes use of it for a while before he thinks it's time to get to the point.

"So, you're interested in that gun, right?"

"Yes."

"There was a break-in quite a while ago. It's hard to be sure, after so many, but guns are a bit special. Not that many around. Some, of course. Old gun, wasn't it?"

"From the war, I think."

"PK's bloody good at that kind of job, but he's got such a bad short-term memory. Could well have been him, but it ain't certain. I've talked to three or four others who remember a bit better, to try and jog his memory . . . It's just that he's stony-broke at the moment, so . . ."

"Of course," I say.

Bjørn goes away for a bit and then returns with another beer.

"He should be here now, really. It's OK, we can go on up to his place. But I think it's best to arrange things now, so maybe you've a hundred or two?"

PK lives in the basement below his parents' small house on the outskirts of Asker. But he's not at home.

We go round the house to the other entrance, the one his parents use.

His mother, a little woman with long grey hair in a thick pony-tail, looks at us with tired eyes and asks whether we know where he is.

"No," says Bjørn. "I spoke to him yesterday and he said he'd turn up at the Cellar, to meet these two. But he must've forgotten."

"Well, I don't know where he is. He never tells me anything, and I can't go on looking after him for ever."

"No, 'course not," says Bjørn.

"We'll try Arild's," he says, with undimmed enthusiasm, as we leave. The angel seems to have taken us under his wing.

Arild lives in his girlfriend's flat in one of the new blocks just outside the centre of Asker. From a distance, the apartment blocks look like green-and-brown checked tea-towels; inside the flat it's some time since anyone did any washing up.

A few of Arild's mates are there, but no PK. Bjørn sits down to discuss some other business, while Tom and I stand rather helplessly in the hall.

The smell of dope arouses old memories, as does the music – some people never moved on from the Doors. Tom and I sniff the air and smile at each other. Of course, Tom has been to Jim Morrison's grave in Paris.

"It's getting to be a few years ago," he says.

"I was there last year," says a dark-haired girl on her way to the toilet. "But we didn't manage to get right in. It was too damn hot."

Bjørn looks a bit at a loss when he joins us again.

"Can't think what PK's up to," he says. "He knew Arild was having people in tonight. And he doesn't usually say no to a free drink."

The dark-haired girl has finished in the toilet and is standing in front of the hall mirror. The mirror looks tipsy, but so is the girl, so presumably it doesn't matter.

"You looking for PK?" she says, catching Bjørn's eye in the mirror. It's far too cramped with four people in the hallway, and her elbows come menacingly close to Tom's nose as she starts to arrange her mane of hair.

"He's off his head at the moment. Christ knows what kind of trip he's on, but it's not a good'un. I met him this morning and he looked really freaked out. 'Something wrong with my face, or what?' I asked him – it looked as if I'd frightened the life out of him."

"Where did you meet him?"

"Down by the playground. Swaying about on the pavement there. Maybe he's gone back to his childhood!"

She laughs at the thought before making a face at herself in the mirror and going back into the living-room.

Tom is driving. I daren't after all the red wine we've drunk, but Tom says it just improves his Russian accent. It seems to be true. Gorbie doesn't make the slightest protest on the way to the playground.

There's nothing to be seen apart from slides and climbing frames abandoned in the thick snow, looking like relics of the past, remains of skeletons in a frozen desert. But there are footprints in the snow, zigzagging between the buried apparatus; they look lonely and pathetic, as if someone has been looking for a long-lost summer, a childhood buried by more than snow.

"He can't be here," says Tom. "He'd have frozen to death ages ago."

A single set of prints leads to a little shed in one corner and Bjørn goes to investigate.

"He must've jumped a helluva way if he came out again," Bjørn whispers.

He must have heard us, despite the whispering, for as Bjørn puts one foot on the snow-covered steps leading into the shed, he yells from inside.

"Get the hell out of it! I wanna be left alone, OK?"

Bjørn recoils and looks taken aback.

"PK?" he says cautiously.

No reply from the shed.

"PK, it's Bjørn. Relax, eh? I just want to talk to you. Nothing's up – no one's after you."

Silence.

"Got a bit of fodder for you. What d'you say to that? You'll freeze your arse off in there. Wouldn't it help to have something to puff at?"

A sort of growl comes from the shed, but it does sound a little more friendly.

"How are you keeping warm in there?"

"Blankets. Got some blankets."

"OK if I come in?"

There's no reply, but the door is pushed open a crack and Bjørn goes in.

"Only you, Bjørn," PK shouts. "I don't want nobody else in here."

It's quiet for a moment. Then there's a violent crash and a stream of curses from Bjørn.

Tom whips open the door, but neither he nor I can see anything inside.

"Sod off!" shrieks PK's voice. "I said no one but Bjørn. Get the hell out!"

Bjørn is the only one I can see when I hold up my lighter,

which casts an incongruous, cosy light over the shed. He's extricating himself from a heap of plastic buckets and rocking horses painted in bright, cheerful colours.

"Tripped," he says, somewhat unnecessarily.

What looks like a heap of rags in the far corner giggles a bit before the laughter turns into a racking cough.

"We must get him out of here," I say to Bjørn. "Give him what he needs, but not here."

"Piss off!" hiccoughs the heap of rags.

Tom and I wait outside while Bjørn works on PK. We can hear him talking in a soothing, gentle voice, as if speaking to a child, although we can't make out the words. Bjørn knows how to do more than just change his kid's nappies. PK's protests become fewer and less shrill, then they stop completely.

They come out in the end, Bjørn with his arm round the blankets covering PK's thin body, and he half carries him across the snow to the car.

Gorbie's heater has never been super-efficient and is not up to thawing PK's rags. He is shivering so much that he and Bjørn make the back seat shake; Tom and I take off our jackets and put them over him, but even that doesn't seem to help.

"We'll take you to your place, OK?" says Bjørn.

PK utters a lengthy stutter in reply.

"C-C-cigg," finally emerges from his thin blue lips, but he's in no state to hold a fag himself. Bjørn feeds him with it as if it were a baby's bottle.

At the house, I help Bjørn carry PK wrapped in the blankets past his parents' entrance and to his own door.

We put him on the shabby sofa and cover him with as many layers as we can find, including a smoke-stained tapestry off the wall above him.

He's no longer bothered by Tom and me being there. Now that he's beginning to thaw out, he's captivated by his own trembling.

"L-l-l-look at this!" he says, holding out a bluish-white hand shaking like a spastic eel.

I express my admiration and am rewarded with several demonstrations of how different parts of his body are shuddering. Meanwhile Tom goes into the kitchen to make him tea, and Bjørn gets down to the equally important task of fixing him a joint. PK's spasms abate a little as his eyes follow Bjørn's calm movements as he rolls the dope.

The tea appears to help some, though it has little effect on PK's corpse-white face. But, then, his pallor is the result of other, long-standing habits, just as it isn't really the cold that makes his nose run.

We gallantly refuse to share the joint when he has eventually recovered enough to take a satisfied drag. From each according to his ability to each according to his need. He's propped up on the sofa now, peering at us through his greasy fringe, almost contented. We sit looking at him, like anxious relatives visiting the sick.

Then he frowns.

"Ain't a trick, is it, Bjørn?"

"No! Are you crazy? Just got worried when you didn't show up at the Cellar."

"Couldn't come. Not poss, see?"

"No. I suppose you were too busy on those climbing frames. What the hell were you doing there?"

"Nothing to do with you."

PK straightens his narrow shoulders and looks sourly at Tom and me.

"Come off it," says Bjørn. "I don't believe you were there playing in the sandpit. Who the hell were you hiding from? Not me, eh?"

"What do them two want?" says PK, nodding at us with displeasure.

"They're OK. Friends of mine. The ones I told you about, remember? They're interested in that gun."

"Don't know nothing about no gun."

"For God's sake, PK, I told you – a bloody break-in months and months ago. Why are you so jumpy all of a sudden?"

"Don't know nothing. Don't remember nothing."

Bjørn looks at him long and hard.

"Somebody scared you, or what? Threatened you?"

"Christ, Bjørn," PK wails, "I didn't know that gun meant anything. I wouldn't've talked to you at all if I'd thought the fucking thing was so important. Then that vile little shit comes along and talks about punishment and revenge, and Christ knows what else. I don't fucking well arrange that kind of thing. You think it was fun lying in that shed, do you?"

"Take it easy, PK. One thing at a time. Were you in on that break-in, or not?"

"Maybe."

PK looks rather vague and his shoulders twitch.

"OK. Who's this guy you're talking about?"

"None of your bloody business."

Bjørn sighs. I imagine that's the sound he makes when he finds his kid has filled his Pampers and the famous absorbency has failed yet again.

"Now listen, PK," he says, "we've got you out of that icebox, haven't we? We've brought enough fags for several days and Igi here is thinking of forking out a couple of hundred so you can buy some you know what. Don't you think it's time you realized it's not us you should be mad at?"

"Oh, no?"

PK looks almost belligerent as he stretches his thin neck and fixes his eyes with their pinhead pupils on Bjørn.

"If it hadn't been for you, then that little shit wouldn't have showed up at all, would he? He'd heard you were going around asking about a gun. He's not stupid, that guy, even though he looks a twat."

"PK, if somebody's threatened you – and it damn well sounds like it – then you must tell me who it was. Maybe I can get him to lay off."

"It really put the wind up me," says PK, blinking his pinhead eyes. "Never been in anything like it, not since I was a kid and had to hand over my pocket money to escape being done over on my way home."

"He threatened you?"

"Did he, hell! I didn't know what he was babbling about to start with. Keep your mouth shut, he said, say fuck all about the break-in."

"Was he the one you did the break-in with?"

"No. You crazy? And don't call it break-in . . . but if I did it, then I did it alone, OK?"

"OK, so you just came across this gun?"

"That's right: I came across the gun. Thought it was quite something, but what the hell could I do with it? Then some twat said he wanted it. Paid good money for it, too. You know who I mean, Bjørn? Weird little creep. Wanted to add to his collection, I reckoned, something to wank with. Hooked on guns, he is. Then I forget the whole thing. Right until yesterday, when that little rat comes here promising me more shit than I could dream of if I says anything."

"Can't say I know who you're talking about, PK," says Bjørn.

"You know, the little spotty guy. He's got those small, pinhead eyes, like he's on speed. Doesn't touch the stuff, but he's off his head, even so. Trains that scrawny body of his so hard, he's bloody strong. Backed me up against the wall here and hissed in my face."

"No wonder you were scared . . ."

"Wasn't really that what scared me. Sure, he could beat me up, but wasn't that . . ."

PK snivels and wipes his nose on the sleeve of his sweater.

"What was it, then?"

PK's voice disappears into the sweater and he has to repeat it twice before we grasp what he's saying.

"That Charles said they would set the devil on to me. Him and that magician he goes around with. The magician was going to set Satan on to me if I split on him."

And then he starts crying.

15

BJØRN IS OUTRAGED. He suggests we go out to Heggedal, there and then, in the middle of the night. He's sitting beside me in the back of Gorbie, and his face has a bitter, adult expression, as if he were a stern father on his way to teach a lesson to the bad boys who have made his little boy wet his pants.

I understand him. To threaten PK with the devil is the equivalent of bullying a six-year-old. His ruined brain is more receptive to that sort of suggestion than to physical threats, and the nightmares will probably gang up on him for a long while. It wasn't just the cold that made him tremble like a small animal before Bjørn calmed him down and we left him safe in the care of his partner and their kid.

All the lights are out at the farm, which is not surprising, since it's almost four in the morning.

Bjørn stumps straight up to the front door and thunders on it as if that was what he was angry with. I hope he works off the worst of his fury – I'm not looking forward to seeing what he does to Yngve. I don't believe that Caspari's dark powers will be much help in the face of this angel's holy wrath.

No one answers, and although Bjørn shakes the door much harder than I did, it doesn't give.

Bjørn takes a few steps back and shouts, and I have a go at the door myself – without success. Despite his indifference to manual labour, Yngve must have had it mended, or else put something heavy against it. It's bolted and barred.

"Get up, you bastard!" Bjørn shouts. Tom gives me a resigned look. This is beginning to be a bit much for him, and I agree.

I let Bjørn shout once or twice more, and then I ask him to stop.

"I don't think anyone's at home," I say. "We're only risking one of the neighbours hearing us and phoning the police."

"What neighbours?" says Bjørn, still angry. "He's in there and just doesn't dare open up, the cowardly bastard."

Not a sound comes from the house. Bjørn makes his way round the corner and I follow him. The curtains are drawn firmly across the windows, and it's impossible to see anything inside. At the back of the house some snow-covered steps lead up to a narrow door, probably the kitchen door.

Bjørn bangs on that, too, shaking it and tugging at the handle, but it's equally useless. If Yngve Caspari is inside, he must be determined to be left in peace.

"Could smash a window," Bjørn suggests when we've been right round the house and have rejoined Tom.

"Christ, no," says Tom. "That's enough now, Bjørn. I'm knackered and this is getting silly."

"If only I knew where that Midge is," growls Bjørn.

"But you don't, and there's nothing we can do about it. I want some sleep. Now."

I think I know how to get hold of Charles the Midge, but I'm not going to tell Bjørn.

He throws snowballs at the first-floor windows as a parting shot, but I'm the one who sees what looks like a bluish face in one of the windows as Gorbie's engine starts up. I wonder what Yngve Caspari makes of our angel-raid in the dead of night.

Sometimes the apple does its best to fall far from the tree. Mrs Falk answers me on the phone the next morning in the kind of crisp, educated Norwegian you only hear at the National Theatre or at the Conservative Party conference; it's as far removed from the way her daughter speaks as you can get, but it certainly isn't her mother tongue.

I don't think Mrs Falk has acted at the National Theatre, but, to judge from her accent, she may well have a future in the Conservative Party. Her daughter is not at home, she says, and she is strangely unwilling to tell me where she is, although in the end she does give me a telephone number.

"Hello, you are through to Metal Mystery," a guy says through a wall of music. No wonder Mrs Falk was embarrassed. I don't suppose she phones her daughter at work very often. However, I get Elisabeth on the line and arrange to have lunch with her at twelve.

The heavy-metal music shop she works in is in a department store behind the Oslo City shopping complex, so we agree to meet in the "genuine French" café there.

I usually avoid Oslo City, and when I do have to go there, I remember why. Beneath the pretentious atrium, the muzak resounds like church music – a commercial mass for dead souls swelling up towards the dazzling lights and blessing the pious congregation of young consumers with vacant eyes. Every so often the mass is interrupted by the dulcet tones of the tannoy informing us that a special offer is on at Cubus on the second floor.

There's not much that is genuinely French about the café downstairs, and twenty-two kroner for a tepid café-au-lait doesn't strike me as an EU-adjusted price. But I guess for Elisabeth Falk this is dream city – she arrives ten minutes late because she had to go and look at a pair of dead smart shoes.

"So you're into heavy metal, are you?" I say once she has ordered a genuine Norwegian baguette with cheese and ham.

"It's not so much that, but I know someone who works there and I just landed the job. Not much fun staying on at school if you don't get high marks, is it? Bad exam results don't do anything for you, so I quit. The job's fun."

She takes two small bites of the baguette before she gives up and asks if she can borrow a cigarette.

"Do you know much about that guy who always seems to be at Yngve's?" I ask, handing her the packet. "The one called Charles something or other."

"The Midge? No, not really . . . and he's not there much any more, either. He and Yngve had a big bust-up."

"Oh? What about?"

"I think it was about Siv. The Midge was awfully jealous of Yngve, you see. After all, he's not exactly attractive."

"So he was in love with Siv?"

"Oh, God, yes. Well, I suppose he would've had anyone – if anyone'd wanted him."

"I'd really like to talk to him."

"Christ, I'd never have thought that."

124

She obviously thinks I want to give him the once-over.

"Do you know where he lives?"

She shrugs.

"Maybe."

I sigh, rather like Bjørn the angel. Little children can be very wearing at times.

"Could you tell me where I could get hold of him?"

She gives me an address in Asker and I write it in the outsize diary Mother gave me for Christmas, which, against my better judgement, I have come to quite like.

"Listen," I say, "are you sure you were with Yngve the night the church burnt down?"

"Course I am."

"And Charles was there, too?"

"Are you dumb, or something? I told you so."

Elisabeth forgets to thank me for the meal as she leaves.

I try to ring Bjørn, but only his girlfriend is in.

When I get to Charles the Midge's house, it's clear that the angel has already tracked him down. The door is wide open and inside is an overturned clothes rail. I begin to feel I should head straight for Yngve's place, but I must have a word with the Midge if he's still at home.

The avenging angel has also ripped down a couple of posters — half a gleaming tit is lying on top of the heap of outdoor clothes, which I step over, and the rest of the pin-up is scattered over the wall-to-wall carpeting in the room beyond. No doubt he tipped over the chair and table in there, but the tangle of bedclothes on the sofa-bed is perhaps Midge's own doing. I find him sitting in his underpants and T-shirt on the edge of the bed, his hair on end and in a state of shock after the morning's visit.

"Who the hell are you?" he squeaks in a voice matching his scrawny body, then he clears his throat and says more gruffly, "You can't just walk straight in like that!"

"I'm a friend of Bjørn's, who I imagine you've met," I say, stirring the remains of the pin-up with the toe of my boot.

Violence can certainly make an impact — I doubt that the Midge would have been as cowed by my appearance if the angel hadn't dropped in before me. Charles looked a lot tougher last time we met, whereas today I don't think he'll try his stranglehold out on me.

"We've met before," I say. "At Yngve's."

Maybe he remembers, but he just grunts.

"It's about that gun," I say, setting his chair straight so that I can sit down. "The one you bought off PK, remember?"

No reply. Perhaps he has to save his voice to make it deep enough each time he speaks.

"The gun that killed Siv Underland," I add helpfully. "I was wondering how it came to be in the snow with her."

"Wasn't mine."

"No, it wasn't. It was stolen. But you knew that when you bought it, didn't you?"

He says nothing.

"You did buy it, didn't you? I think the police might like to know that."

"It was nothing to do with me!" exclaims the Midge furiously. His eyes do look as if he's on speed. "He was set on having a gun. I just got hold of it for him."

"Who? Yngve?"

He nods.

"You bought the gun for Yngve?"

"Yes, for Christ's sake."

"When?"

"Can't remember. A few months ago."

"What did he want it for?"

"Don't know. Just to have it, make him feel tough, I guess. He didn't have any use for it then."

"Not then? You mean he's had some use for it since?"

He doesn't reply, just stares sorrowfully at a piece of the pin-up's red-painted mouth lying abandoned by his bare toes. I don't like doing it, but I try a little blackmail.

"You might as well answer," I say. "I don't suppose you want another visit from Bjørn?"

"He's got enemies, hasn't he?"

"Yngve?"

"Who else are we talking about?"

126

"What kind of enemies?"

He leans over and rubs one leg. He doesn't like this much.

"Enemies. Those fools who left. Set up their own shop, sort of. Damned idiots."

"Left what?"

"They wouldn't accept that Yngve was the boss. They were jealous. Thought they could start their own order, without him. They don't know half as much as him, so they made right fools of themselves, but Yngve was fucking furious with them."

"What do you mean, an order? Is it a kind of sect he runs?"

He looks at me with contempt in his eyes.

"You haven't got a clue, have you? If they were the ones who sent you, I can assure you it doesn't pay to be an enemy of Yngve's."

"No one sent me. So when did that lot leave? Recently?"

"No, last summer, after the feast of the solstice. The orgy."

"The orgy?"

"Yes, there's always a wild party at Yngve's on midsummer's eve. Nothing special, just a maypole decorated with leaves and boozing and fooling about in the bushes afterwards. But the last time there was a bit of a bust-up, with these people picking a fight with Yngve. I chucked them out in the end. The women were crazy."

"Siv?" I say.

"Her, too. But I couldn't chuck her out, only the others . . ."

"They're the ones who've started up on their own?"

"Yeah."

"If it's true you bought the gun for Yngve, do you know where he kept it?"

"He just left it lying around in his room. Tidiness isn't his strong point, although he's not muddle-headed in other ways."

"Can you remember where you saw it last?"

"No. Don't know. I cleaned it for him a few weeks ago, maybe. When she and Yngve were rowing so – before she moved out. They were having a row and I was cleaning the thing."

"Is that the kind of service you do him?"

He reacts as if I'd trodden on one of his bare toes – a tender one at that. He half gets up from the sofa-bed and clenches his little-boy fists at me.

"What the hell d'you mean by that? I'm his second-in-command. Just piss off!"

He must have forgotten about Bjørn for a moment.

But I decide to leave him to it. As I step over the heap of clothes on the way out, I bend down and pick up the pin-up's tit.

"If you're in luck, you'll find the other one," I say, and throw it in to him.

He looks at the bit of poster in some confusion. Maybe the little second-in-command of Yngve's order wasn't the one doing most of the fooling about in the bushes after the sacrifice.

16

NO ANGEL HAS descended to wreck the farm. If he had, he would have had to use the chimney, for the door to Yngve's place is as firmly closed as it was last night.

The indefatigable winter sun is bathing the farm in picture-postcard light – it looks almost idyllic nestled between the gleaming white fields.

I knock. I hammer on the door.

I go round the house banging on every window as I try to raise him.

"He's barricaded himself in," Elisabeth Falk told me.

I hope she's right, because if he's just nipped out to the shops, he'll think I do nothing but break into other people's property.

I consider smashing a windowpane, but first decide to see if I can find a useful tool in his outhouse.

There's nothing much there – a few cardboard boxes full of yellowing newspapers, some cans of paint so old they must have been there when Yngve moved in, two broken chairs. No tempting tool-box – that was too much to expect – but a spade with a broken handle is just what Igi the Burglar needs.

The kitchen window is the right height from the ground, and, with the spade as a lever, I can easily prise it open. It's harder to heave myself up, but after a minute or two scrabbling with my legs against the wall, I manage to wriggle in and on to the filthiest sink unit I've ever seen. Two greasy plates get smashed in the process, but no one comes to investigate. I begin to think Elisabeth was wrong: Yngve has probably gone to the shops after all. I just hope it's detergent he's gone to buy.

If this is where Yngve cooks his food, he must have an almost supernatural indifference to trivialities like hygiene. The kitchen looks as if it hasn't been cleaned since that midsummer sacrifice, if at all since he came to live here. The sink in particular has a vintage quality, but the bouquet is far from refined.

The hall is empty, no one answers when I call, no one grabs me round the neck when I go into the living-room. Nor is anyone lying in bed in the small room upstairs.

I return to the living-room and stand for a moment in front of the tapestry covering the door to Yngve's temple. I don't particularly want to open it, but the sun's shining through a slit in the curtains and I tell myself it's broad daylight outside – no reason to be afraid of a little tawdry mysticism.

He's lying in the middle of the floor.

His legs are slightly apart, one outstretched hand bathed in a ray of light.

As I walk round him, I see he's even paler than usual, his face a horrible yellowish-white. The long brown hair flopping over his forehead looks damp and his eyes have rolled up into his head, so only the whites are showing.

He bloody well looks dead to me.

Just as I'm about to bend down to feel his pulse, I notice a slight twitch in one leg, the same spasm I've observed before.

The skull on the altar is grinning at me.

With some effort I manage to prop him up in a sitting position against the wall. His head hangs limply to one side and a thread of saliva dribbles out of one corner of his mouth. I wipe it away for him, and he mumbles something. His hands are icy cold, but his face feels burning hot, despite its yellowy-white pallor. A film of sweat breaks out on his forehead and his leg starts to twitch again, stronger now.

Suddenly he tips forward and, retching again and again, vomits all over his trousers – glistening threads of the viscous slime cling to his smart shirt. The vomiting seems to rouse him, his irises reappear, but he's still not able to focus.

His slack lips begin to mumble again, quietly and indistinctly at first, then louder and more insistently. He repeats the same words over and over again, but they're meaningless to me. It sounds a bit like someone attempting tongue-twisters to show they're not drunk. Yngve may not be drunk, but he's certainly out of his head.

I bide my time, crouching down in front of him and his altar. The shadows gather round us. He's on the verge of losing consciousness again, so I shake him gently and, with reluctance, put a firm hand on his chin. His swimming eyes slowly focus on me and then he starts. His arms thrash around in the air before he manages to grab me and push me away.

He then tries to get up, but his legs give way and he collapses against the wall, his eyes fixed on me.

In a calm voice, I tell him who I am and where he is. I have to repeat it several times before the fear in his eyes evaporates and his breathing returns to normal.

After a while I can help him into the living-room and lower him into the chair by the stove. He grimaces as I switch on the light, so I direct it away from his eyes.

He doesn't address me until I'm heading for the kitchen door.

"No, no," he whispers. "No admittance. Especially not to women."

I smile at his unexpected vanity.

"I've already been in there," I say, "and survived. I also think you need something to drink."

"Brandy," he whispers, wafting one hand towards a bookcase, where I find a half-full bottle and two filthy glasses. He'll have to put up with me going into the kitchen after all. The acrid smell of bile all round him is bad enough, but at least my glass is going to be clean.

He has pulled himself together when I come back and is sitting straighter in the chair, but his trembling hands keep smoothing the rug I've put over him.

He takes three cautious, rapid sips of brandy, then leans his head back and waits for the effect. There's an almost humorous glint in his eyes when he looks at me again.

"Hangover?" I ask disingenuously.

"Certainly not. I don't think I've ever been so clear-headed."

"You didn't look all that clear when I found you."

"I suppose not." He laughs. "Did I frighten you?"

"A little. I wondered whether you were having a fit or something."

"No. But you know epileptics are often shamans in some cultures?

Outwardly they can easily be confused. But this has nothing to do with a fit of any kind. You could call it concentration. Powerful concentration."

"Perhaps it's just as well I didn't phone for a doctor."

"Indeed. There have been quite enough nosy people at the door. I bet those sensationalist hacks would have liked to have been the ones to find me. And you wouldn't believe how much weird mail I've had!"

"Is that why you won't let anyone in?"

"Where did you hear that?"

"Elisabeth."

"Thought as much. Cheers."

We drink in silence while I try to analyse his expression. It looks very like happiness, as if he had passed some test with flying colours.

He goes upstairs to change and when he comes down again, he seems different, as if he has changed his face as well as his clothes.

"I think I'll have one more glass," he says. "And if you look down by the stove, you'll find a cigar."

"Do you think your stomach will take that?"

"It'll take absolutely anything now."

"What exactly are we celebrating?" I ask as I light his cigar for him.

He lets out a great cloud of smoke. The cigar is not such a bad idea – the smell of gastric juices from the next room is soon neutralized.

"A homecoming," he says, nodding. "Yes, the hero's home-coming, we can call it."

"But as far as I know, you haven't been out of the door."

"Correct."

"Yet you've been on a journey?"

He nods, beaming. I think he deserves some encouragement, so I pile on the naïve ignorance.

"Where? In never-never-land?"

"You could call it that. Though ever-ever would be more accurate – it's always there, for those of us who have access."

"It looked like an exhausting journey. Lot of trouble with customs?"

"Very funny."

"So what did you do on this journey?"

He looks doubtfully at me.

"I'm not sure I feel like telling you. You could say it was a . . . meeting."

"With whom? Beelzebub?"

Now he thinks I'm really stupid. And that suits me fine for the time being.

"How is it people who haven't the slightest knowledge of these things are always obsessed with Satan? It's so primitive, so boring. Can't you see it's rather absurd that people with no interest in God should suddenly start worrying about the opposite power? They call me a Satanist – whatever that means. Satan is only the face that appears when Father Christmas takes off his mask. Nothing but a bogeyman for kids. I don't play childish games. But I don't suppose you understand that."

"No, I probably don't."

"Thinking doesn't always get you that far. There are certain insights which are only obtainable in other ways – by means which may seem strange to outsiders. That has always been the case – it's nothing to worry about. Mysticism has never been for everyone; it's not terribly democratic. The main thing is that it works, isn't that right? And it does."

He reminds me a little of Siri Ekelund now, her dark twin, perhaps.

"And did you obtain the insight you were seeking?"

"Yes. Oh, yes."

"But I presume you don't want to share it with me?"

"Another time, perhaps. When I know what I shall use it for."

"In fact I didn't come here to see you on an astral plane, either. I've talked to Charles – your second-in-command, as he calls himself."

"I'm sure he does, the idiot."

"It's not entirely clear that deep down he shares your spiritual interests."

Yngve laughs. He's not quite so pale any more, and has regained control over his trembling hands. When he laughs, I can suddenly see the straight property developer he might have been: a man who would satisfy his need for excitement by rock-climbing, or sailing, and who would form his opinions from what he reads in the newspapers. Maybe Yngve hasn't made such a bad choice after all.

133

"There is nothing remotely spiritual about Charles's interests, or his abilities for that matter. He just needs someone to serve, in a way."

"I thought you didn't like people who needed a father figure?"

"No, I don't. You end up with so much opposition after a while – liberation and all that. What Charles wants is a general, and that's rather different. He's not the type to start a mutiny, or whatever."

"Is that why he likes weapons so much?"

"Some people are more obsessed with weapons than he is. But he has some, yes."

He gives a big yawn, but I don't think he's the least bit tired.

"Handguns?"

"Yes, I think so, but I don't pay much attention to that kind of thing."

"No?"

"No. Is there anything that makes you think otherwise?"

"Only the fact that Charles claims he bought a gun for you. It used to lie around in here, he said."

"Did he? Then he was wrong."

"He said you had enemies, and that was why you needed it."

"Oh, that. Charles was terribly upset about it at one time. There were some . . . defectors from the order. He thought I shouldn't have allowed it. But what good were they to me? I can't stand that type. You know, vulgar people, the kind who think burning down churches is fun."

"Oh, really? So do you think they were the ones who . . . ?"

"I don't know. Charles thinks so. He had a good mind to tip off the police about them, but I didn't want that. We had a disagreement over it, Charles and I. Perhaps that's why he's lying about the gun."

"He told the truth about everything else, as far as I can make out – that he bought it off a guy who stole it from Leonard Holmgren's house."

"Really?"

"So we're talking about the gun that killed Siv Underland, but I presume you realize that."

"I'm not a fool."

"And if she did commit suicide, she didn't get the gun from Holmgren's."

"You mean she got it from Charles? For all I know, he may well have left it lying around here, without my ever seeing it." He makes an expansive gesture. "You must have noticed that housework is not exactly my main interest. And neither of us believes she killed herself, do we? But in any case, he did not buy it for me. If I have enemies, I have other means of dealing with them."

"Is Elisabeth Falk wrong, too, when she says that Siv was more than what you call a disciple?"

"No, not entirely."

"And is she wrong when she says it wasn't you who finished with Siv – it was the other way round?"

"I'm not a monk. And I'm not a believer in purely fraternal relationships. Siv . . . no longer wanted anything more."

"You mean, she no longer wanted a sexual relationship?"

"Yes."

"And how long ago did she decide that? When she found out you had known Petra Holmgren, or what?"

"We-ell. I think this is getting rather private."

But he doesn't look as if he wants to throw me out yet.

"As far as I can make out from Charles, you had a major bust-up before she moved out."

"Charles has no idea about that kind of thing. His sexual life is utterly asocial. What he fantasizes about, I have no idea."

"So there wasn't a row?"

"Yes, there was."

He falls silent. The cigar has gone out and he's holding it in a place which would have amused Freud.

"As I said, I'm no monk. But I realize it's not usually a coincidence when a grown woman no longer wants . . . It's hurtful, upsetting. I may well have given the impression that I didn't mind her moving out. To Charles, for instance. Or to Elisabeth. Charles always took a slightly prurient interest in my relationship with Siv – in the sexual side of it. Do you understand? I've never been in the army or in the kind of places where men talk like that. It doesn't seem natural to me."

I can well believe it. Nor can I see Yngve telling a really dirty joke.

"But you're wrong if you think she imagined I had something

to do with Petra, or with her disappearance. She suddenly got it into her head that I was dependent on my father. Me! I never exchange a word with him unless it's absolutely necessary."

"So why did she think that?"

"She got hold of the idea that he paid the rent for me here. I explained that is out of the question, since there is no rent to pay. But that didn't make her any less uptight."

"I can imagine."

I remember thinking it most implausible that Leonard Holmgren should allow Yngve to live in the farmhouse for free.

"Of course it was my father who fixed it, I regret to say. I don't know how come, what hold he had on Holmgren."

"And you have never asked him? Not even after the row with Siv?"

"No. We speak as little as possible. He's an idiot, and vulgar enough to be a Freemason. I can't stand people who mix what they call spirituality with business."

"But if you'd asked your father, he might have told you that he helped Holmgren by paying off his gambling debt."

"Oh, really?"

"And so it may not be the case that Holmgren allows you to live here for free because your father has some hold on him."

"But . . ."

"But it's not certain Siv knew that. What you said to each other during that row is rather important, in fact."

"I realize that. We were both pretty uptight, I guess. It's not easy to remember everything perfectly clearly. I was . . . angry that she was rejecting me. And she . . . she used that business of Father's Freemasonry against me. Said I was no better than he was – something like that – and that men are so childish."

"So she knew that your father was a Mason?"

"Oh, yes. Her father is too."

"And was Charles here then?"

"Yes. He was pleased – to see her go."

"Could that gun have been lying around that day?"

"I've really no idea."

"Charles thinks so. He even says he was sitting here cleaning it at the time."

"I don't know. I certainly don't remember it."

"But Siv left here in a rage, is that right?"

"You could say so, yes. And . . . I didn't really understand what was going on in her head. Sex is never easy to talk about, is it? Like my rituals – they're best experienced."

"But you said she was in a state about the business of the rent. So she left here with the idea that your father had something on Holmgren."

He's tired now and is sitting slumped in his chair. He no longer matches the elegance of his clothes.

"One more thing. That phallus at Siv's place . . . what was it you called it?"

"A lingam."

"Had she had it long?"

"I didn't know she had any such thing. As far as I remember, she thought it rather ridiculous."

"So you didn't give it to her?"

"No, no."

"Isn't it a bit strange that she should have acquired it, if she had such an aversion to sex?"

"Yes."

He falls silent, then he turns his face away from me towards the door which leads to his temple. It's dark in the room now, the light from the lamp in front of us doesn't reach that far. But when he turns back to me, I realize that he wasn't trying to look at his temple. His eyes are red and he has to blink away the tears. He has more in common with Siri Ekelund than I thought.

"Most probably she didn't acquire it herself," he says after a moment. "I ought to have thought of it before. You remember her door was forced?"

"Yes."

"Excuse me." He wipes his eyes, rather clumsily; like most men, he's not sure how to handle tears, whether his own or other people's. But his voice is no longer trembling when he speaks again.

"It's just the kind of thing Charles might think of doing – with that infantile sexuality of his: putting something he sees as nothing but a big prick on her altar."

"Do you think he broke into her cabin? Or do you know that he did?"

"I think so. I know him. But you must go now. Really."

And as if he was suddenly reminded that a cigar can in fact be a cigar, he lifts it up to light it.

As I leave, I wonder just how infantile Charles is: infantile enough to set fire to a church, or only if ordered to do so?

When I go to bed I take my little time-bomb with me. Dad's toothglass is still on the shelf in the bathroom, and I can't bring myself to leave the small plastic jar beside it, so I put it on the floor under the sofa. I hope the vibrations from the bass upstairs won't tip it over, even though the lid is screwed on firmly, so it's not as if the urine would run out.

There I am, lying awake and waiting for that soundless chemical clock to run its course.

I have suspected it for a while. This time it's not just my body deceiving me with its irregularity.

"Dad," I whisper. "I'm pregnant. By the greatest transvestite this side of Dame Edna."

17

SAM HANSSON PHONES me the next morning and it sounds as if he is suffering from full-blown flu. He's bound to have forgotten to take his cod-liver oil, now his wife is away. He has a magnificent smoker's cough and I stare longingly at my packet of cigarettes. Forbidden fruit – at least until I know what I'm going to do with the stranger inside me.

"What do you do when you talk on the phone?" I ask Samuel.

"Talk, of course," he snaps.

"I mean, what do you do with your hands?"

"Nothing."

"Don't you doodle?"

"No."

"I think from now on I'm going to have very small phone bills."

"What?"

"Nothing."

No doubt it would be very simple just to tell everyone I've stopped smoking, but someone might then ask why. Half the page in front of me is already covered with doodles, and Samuel still hasn't got to the point. My paper bills will no doubt make up for what I save on the phone.

I tip him off about Yngve's enemies, and he has some news for me.

Samuel has been talking to his mates in Special Branch and various other people – probably Johansson's defence counsel, but he indicates that very discreetly.

Johansson has changed his story. He now maintains he was not outside Petra's house at all the day she disappeared. He was busy doing a break-in at the offices of a small advertising company and stealing people's wallets while they were in meetings – at exactly three o'clock.

"Oh, so Siv couldn't have seen him on that day?"

"No. He claims that at first it suited him perfectly that she thought she'd seen him there. It gave him an alibi for the break-in, didn't it? So he went along with it, saying that he took Petra to Østfanestasjon. He maintains she'd talked to him about wanting to leave home, because it was so unbearable."

"What does he mean by unbearable?"

"He doesn't know any more, he says, just that that was what she used to say. He also claims she wasn't really his girlfriend. He reckons she was using him, so she could pretend she had a boyfriend too. She only went out with him once in a while, no more."

"So he isn't implying that she had another boyfriend?"

"No, but she was secretive. And she was determined to leave home."

"Isn't it rather fatal to change your story?"

"It's a fairly human thing to do."

"Then what about Siv's testimony? Why should she lie about seeing Petra getting into the car?"

"Well, she was very fond of Petra. Maybe she was rather jealous of Johansson."

"And so lied to cast suspicion on him? That sounds very sophisticated for a seven-year-old."

"Yes, it does. When she was questioned, she said she liked him, he took her for rides in the car and bought her hot-dogs. Details like that make her testimony seem so plausible, don't they? And everyone believed the thefts at the advertising company were done by an ex-employee."

"Can the exact time be established?"

"No."

I'm dying for the call to be over. I can feel a thread of excitement in my stomach, so thin I can't mention it to Samuel, so tenuous my hands are clammy. But now I know what I overlooked when I last spoke to him.

The circumference of the earth measures 24,900 miles, according to official figures. That isn't true. No one can say for certain what the circumference of the earth is. It depends entirely on what scale is used. Instead of measuring it in miles, you could use kilometres, decimetres, centimetres, inches, feet, yards. If you walk round the earth with a ruler, you'll arrive at a figure that is not the equivalent of 24,900 miles, because the earth isn't a glass marble. Far from it: the surface is full of irregularities – mountains and boulders and tree roots – which you take into account with your little ruler, but which are imperceptible to a satellite taking measurements out in space. All the major and minor irregularities are undoubtedly part of the surface, and in relation to your ruler some of them will seem quite large. If you choose a smaller scale, they will seem enormous. As you change scale, you will come up with a different figure altogether. The boulder you've just measured with your ruler is itself irregular. If you take a magnifying glass, you will see that the irregularities, and thus the uncertainty about the result, continue down to the microscopic level. So it's impossible to determine the exact circumference of the earth; it can only be determined relatively, in relation to the instruments we use.

I rather like that idea. What is important? The great chain of mountains or the little stone? The scale decides.

Right now, I'm off in search of a grain of sand.

It's five o'clock – time for a beer before dinner, so Tone Indrelid won't be at home. On my way to Schou's, I notice two bulging pregnant tummies and five prams.

The guy she was with last time is sitting in the haze of smoke. He's not staring into his beer quite so fixedly, and he can actually speak.

"Haven't seen her today," he says. "Maybe at Becker's."

A bitter wind is blowing up Thorvald Meyersgate, and my eyes are watering by the time I get to the Becker. The clouds of smoke inside don't help either. I look forward to the day when cigarette smoke will smell vile instead of tempting.

Tone gives me a big wave from a table at the back of the pub. She's with a bunch of friends this time, all in various stages of inebriation, and she introduces me at length in a loud voice. We are more or less bosom pals since last time.

After a rather strained round of chat, I ask if it's all right if we go and sit at another table for a few minutes. Tone is ready for anything, so that's no problem. She collects her things – filter cigarettes as well as roll-ups, the rolling machine, a limp packet of tobacco, lighter, wallet, glass, handbag and quite a lot of outdoor clothes. She has to go back and forth three times to collect everything, even though I say it's not necessary, as we won't be long. Maybe she thinks someone will nick her scarf if she leaves it there.

"Remember you told me about how Siv was once off school, but sneaked over to your house?" I say, the thin thread of excitement in my stomach pulling tight.

"Yes," she says rather uncertainly. "Well, we weren't that old then. At primary school."

My hopes sink because of her hesitation.

"Can you remember when it was?"

She laughs loudly.

"You must be crazy! I can't even remember what I did at the weekend. But I guess I was about nine or ten."

"And Siv?"

"She must've been seven or eight. Round about."

Round about is not good enough. Not by a long chalk.

"When I talked to you last time, you said you kept a diary when you were younger."

"God, yes. Right up till I was about twenty. Don't know why I stopped, really. I suppose because I ended up writing about the same thing again and again."

"Did you write every day, or just when something special happened?"

"That's what's so blooming sweet. I wrote every bloody day, certainly for the first few years, and every day I began with 'Dear Diary . . .'"

I could have kissed her, but Becker's isn't a gay pub like the London, so I don't.

We laugh, and a lot more colour has come into her face, not just a beery flush, and her eyes are sparkling with something other than alcohol. What is left of the little girl who was Tone Indrelid is looking at me now.

"Maybe we could take a look at them, to see if you wrote anything that day?"

"Yeah, maybe."

"I can pick up some beer on the way. You might enjoy looking at them after all this time."

142

She lets herself be talked into it, either because the chance to go over the good old days appeals to her, or because there's a point to be scored by leaving the premises with a stranger. Anyhow, she makes the most of her exit, going back twice to the table where her friends are sitting to make sure she hasn't forgotten anything. I wait patiently by the door.

I am not quite sure how many beers she needs, so I put a generous amount in the trolley at the supermarket. She thinks I'm overdoing it.

"Take it easy. I wasn't planning on getting pissed."

"Maybe Rolf'd like one," I say.

"I'll chuck him out if he's there. He can't stand me taking an interest in things that happened before I knew him. You know what blokes are like."

But he's not in. Their two-room apartment is rather dark, but painfully tidy.

On the polished teak coffee table there's a gossip magazine and one about cars. Apart from some sad, old-fashioned pot plants they are the only indication that anyone lives here at all; no pictures on the grey hessian walls, no cushions on the brown check sofa, none of the clutter that normally lies forgotten on every available surface – pens, lighters, books. I think of all the junk in my own apartment and conclude that I've become a materialist.

"It's Rolf," says Tone. "He can't stand things lying around the place."

I wait in the living-room while Tone goes to dig out the diaries in the attic. I nip into the kitchen while she's away and find a plastic ashtray with a few burnt black patches. "Ringnes Pils" it says on it. Only when I've sat down on the sofa do I remember that I no longer have any use for it.

Tone flicks through the diaries while I wait, reading a bit out loud to me here and there, but mostly just humming to herself. I give her all the time she needs. I've already pushed my luck pretty far and I have no right to hassle her now.

Finally we get there.

"'Dear Diary'," Tone reads. "'Today Siv and I have played at ranches' – that's what I've written, ranches – 'in my room. Siv is home on the ranch' – and here I've spelt it quite differently! – 'she's up in my bed while I'm out seeing to the cattle. I have a horse called . . .'"

Tone burst out laughing.

"To think she put up with it! She just sat up on the bed the whole time while I was out shooting and plundering. She was two years younger than me, that was why I could push her around. 'I have a horse called Bonzo. It's white with black spots.'"

She's really trying my patience now and my longing for a cigarette doesn't improve matters.

"Here it is: 'Siv came over to my house after school, although she hasn't been to school today because she's off sick. But she had to go at five o'clock before her mother came home, so I had to clean up the rantch all on my own. That was really mean of her, I thought.'"

"And the date?"

She shows me the book. At the top of the page she has written painstakingly, 28 August. The year is on the first page of the book. "This diary belongs to Tone Indrelid, Borgenveien 18, Asker, Norway, Europe, The World, The Universe, 1979. HANDS OFF."

He doesn't even frown while he's reading. As my father's daughter, I'd hoped to see his face overshadowed by bitter defeat, but Hans Ivar Søreid remains vacantly polite when he puts the diary down.

"Hm," he says, considering his spotless nails.

He cuts the kind of cultured figure I've seen hundreds of times – behind the counter in banks, leaning stylishly on his sticks out skiing, in cafés that are not too trendy, sitting in the middle of the stalls at the theatre, not to mention the younger version you find in the reading rooms at law school. My prejudices about that type of man are so deep and ingrained, I'm a little disappointed to find I don't dislike Søreid more – he's too dull to arouse passions that match the strength of my prejudice.

"Thank you very much," he says. "You were quite correct to bring the book to us. And naturally we shall take it into consideration when we investigate matters further."

I imagine "quite correct" is high praise indeed from this man in his pin-striped shirt, so I feel I have to behave rather less correctly.

"Take it into consideration? What the hell do you mean? It pulls the carpet from under your whole case, and you know that perfectly well."

He tightens the corners of his mouth in what must be an attempt at a smile, but he'll have to practise for a few more years before he gets the hang of it.

"That's going rather far. But, as I said, we shall investigate it further."

He takes off his steel-rimmed glasses — modern, but not too modern — and carefully breathes on them before polishing them thoroughly with a snow-white handkerchief.

"Johansson was at work all day, and his friend met him at half past five. After that they were together the whole evening. That leaves very little time, and, as Siv's testimony no longer stands up, there are no more grounds to suspect Johansson than any other man who knew her. Moreover, it has been shown to be inappropriate to put such great weight on children's testimony," says Hans Ivar, blinking. Presumably he doesn't realize how naked he looks without his glasses. "Experience teaches us that caution is required in such instances. But this is our case. You can rest assured we shall get to the bottom of it. In our way. And, as I said, we do appreciate your helpfulness. I was sorry to hear about your father," he adds as he opens the door for me. No doubt it is the perfectly correct parting remark.

Or does he perhaps have a crumb of a sense of humour after all, a slightly malicious, subversive humour?

But Samuel is enthusiastic.

"Brilliant," he says jubilantly when I phone him from a phone box, and I am grateful for the pat on the back. Igi's ego purrs like a cat. I need it, for I know that once Samuel has finished listening to Hans Ivar's little defeat and can go back to nursing his cold, I'll be on my way again. And then I'll be forced to confront the fact that the only thing I have proved is that Siv Underland, the little girl of seven, was lying.

I don't like the truth one bit. For I've inherited her dreams. She has drawn a picture I can't get out of my head which wakes me up night after night. Naturally the face of the man is no longer an empty oval, but has become father incarnate – my father and Petra's father and Siv's father.

Having discovered that the seven-year-old was lying, I suddenly realize that I have a duty. Not to something abstract called the truth, not to my need to be certain that my father was run over by some drunk, or to my or Petra's or Siv's stolen dream of a father, but to a seven-year-old girl who felt she had to lie when the person who was almost her big sister went missing.

And I don't need Siri Ekelund or my gut reaction to Siv's drawings to tell me that she must have had a hell of a good reason to do so.

18

MY KITCHEN, OUR kitchen, has decided I don't live here any more.

Benny's basil plant in the window is flourishing, bursting with good health as if happy to be alone with him at last. The spice rack has been washed and it looks as if the jars are arranged in alphabetical order, and someone, perhaps the besotted basil plant, has bought a load of garish new tea-towels.

When the wife's away . . . our flat has become as tidy as Samuel's has become messy.

It looks as if he's polished everything with one of those bright tea-towels and then thrown it away. He's even bought some luxuriant orchids which are gazing at their reflections in the shiny polished surface of the kitchen table. Or perhaps he didn't buy them. Perhaps he's been given them by someone who is as much in love as the basil plant.

I can't very well throw the damn plant out just because it is at last happy, and I can't even try to smoke it out. Instead I lay into the dish of delicious fruit Benny has put on the kitchen unit in order to deaden my hunger for nicotine.

It's hellish trying to think without smoking. I've peeled five mandarins and picked his decorative bunch of grapes to pieces before I have done much more than written "After Johansson – what next?" It sounds like the epitaph for a politician who has resigned, and that doesn't get my brain cells going.

One more mandarin. Siv lied. Probably – if you can trust a nine-year-old's diary.

Why did she lie? To put the blame on Johansson for a crime she did not even know had been committed? As Elisabeth Falk would put it, that's dumb.

So she lied to protect someone. Who?

And Siri Ekelund's mild voice comes back to me: "*Fathers, grandfathers, uncles, brothers, neighbours, teachers . . .*"

This whole loathsome mess of guilt, desire and evil can only hang together and make sense if Siv's childhood, and perhaps Petra's, were overshadowed by those dark secrets we see reported in the tabloids: a childhood shattered by sexual abuse.

I strip the remains of the bunch of grapes and make a list:

Yngve Caspari: one of Petra's classmates. Siv sought him out as an adult and then suddenly acquired a sexual aversion to him.

Øyvind Underland, Siv's father: his daughter signed petitions about him in the local paper; he gave Leonard Holmgren jobs for the boys at Dikemark.

Leonard Holmgren: a neighbour, and father to Petra. He was almost more fond of Siv than of his own daughter, and took all those photographs of the two girls. He built a house for Siv's father for nothing.

And, after peeling the last mandarin, I add the two women: Laila Holmgren and Ellen Underland. Laila hasn't told her husband that Siv came to see her a few months ago. And Ellen moved away with her daughter because the neighbours were "rather different to us".

"*Fathers, grandfathers, uncles, brothers, neighbours . . .*"

I contemplate the segments of mandarin in my hand. Why should I, who can't bring myself to go into my father's bedroom, feel such fierce loyalty to a seven-year-old who is compelled to lie?

Don't be so hypocritical, Igi. It doesn't surprise you, of all people, does it, that children lie?

I know children lie. I told blatant lies myself, when my mother found money was missing from her purse and I was the only person in the whole world who could have taken it. I lied, earnestly and to her face. And I never, never retracted it.

Never mind what they accuse you of, deny it. Every defence counsel knows that. Where did I learn it?

The appalling scenes of Mother bestowing forgiveness on me, repeated until I could bear it no longer, float before my eyes and make me jump up to see whether Benny, that paragon of domesticity, has remembered to buy wine. He has.

A glass of white wine can only do mother and child good, can't it? That's right, says the basil plant silkily.

I pour out a glass. And take one of the ultramild cigarettes I happen to have bought.

Who was it I was protecting when I lied?

The white wine gives me the eternal reply: only myself.

Only my own thieving, only the lie I had begun with. The one lie I had to stick to. Why? Mother wouldn't have hit me. She wouldn't even have kept me in, the standard punishment for lying, which was quite unknown to me but sounded like the pits. What would she really have done? Been disappointed? Felt sad, depressed? I've no idea. All I know is that regardless of what it was, I couldn't risk it. As a child I lied simply to preserve my own dignity.

"Cheers," I say to the basil. "I've just found out that Siv killed Petra herself, inducing a schizophrenic need to expose the murderer in her, which she satisfied by killing herself . . . by a double murder, in other words: Siv shoots Siv, hence the two shots."

The basil nods eagerly, and wants me to have another glass. The shameless hussy — it must be a woman as she needs so much looking after — is egging me on to have an abortion as soon as possible.

There's not a single grape left when Benny lets himself in.

The dandy has bought himself a new leather jacket that he can't possibly afford, and it suits him like everything else he ever wears, whether it's men's, or women's, clothing.

"For you," he says, pointing at the orchids.

"Come off it, smart-ass," I say. "You didn't know I was dropping in today."

"Didn't I? How many times do I have to tell you that I'm telepathic when it comes to you?"

I hope he's not that telepathic. I haven't considered telling him why I've given up smoking. Not yet.

He smells of new leather as he leans over and gently kisses me right by my eye. His lips are soft against the delicate skin of my eyelid and they stay there a long time, still, very still.

I never imagined it could be like this. Equally, making love isn't something you should plan. To start with we were both fumbling like beginners — but slowly we are coming home.

"You said something," says Benny afterwards. "Just when . . ."

"It was nothing," I say.

We don't talk while he's making a large Spanish omelette as a late dinner.

I look at his back, bare above his jeans. I wonder how much I'd miss that back if I did leave him for good. I know it so well, every muscle, every sinew, the shoulder blades slightly too big for his slim body, the soft hollow in the small of his back in which I can rest my hand.

I only have to glance at that back to know exactly how he's feeling. There have been times when I've wept over his back, so defenceless and slim, but right now, standing at the kitchen unit, I can tell things aren't too bad for him.

The telephone rings and he answers it, speaking in that loud, enthusiastic, post-lovemaking tone of voice which anyone who has ever had sex must recognize immediately.

Mother has only ever paid us one surprise visit, and I know why she hasn't repeated it. Benny can't help himself; he trips around, dances, suddenly roars exultantly and loves the whole world when he's made love to me.

"No, how lovely!" he cries into the phone. "Long time no see! Igi, it's Tom on the phone! Tom!"

I smile back inanely.

Then Benny starts a long, happy, haven't-seen-you-for-ages conversation. He sounds like Winnie the Pooh who's just found the largest pot of honey in the world and is trying not to let on where it is.

I can virtually hear Tom sweating at the other end.

"Yes, of course you can talk to her!" hoots Benny at last and gives me a resounding kiss as he hands me the receiver.

"That was a bit heavy!" says Tom. "I'm quite shaken."

"Me, too."

"I don't think I've the nerve for that kind of thing any longer."

"Nor have I."

"Are you going to stick to that kind of answer, or what?"

"At the moment, yes."

He sighs.

"You remember PK?"

"Of course."

"I dropped in on him today, just to see how things were – to check the angst and paranoia aren't getting too much for him."

"Mm."

"Well, I'll only tell you this if you promise not to hand him over to the cops. He couldn't take it now, you know. He'd piss himself with fright. OK?"

"Sure."

"He said he knows who killed Petra Holmgren."

"What?"

"Yes. Could be the speed talking, of course, but he seemed fairly coherent. Someone told him, he says."

"And who was it who told him?"

"Only knew his first name. PK was rather reluctant to tell me, but I got it out of him. You see, occasionally PK roams around up in Sofienberg park. I presume you know what that means?"

"I hope for PK's sake it only means meeting boys he likes, but the way you put it, I assume he sells himself. Sometimes."

"Probably. Anyhow, that was how he met this guy, Harry, his name is. And he's old, you see, so no doubt he paid."

"And he knew something about Petra?"

"That's what PK says."

"It's beginning to sound like Chinese whispers."

"How do you mean?"

"You know, a rent-boy on speed has heard from an old client that . . . How am I supposed to find this Harry? In Sofienberg park? Maybe I could try turning myself into a pretty young boy?"

"You could ask Benny to help you. PK thinks Harry usually hangs out at the London, so you could try there. There can't be that many old buggers called Harry, can there?"

But Benny can't help me. He's hurt because I haven't told him about the find-yourself-a-lover strategy, and as there's also something much more important I haven't told him, I behave as if I'm hurt because he's hurt and slam the door behind me when I go. Only kids are more childish than lovers.

* * *

It turns into one of the longest evenings of my life.

The barman at the London hands me the bottle of mineral water and asks me if I'm looking for anyone.

"Yes," I reply.

He clears his throat and leans across.

"The girls mostly stay upstairs," he says kindly.

"I know," I say. "But I'm not waiting for a girl. I'm looking for a guy called Harry. Do you know him?"

"Elderly guy?"

"Yes."

"Yeah. I know who you mean. He comes in fairly often. But usually a bit later."

"Tell me when you see him, if it's no hassle?"

He agrees, but hours go by and all he gives me is more mineral water.

The barman is not the only one to think I've come to the wrong place. So do the three or four guys sitting on their own among the groups of girlfriends upstairs. Benny usually laughs at these men: it often takes them several hours to realize the girls aren't just playing hard to get by preferring each other's company to theirs.

The pub's busy in the hours around midnight. A feeling of restlessness pervades the place as the boys depart in small groups or alone. I know the feeling – now is the time when the Black Widow starts to get crowded.

I stay where I am. A club like the Widow is no place for men of Harry's generation. The leather bar and whiplash rhythms in the discotheque would probably scare the life out of him, even if they did stir his deepest desires. The barman agrees: there's no point in looking for Harry there.

Maybe I'd have bumped into him in Sofienberg park, but that's no place for girls, and even if I'd gone there, there would have been no way of striking up a conversation.

So I stay where I am until closing time, then I head upstairs. In the bar on the ground floor, two girls are locked in an embrace on one of the sofas, refusing to be disturbed by the barman pointedly banging the chairs on top of the tables around them.

I smile to myself, despite the cold blast that meets me in the doorway, and button my coat up tight.

19

THE NEXT DAY I have better luck. Tuesday tends to be a bad night for pubs and cafés, though less so for gay joints whose clientele is not so bothered about whether it's the weekend or a weekday.

Harry shows up around eleven. He's a bit pissed already. His suit is a bit big for his scrawny body, and his flamboyant tie is askew and stained with I don't know what. He hasn't much hair, but, even so, his jacket collar is flecked with dandruff. There's an air of poorly concealed loneliness in his great eyes. He hoists himself up on to one of the high bar stools and orders a beer.

He struggles with his box of matches and looks apologetically at me as I light his cigarette with my lighter.

"Cheers," he says, taking a cautious first sip of his beer. The glass looks too big and heavy for his old-man's hands. He looks about seventy, but perhaps he's old before his time.

We're alone at the bar, and he isn't sizing up the five or six guys at the tables behind us with the predatory look that's common here. He's probably given up, so, despite my sex, it's not difficult to start a conversation. And, like someone who mostly talks to himself, he doesn't mind continuing his monologue.

He usually comes in here for a chat with Jens, the man behind the bar. Nice guy, according to Harry. Harry worked in the business himself, so he knows what he's talking about – he worked at the Fallas inn in the fifties.

"But, of course, you wouldn't remember that."

"No, unfortunately. But I've heard of it."

The Fallas, known as the Phallus, was the only place for gays at the time, famous as well as notorious.

"There weren't many girls there, either."

It suits me fine to be accepted as someone who has something to do with this place.

"Do you still work as a waiter?"

"No." He leans closer and I catch the sharp, sad smell of old man and cheap aftershave.

"I'm on invalidity benefit. Have been for a long time now. Trouble with my nerves, you see. It's not too bad, but the days can be a bit long. Mustn't complain, though. Seen a lot of good things. Lots have had a much tougher time than me. Things're much easier now – the young don't know how hard it was in those days."

"No," I say. "You probably weren't the only one to have trouble with your nerves – if that was the reason."

"I don't know about the reason – it's not easy to say. But we were trash, you know – sick and dangerous, people thought we were. Just because we were . . . different."

He takes a gulp of beer and looks at me with his big eyes; the whites are yellowish and bleary.

"I was in hospital for a few years. They thought I was mental just because I was . . . that way inclined."

His gaze is intense now. It's important to him that I, a representative of the young for whom things have been so easy, should understand the extent of what he's saying, understand what it means to be "that way inclined", the euphemism for the word he still can't bring himself to use.

"So when was it?" I ask. "It must be quite a while since homosexuality was considered a mental illness."

"Oh, yes, yes. It was more like a symptom – part of the package, as it were. But if you weren't mad before you were put away, you soon went mad inside. Though Dikemark wasn't the worst place, from what I've heard."

I can't help myself: I light a cigarette, and hold it between my fingers to give me something to cling to.

"Were you there long?"

"We-ell." He searches his memory for a moment, "From '67 to '75, on and off. And another spell later. I was a bit depressed at the end of the seventies. Things hadn't improved much then."

I push the tip of my cigarette around in the ashtray.

"So you were there when that girl disappeared – the one that's in the papers. Petra something."

"Mm."

There's a trace of a smile on his face, but he doesn't say any more.

"But maybe you didn't read the papers there."

"No, that's true. But I did hear a bit of this and that all the same."

I wait. He won't be able to keep it back. The way he straightens his back, and the smile, which gets more crooked and knowing, give him away.

"That Johansson they keep writing about – I don't believe it was him for a moment. Not for a moment."

He asks for another beer and doesn't even blink when I pay for it. I reckon he considers we owe him that much, the generation that's cleaned up on all the fun.

"You came across one or two there, you see. Most were well out of it, of course, had enough to cope with what was going on in their heads. And that guy was like that, too, really. Very posh, I thought he was. It wasn't obvious why he was there – he didn't seem all that disturbed to begin with. Nice manners, mostly sat on his own and read and read. I like people with nice manners.

"Some of them thought he was real brainy – you know, the kind who thinks so much with his head, it all goes wrong in the end. But that's what people said. Stories like that are popular in loony bins, 'cos then you can believe it's not just nutters like yourself who go crazy. It doesn't matter so much.

"But he had something eating him, I think. It's often like that. No use talking to him. He was on an open ward, after a while, on the way out, you see. But then he came back. And then he was real bad. Doped up to the eyeballs to start with, face white as a sheet whenever he dared go out of his room. Stick thin. Didn't read no more. Just sat in a corner by himself. I felt a bit sorry for him, so I tried to talk to him. It was useless, for a long time.

"Then one evening I was playing patience. Nothing else to do, you know, except play patience and smoke. We were allowed to smoke – you have to be in a real state for them to take away your fags and matches . . . That wasn't what I was going to tell you, was it? It was about this guy. That evening he was sat in the chair behind me, so I asked him if he'd like a game of cards. Not because I thought he would, but to be polite. He was sitting there staring at his hands and whispering something I couldn't hear.

" 'What you saying?' I said. And his answer was real nasty.

" 'Can you see the blood?' he said. And he held out his white hands. 'Can you see the blood?'

" 'There's no blood there,' I said. 'Relax.'

" 'Blood came out of her head,' he said. 'It got on my hands and my face. Masses of blood.'

" 'What're you talking about?' I said, rather frightened of him now.

" 'That poor girl,' he said. 'Poor Petra.'

"And then he began to shake terribly, so I fetched a nurse. He was put in a strait-jacket then, in isolation, for a long time. I thought he was just rambling, but I asked one of the nurses if he knew anyone called Petra. And he told me about the girl who ran away from home. I thought he must've heard about her, too, and started fantasizing. But now they've found her, with a hole in her head, haven't they? So that set me thinking again."

"What happened to him?"

"No idea. I went on to an open ward not long after that and spent a lot of time getting myself out. I didn't see anything of him . . . and I didn't think much about it, either. I had a tough enough time with myself."

"Do you remember his name?"

"Oh, yes. Not easy to forget. Such a nice name: Georg Fredmann, it was."

We talk about other things for a while. Harry's become really talkative now, and I feel he deserves something in return for the evening. He probably doesn't often have such an attentive listener. I don't hear a word of what he's saying, though. I just nod automatically and mumble agreement as my heart thumps away.

He leans on me on the way home, and thanks me effusively when I leave him at the entrance to a run-down block of flats in St Olavsgate.

I discover I'm a dab hand at forgery.

The list of patients' case notes provided by Dikemark for my thesis is produced by a different kind of computer, but mine does have the same typeface. I work out where on the page I'll add his name, below the others, and then I type "Georg Fredmann" on the screen. I have to print it out three times before I get the position just right, and my stomach is tense as I push the list from Dikemark into the printer.

But it's spot on. The letter signed by medical director Underland's secretary now has one extra name. Neither size nor typeface is different and you'd have to examine the page very carefully to see the tiny differences in the print. If I'm in luck, she'll just look at the letter I give her and won't compare it with her own copy. I choose not to think about what would happen if I'm out of luck.

As she leans across the desk to take the list, a ray of sunshine strikes her short hair and I can see she dyes it – the henna is bright red in the sunlight.

"I wondered if I could have a copy of his case notes. They weren't with the others, you see. Not that I've needed them yet," I say, "but they might be useful."

She looks at the list and frowns a little.

"I had an awful lot to do at the time," she says. "I had a new assistant in the office and . . ."

"Of course," I say reassuringly. "You must have quite enough to do without people like me coming and bothering you like this. And, as I said, it hasn't been a problem."

She takes the list away to one of the huge filing cabinets and spends some time searching.

"Funny," she says. "I can't find him. Of course, some of the files are in the medical director's archives. Now let me see . . ."

She gets his name up on the computer. My stomach is a hard, compact ball and my hands are clammy.

"That's right," she says. "The case notes have been transferred to Dr Underland's archives, together with those of other patients under Dr Østgaard. That must have been a doctor who worked here before my time. Do you want me to ask Dr Underland if you can have the notes?"

"No," I say. "If they're not in the files here, then that's probably the reason why I didn't get them. His name has just got left on the list by mistake."

"I could ask Dr Underland, but he's not here at the moment."

I know — I made sure by telephoning the switchboard before I came.

"There's no need. I've taken up quite enough of your time as it is. It's great to have cleared up why the case notes weren't included. I've got my work cut out with those I already have," I say and even manage a little laugh.

And, thank goodness, she laughs too, and I can leave the office with my forgery in my hand.

My knees are knocking as I go down the stairs.

At first Tom refuses point blank.

"No way," he says. "Besides, I've no access to the keys to Underland's office."

But I manage to lure him into toying with the idea, and then my eager eyes see the little smile hovering at the corner of his mouth as he rubs his stubble.

"The cleaners have a key," he mumbles. "They clean the offices in the evenings, after the staff have left . . . Could be that I know one of them."

Then he laughs, the good old Tom laugh.

"Damn it, Igi," he says, "I can't just borrow a key from them."

"Isn't there a master key?"

"Maybe the caretakers have one, I don't know."

"Could you get hold of it, if so?"

"They keep a hell of a close eye on them," says Tom. "The place is stuffed with drugs, you know."

"Not the administration offices, surely?"

"No, but that's where the most sensitive information is kept. As you know."

"Well, what about the cleaning staff? Don't they have a staff room where they have their coffee or something?"

"Sure. I could pop in for a bit of a chat . . ."

"You're so good at that. Then if someone put a key into his coat pocket . . ."

"Or I could put my keys down on the table, beside his . . ."

"And then you just happen to pick up the wrong keys! Before you go home."

"This is wild," he says, grinning. "It'd have to be when the cleaner has finished for the day and couldn't be contacted at home afterwards."

"Of course," I say. "Because you'd be helping me by letting me in."

"No bloody way!" he says. "If I manage to get the keys, then you've got to go in there on your own."

"OK," I say, "agreed. And if I'm caught, I stole the keys from you at your place."

He's in luck first time round, as it's a girl who cleans the offices on Underland's floor, and she's keen on having a coffee with Tom. But she keeps her key-ring attached to her belt.

"I couldn't very well take her belt off, could I?" he says on the phone, clearly relieved.

"What's happened to your powers of seduction, Tom?" I ask. "Maybe she takes the keys with her when she goes home. Ask her out for a beer."

And he does just that. The following evening they go to the pub, the Corner, at about seven and sit down at a table next to mine. Tom and I are sitting beside each other on the same sofa, but Tom doesn't so much as glance in my direction.

My questioning his powers of seduction must have stung a little, because now he really gets going and the girl with curly hair laughs so that her round breasts bounce as he gesticulates and talks.

Don't overdo it, I think. She must have time to drink a little, too. The same thought occurs to Tom and he gallantly raises his glass to her. She takes a tiny sip.

I needn't have worried. The laughter has the same effect as the beer. She gets up to go to the toilet, probably to check on her mascara, but she takes her bag with her.

Ah well, I think, and prepare myself for a long wait.

But Tom is busy feeling her coat pocket. He pushes a bunch of keys towards my leg, and I put my thigh on top of them. Looking straight down at my newspaper, I cautiously pull them out between my legs and put them in my pocket.

The girl is back by the time I've finished my drink and get up to leave.

20

I STOP THE car in an empty street and pull on the blue overalls, which Tom has filched from the laundry. Then I drive on to the hospital, keeping nicely below the speed limit. I leave the Lada in the staff car-park and walk over to the administration block, slowly, so as not to appear any more out of breath than I already am. Before I get to the door, I cool my face with a fistful of snow and wipe it dry with my sleeve. I know it doesn't do much to reduce the redness of my cheeks, but it makes me feel a little better, and I need all the moral support I can muster.

I panic for a moment when I think I've forgotten the code for Tom's plastic card, but then it's in my head, four numbers which I tap out on the keypad by the door. The green light comes on and I can push the door open.

There's no one in the entrance hall apart from a security guard sitting with his nose in a newspaper.

"Hello," I say, nodding in his direction. He nods back, looking at me without interest – it must be the overalls. I'm glad I don't have to come out with the crazy explanation about how I've forgotten something up in one of the offices.

I try three keys before I find the right one.

The front office is pitch dark and I'm not sure whether it's better to use the pocket torch I've brought or to switch on the light. I decide on a compromise, fumble my way over to the secretary's desk and switch on the desk lamp. By its yellowish light I can find the door to Underland's office, but it casts deep shadows that set my heart hammering faster than ever. I regret not taking off my trousers and sweater before I put on the overalls – I'm already sweating profusely.

The door to Underland's office is locked with the same key I've already used. Then there's an inner door without a keyhole, designed to help make the room soundproof.

I stand in front of the door for a moment to allow my eyes to adjust to the darkness. I can just make out the windows, and I remember they have thick curtains, presumably so that he can create a warmer atmosphere for patients who need it. Gingerly I pull them to, but am startled by what a loud noise they make. Then I switch on my torch. If someone should come in, it'll be easier to switch off than scrambling over to the light switch on the wall opposite the filing cabinet, which is tucked discreetly in one corner below a Widerberg print.

I don't bother with the key-ring when it comes to unlocking the filing cabinet. Instead I fish out my father's small bunch of picklocks. It is a very long time since I last played with them, but I tried them out earlier in the day, and the lock on the cabinet doesn't look all that sophisticated. Why should it be, when the office keys are guarded so well?

I fumble. My hands are shaking in the beam of the torch I've balanced on the cabinet, and an eternity seems to go by as I force myself to take a series of deep, calm breaths.

I make myself wait for thirty seconds before trying again. Then the picklock turns right round.

The metal drawers of the cabinet run on almost silent rollers; I blink hard to focus between the beads of sweat that run from my forehead, and I pull out the drawer marked F on the outside.

No Fredmann. I have made a list of words it could be filed under, but the next one I try, Østgaard, yields a fat file containing several sets of case notes. I leaf through them. Twenty or so patients, all admitted at the end of the 1970s. The yellow folder marked Fredmann is the last and the only empty one. Inside is nothing but a brief note: "Transferred to Gaustad, February 1980", it says above Østgaard's signature.

I glance at my watch. I ought not make Tom wait too long, but I allow myself a few minutes to riffle through the other notes. They seem to have been a colourful bunch, all different ages and with different diagnoses. Some were admitted for a long time, others for short stays. The only thing they seem to have in common is that their medication was fairly heavy, but that's not unusual. I decide to photocopy one, together with the note about Fredmann's transfer. It's normal practice to keep a copy of the case notes after a patient has been transferred, and I wonder why that hasn't been done.

I put the other notes back, open the curtains and am just about to leave the inner office when I hear a sound outside the soundproof door, which I left half open.

I switch off my torch and slide down behind the desk, caught in an idiotic trap. The situation could not be more humiliating: I can picture Underland, or whoever it is, leaning over the desk and staring down at me as I get up, scarlet in the face, a schoolgirl caught stealing apples.

Another sound . . . footsteps, someone walking calmly across the outer office, heading straight for Underland's door.

The key is turned in the lock and now I'm not just sweating under my arms – my whole body is drenched and I'm boiling hot.

A narrow strip of light falls on the floor as the door opens. I can see it getting wider, and then the shadow which almost covers it. Someone stands there breathing calmly; I am sure that he must be able to hear my heart beating, or perhaps he'll catch me by the overwhelming smell of sweat.

Then the door closes again and all sounds fade. I can't hear his footsteps, or whether he locks the door behind him. I stay crouched behind the desk for a long time, certain he's standing outside waiting for me.

At last I regain my ability to think. It must be the security man on his rounds. He didn't even bother to switch the light on in here; if he'd suspected someone was in the office, it would be strange to just stand outside instead of checking properly.

There's only one explanation why I didn't hear his footsteps recede, I say to myself, slipping as quietly as I can over to the door. I'm right. The soundproof door has been closed. Security staff are orderly people.

I have convinced myself, yet I stand by the door for several minutes before I dare to open it. If there is anyone in the outer office, he'll hear me opening it – in my overheated imagination the sound is as penetrating as a scream.

It is pitch black because the desk lamp has been turned off, but there's no one breathing óut there, at least not loudly enough to be heard above the thumping in my ears.

I stand still for a minute. Two minutes. Three. Then I fumble my way over to the desk and switch on the lamp. Of course there's no one there – no one behind the curtains, no one in the corner where the photocopier is.

I've forgotten how long it takes to warm up those machines. A couple of lights blink, it growls, thinks a bit, growls much too loudly, thinks again, blinks.

That's when I hear the voice. First a high-pitched tone which makes me jump a foot or two in the air, then Øyvind Underland's voice. Behind me.

"Listen," he says, "er, I forgot to tell you I'll be in a bit late in the morning. I'll go to the department straight from home, and then I'll come in for that meeting at eleven. Cheerio, then."

Then another ear-splitting tone before the tape stops.

Answerphone.

I pour curses upon all technological aids and am almost weeping by the time I've copied three pages of the case notes. The photocopier chooses this moment to address me, with the help of its green display signals – thank goodness it hasn't yet acquired an audible voice. "Error. Paper jam. Press again for instructions," it informs me eagerly.

I'd like to just switch off the whole machine, but I can't leave it with a half-copied sheet of a case history jammed inside, so I have to follow its instructions, which involves opening the door to the innards of the machine, then, with shaking hands, freeing the remains of the paper stuck between the rollers.

I send up a quick prayer before I press the start button again, for I can't leave the machine not working. It growls. Another prayer. It blinks. The answer comes not from God, but from the display: "Error. Paper jam. Press again . . ."

I feel like hitting it, but I repeat the whole procedure. My hands are shaking almost uncontrollably by now, but in the end it delivers page four of a set of case notes I no longer give a damn about.

Thank God it's much quicker to turn the machine off than on, so I'm soon back in Underland's office replacing the file, locking the inner door, turning off the desk lamp. I take ten deep breaths before I open the door to the corridor.

The harsh light makes me screw up my eyes, but there's no one outside, no footsteps in the distance. I make sure I've got the four sheets of meaningless case notes and also the torn bits of paper that had stuck in the photocopier, then I carefully lock the door behind me.

I suppress the urge to run down the stairs and try wiping the worst of the sweat off on my way down instead. If the security man at the reception desk in the entrance hall notices me at all, my face can't look much redder than when I came in, and I manage to appear reasonably calm as I walk past him. Only when I get out into the marvellous, heavenly cold do I give way to the pressure in my bladder and walk bent double to the car-park. I pee in the snow behind the Lada. There's no one around and, if there had been, they sure as hell must be used to worse.

On the way into Asker, I shout and sing in the car, a kind of hysterical reaction, an urge for relief like needing to pee in the snow.

I don't know whether my break-in has achieved anything, and right now it doesn't matter. I got myself out of there: can't think beyond that at the moment.

But it's not quite over yet. I stop the car, tear off the overalls and put my coat on as I walk towards the Corner.

The seat next to Tom is occupied, but as soon as he spots me he gets up and makes for the toilets. I give him the keys in the corridor. When I come back out of the toilets, I see the girl's smiling face turned to Tom as he leans over the back of her chair. I can't tell whether he's just whispering in her ear or is kissing her, but his hand is hovering over her coat pocket.

The adventure must have left its mark, because when I meet two young men on the stairs, one of them puts a hand on my arm.

"Good vibes up there?" he asks.

"No idea," I say and go on.

"What're you grinning like that for, then?"

Once I'm outside, I burst out laughing.

Tom's a hell of a guy.

* * *

He phones later that evening, in the same, almost hysterical mood.

"The trouble was the Corner wasn't really her kind of place, and she was hungry. You seemed to be taking a heck of a long time, and I thought I was going to have to take her somewhere else. I was racking my brains because I couldn't risk her putting her coat on. I know how you girls automatically feel in your pockets to see if you've got everything. I'd used up most of my good stories by the time you got back."

"But you did it!"

"Never again, Igi, never again. Actually, the girl was rather nice."

That's one in the eye for me, I think.

"Good."

"In fact I'm going out with her again in a few days' time."

"Perhaps it'll be the beginning of a lovely friendship," I say.

"Then I'll have a bloody good story to tell, about how we met," he says.

"Don't go telling it yet, Tom. She might not think it that funny. Not everyone has the same sense of humour as you and me."

He laughs so that it hurts my ear. For dilettantes like Tom and me, it takes a few hours for the hysteria to subside.

I make a pot of herb tea and sit down at my father's desk.

I wonder what a young ambitious doctor would do if he found out that one of his patients had committed a murder while out in the community.

Report it to the police, of course.

But if it was only a matter of fantasies, what then? No reason to report anything at all, but it would be recorded as a symptom in the case notes, I assume. The notes should at least say whether or not Fredmann was considered someone likely to commit a murder. Was Fredmann given as strong medication as the other patients? What if he had been given the wrong drugs? Would that negligence lead to the suppression of his notes? Or should he not have been released when he had been?

These are just hypotheses – I have to get hold of Fredmann's notes if I'm to get anywhere, and I have no intention of breaking into Gaustad.

The herb tea is disgusting, but I don't know whether I've let it draw too long or not long enough. That's probably the kind of thing

I ought to spend my time investigating, but I refuse to, at least for the time being.

"I tried that gambit of yours," I say to Astrid when I phone her.
  "What gambit?"
  "The 'find-yourself-a-lover' strategy."
  "Have you been out with Benny's boys?"
  "Not exactly. But you're not far off. Doesn't work, if you ask me. It just complicates matters."
  I relate the telephone conversation between Benny and Tom, to Astrid's great amusement.
  "Benny's still pissed off."
  "Welcome to the real world," she says. Astrid grew up in the 1950s, so she knows what she's talking about.
  "I'm really phoning to ask if you'd do me an enormous favour. With all your excellent contacts, can you get hold of the case notes of a man called Georg Fredmann? He was in Dikemark until February 1980, but was then transferred to Gaustad, so they've probably got his file."
  "Does this have something to do with the suicide you were talking about?"
  "It may do."
  "Aren't you getting a bit carried away, Igi?"
  "Probably. Can you help me all the same?"
  "OK, I'll try."
  "And see what you can find out about a psychiatrist called Østgaard, too."
  "Who's he?"
  "I think he treated Fredmann. He doesn't work at Dikemark any more, and the woman in the office didn't know who he was, so he must have left some time ago."

"He doesn't exist," says Astrid when she rings back. "No Fredmann has ever been a patient at Gaustad. You must have been given the wrong information. Who told you about him?"
  I can't very well let on about my career as a burglar, so I side-step the question.
  "What about Østgaard? Doesn't he exist either?"

"Oh, yes. But he's never worked at Gaustad. And he's no longer a psychiatrist – stopped practising at Dikemark in 1980. He was young and promising, they say."

"And what's become of him?"

"No idea. You know what it's like. Psychiatry is a closed world. Those that disappear are gone for good."

"So no one knows where he is now?"

"He may be dead, for all I know. Aren't you going to thank me? I have a feeling I've done you a favour."

"Thanks. Ten red roses?"

"Five'll be enough. No need to overdo it."

"But they're on special offer. Ten."

"OK, five for me and five for you."

She's always so precise with her dosages, my therapist.

HARALD ØSTGAARD IS neither dead nor missing. Unlike Fredmann, he is easy to find. A friendly woman at directory enquiries gives me his address and telephone number in Åsgårdstrand.

It takes me about an hour and a half to get there, driving south along the Oslofjord. It's afternoon by the time I park the car down by the harbour and find that the bridge the Munch girls stood on was not in fact a bridge but a jetty. The great tree-tops he painted are bare now, the vast filigree of branches spread out against a sky which is slowly turning a deep red. At the edge of the quay the snow is slushy, a couple of forlorn little boats are stranded in the frozen harbour, while out towards Bastøya the ice is covered with grey snow.

The man I have gone to meet turns out to be a fugitive. Not that he looks like one as he gets up from his potter's wheel, a thick layer of clay on his hands and a friendly look in his myopic eyes. We laugh a little awkwardly because he can't shake my hand, and chat about Åsgårdstrand while he washes off the clay.

He gives me tea in cups he's made himself, and then, when he sits down and I tell him why I've come, his eyes become those of a fugitive – hunted, alone. *I'd hoped it was over and done with*, that look says, *but I should have known better*.

Using my thesis as my cover story, I am able to get him to talk without arousing his hostility.

Yes, he used to work at Dikemark. He stopped practising in 1980.

"I was no good. I don't even think I liked my patients much. But it wasn't an easy decision."

He almost seems to smile behind his pepper-and-salt beard.

"It's a hell of a long time since I thought I could repair other people's lives with pills and fancy theories. There's something so damned arrogant in the idea that you have the right to mould people, just because you've read some goddamn books. You have to be either young or stupid to believe it, and I was both."

"And that's why you gave it up?"

He thinks about it.

"I do this instead," he says, glancing round at the shelves of pottery. "They're fit for use, all of them. I've no illusions that they are the most beautiful cups in the world, nor do I believe they change the lives of those who buy them. But they're good to hold and you can warm yourself on them. That's enough, isn't it? It has to be enough."

It's true that it's something, but it doesn't seem to be enough for him and he doesn't sound quite honest.

"So you gave it up to make pottery — because teacups can't do anyone any harm. Is that right?"

He doesn't mean to sound angry, and to start with he isn't.

"I don't think I did anyone any harm. If I'd thought that, I could have gone on believing I could also help. Don't you understand that? They're two sides of the same coin, the reflection of the same inflated self-image: if you have enough power to do harm, then you have enough to heal. It makes no difference either way. No, whoever or whatever I was, nothing had that power. Nothing." He's talking very fast now. "I've made these cups. They stand on the shelf there, whether anyone wants them or not. I've made them. They wouldn't have come about without these hands. The cups are there; I can smash them all, but, even so, they have existed. Do you see? Do you understand that?"

He jumps up and stands with his back to me, looking at the pottery. He's said all this before, I think to myself, if not to other people, then to the cups.

He still has his back to me when he speaks again.

"No, I didn't do anyone any harm. No one except myself."

So that's it. Now all I have to do is wait while the contents of my cup grows cold, and he will tell me.

"I told myself it was to know what I was prescribing, what I was making my patients swallow. It was not true, of course, but that was what I pretended to think. I was so confident, backed up by all my books; I suppose I thought I had enough self-control to handle it.

It's a classic story. They were very kind about it. I was allowed to resign. An honourable discharge, almost."

He starts straightening the cups on the shelf, rearranging them, brushing away invisible dust.

"But it takes time to get rid of an addiction," he says, his voice rising. "It takes almost a lifetime. And, yes, the only way to do it is to find out what a little shit you are. But it hurts. It hurts like hell. And eventually you make some kind of life for yourself, a life suited to a little person. Is that enough?"

He has turned to face me; the cup he's holding in his clenched fist withstands the pressure.

"Do you remember a patient called Georg Fredmann? Or Harry Skau?"

He bursts into loud, uncontrollable laughter, leaning forward, then doubles up as it turns into a coughing fit.

A woman stands in the doorway. Beyond her I catch a glimpse of their kitchen. Her long grey hair falls over a hand-woven purple poncho. Her face is drained of all colour.

She goes and puts an arm round her husband and then looks me straight in the eye.

"I think that's enough," she says, her voice knife-sharp. "I don't know who you are, nor do I care. But you are leaving now. Do you hear me? Now."

I get up, but she carries on:

"Get out! Don't you think we've had enough of this? Don't you think we've been through it again and again? Is it too much to be asked to be left in peace?"

By the time I reach the door, she's started comforting him with small, crooning noises. I'm glad my back is turned, but as I open the door, he answers me:

"No, of course I don't remember him. I don't remember the names of any of them. Not a single name or face of any of the poor bastards who were my patients."

All of a sudden I'm not sure I believe him.

"But Georg Fredmann, whom you don't remember, was trans-ferred to Gaustad ... by you. It's just that he never went there. How come?"

He frees himself from her grasp and lurches towards me. Suddenly

170

he doesn't look like a peaceable maker of teacups. He's heavier and taller than I am, so I back out of the door and raise my hands to ward off the blow.

But the grey-haired woman gets to him first. Operating that loom must have made her stronger than she looks, for she is able to push him to the floor.

I close the door on the sound of him starting to cry.

It's already growing dark by the time I join the E18, and the snow is falling heavily as I catch a last glimpse of the fjord before the Holmestrand tunnel. Through the crackle on Gorbie's radio I can hear some real car music: country and western – sad and sentimental.

My determination to find that kind of music usually drives Benny wild. It's the perfect music for driving in the dark, but tonight everything else is wrong. Although the orange halogen lights on the E18 suit the sound of steel guitar and windscreen wipers, I want it to be summer rain hitting the windscreen. I'm shuddering with cold, but it should be because Benny has wound down the window to smell the earth, not because the heater has gone on strike again.

We drove this way a few summers ago, late one Sunday night to avoid the heavy traffic. It was the first time he asked me whether I thought we should have children. Benny gets just as sentimental as I do driving on the motorway at night, listening to country and western.

"How many were you thinking of?" I asked.

"Eight or nine, perhaps?"

"And what do you think they'd make of their dad's boyfriends?"

"Kids don't have prejudices. Anyway, you have to go to bed so damned early when you have kids, don't you? Flaked out after children's telly."

"So then you might as well stay at home with mother, in the double bed?"

"That's right. Then we could have some more fun when they've grown up and left home and all that."

"It takes time for eight or nine kids to grow up. I'm not sure the boys will be interested in either of us by then."

"Ah, well."

I know he means it. Benny has fairly conventional dreams about twosomeness with small offspring – he just finds it hard not to fall in love at times.

Soon, soon I must tell him that I have begun on the first of those eight or nine.

But not yet. For a little while longer, I can ignore the fact that I wake in the morning sweaty and exhausted after dreaming of puppies and kittens that I lose or forget to feed.

A small red cat's eye winks at me from the desk as I go into the office. Message on the answerphone, which for once I've remembered to switch on. Unfortunately I've forgotten to switch the heating on before leaving, so it's bitterly cold and I stand there in my overcoat as I play it back.

It's a brief, anxious message, whether because Harry Skau is of the generation that thinks an answerphone is rather scary, or because of what he tells me, I don't know. But it could well be the latter.

"I've seen him," he says. "In the street here. It was him – that madman Fredmann."

I spend a freezing forty-five minutes in the office trying to phone him. No answer.

He's at the London, I tell myself, shivering. Go and buy him a beer.

But he's not there. Jens the barman remembers me and brings a mineral water before I have a chance to order something hot.

I mustn't keep looking at my watch. Time goes more slowly the more I look at it. If I don't stop, it'll start going backwards. Harry doesn't show up. I ring again, and get the same merciless tone: no answer. Nothing is so lonesome as the sound of a telephone ringing in an empty apartment.

When I come back from the pay-phone for the fifth time, one of the customers looks at me with pity. He must think I'm expecting the lesbian of the century.

On my way to Sofienberg park, I stop at every telephone box. No answer, still no answer.

There's no sign of him in the park – nor of anyone else, for that matter.

It's too early, I tell myself, and go back to the London.

At closing time, I decide he must have met a guy – a nice, elderly man who may brush the dandruff off his shoulders.

If so, he must be spending the night at his lover's, for his telephone remains unanswered, even when I try one last time at half past four in the morning.

The walls along the street are covered with signs and signatures, spray-can symbols designed by the illiterate so that only the initiated can decipher them.

The graffiti artists draw their own map of the city in this way, marking out their territory as dogs do when they piss in a corner, or as birds do when they sing. You can follow their routes, spot them daring to cross into someone else's territory, the boundaries fought over in a battle of signatures, sprayed on top of each other again and again.

The same panicky impulse to affirm my existence once drove me, as an uncertain, spotty adolescent, to write my name all over the back pages of a tatty notebook. No doubt the grey-suited men in the town hall did the same.

The symbols on the walls remind me of signs you cut in the bark of trees in a forest when you're afraid of getting lost. They're a feeble attempt to besiege the city, to make this street, this stretch of concrete, into something less unfamiliar and threatening, a vain attempt to lay claim to it by those who know only too well that they will never own anything, that this city does not belong to them. The gangs of city guerrillas who piss on street corners with their spirit pens and spray-cans lack the power to make the city theirs. Long ago it was sold off to advertising executives who write their pretentious graffiti on the huge billboards high above our heads, out of reach of the spray-cans. The two languages both rely on symbols; it's just that the advertisements are bigger, are paid for by infinite amounts of money, and express themselves in codes we understand: the commercial language of the city. The fact that we choose to call one vandalism and the other advertising arises from the confusion inculcated by the language of money, which puts its stamp on all of us.

* * *

I turn the corner by Ringstrøm's second-hand bookshop and see the ambulance. Now I know that Harry has not found himself a lover.

I know it, but I pray to God it isn't true.

I quicken my steps, and although I tell myself that it was too dark the evening I took him home for me to see which number he lived at, I know the ambulance and the police car have drawn up right outside his door.

Other people live in the block of flats, and ambulances do more than pick up old men; the police could be here because a neighbour has made another complaint about domestic violence. As I stumble over the treacherous pavement, such reasoning does nothing to dispel the icy knot in my stomach, which tells me what has happened before I've had it confirmed.

"Has there been an accident?" I ask the policeman coming out of the entrance.

"Yes. An old man slipped in the shower and hit his head."

"Is it serious?"

"Looks like it. One of the neighbours called us."

"Is it all right if I go in? I'm going to see a friend of mine."

"You go on in, yes. But don't get in the way of the ambulance men."

The rear courtyard is dark and dismal. The renovation of the city hasn't got this far – which is perhaps just as well, otherwise Harry Skau and the rest of the tenants would never be able to afford the rent.

The stairs from the courtyard are narrower than the back stairs in most other parts of the city, and it's a long time since anyone gave the walls a lick of paint.

On the second floor, I realize this must be where he lives. The door to the flat is open and the frame looks as if someone has kicked the door in. A dishevelled old woman is standing in the doorway, her hands pressed together below her mouth in a kind of parody of fear, or prayer, or both.

The icy lump in my stomach feels harder than ever when I see the tatty card by the door. In thin spidery writing, it says H. Skau, as if he didn't deserve more than this greasy bit of card with half his name on it. Harry Skau hasn't left his mark on that many places in his life.

174

"He didn't answer when I knocked," whimpers the old woman. "And he hadn't fetched his paper. I thought maybe he was ill and needed something. They're in there now, the men with the stretcher."

We are silent as they come out with him.

One of them looks with some concern at the woman beside me.

"I'll make her some coffee," I say.

Then they carry him down. They've covered his face with a sheet.

I help the old woman into her flat. She doesn't wonder who I am; she is merely grateful someone has put her in a chair and is making her coffee.

Her little kitchen is spartan, and the remains of her breakfast are still on the table. She's eaten only half of the thin slice of bread with cheese on it, but I don't clear it away in an attempt to be overly helpful – I know perfectly well she's going to eat it later.

There is a small jar of instant coffee on the table and I spoon some into two small white cups with a flower pattern.

"I don't want to keep you," she says in a thin voice as I bring in the coffee. "I suppose you were on your way up to the fourth floor?"

She sizes me up. She appears to be nervous of whatever's on the fourth floor.

"No, I was coming to see Harry," I say. "Your neighbour."

"You knew him, then?"

"Hardly at all. Did you know him well?"

"No, not really. But we've been neighbours for many years. I grew up in this block of flats. How strange that you knew him. I don't think he had many friends."

"I don't suppose he had many visitors?"

"None," she says in a firm voice, and she looks straight at me. "Not once in all the years he's lived here."

She too knows what it is to have no one coming to see you, nor does she care that I can see that.

"Not yesterday, or the day before? You didn't hear him talking to anyone, by any chance?"

"No, I didn't."

But I suspect she goes to bed relatively early.

"It was terrible," she whispers after a while, her eyes now moist.

"They kicked down his door, it made a dreadful noise, and they found him lying in there, in the bathroom. I've got one of those safety alarms — he should have had one, too, shouldn't he? But I suppose if he hit his head, it wouldn't have been much help, would it? Do you think they're any use?"

"Yes," I say. "I'm sure they are."

I sit there for a long time, stroking her small hand, as fragile as a bird's wing against mine. It's me I'm trying to console.

22

IN THE HALLWAY a locksmith is repairing Harry's door. The policeman looking on is the one I spoke to earlier.

"She's not too bad now," I say, nodding towards the door I've just closed behind me. "But she's had a shock, of course."

"Was she the one you were going to see?" says the policeman, faintly surprised.

"No, I was going up to the fourth floor, but the person was out. Was it difficult to get the door open?"

"No, you only need to push hard on a door like that and the latch gives way. This one was so old the whole thing just fell off."

He shows me the old Yale lock.

"How was he, when they found him?"

"He was dead when they took him out," says the policeman. "Poor old fellow."

In the street the snow is making a renewed effort to create an illusion of cleanliness.

I try to stand outside my own fear, to examine it, as you would evaluate a new and unknown phenomenon, but my attempt at objectivity merely tightens that icy, hard knot in my stomach. The fear feels like an inaccessible, alien presence in my body, almost as if I am possessed by a demon. It seems quite accurate to describe this kind of primeval fear in such terms: something has taken up residence in my body and has no desire to leave it.

My attempts to ignore it are as false and futile as an adult dismissing a child's terror by saying, "It was only a dream." When my head tries to calm my body, it has to rise above it, to disconnect itself from the instinctive wisdom of the body, which always knows best.

I'm scared, and the lump of ice in my stomach tells me I have every reason to be.

It's too late to regret not going to see Harry Skau, the man who didn't think it worth writing more than half his name on his door. He may not have wanted to leave his mark on the world, but surely he deserved the odd visitor?

He did have one last visitor before he died, of that I am certain, but I wish it had been me.

Blinded by the snow, I walk on in a white city. Bathed in oblivious, still sunshine, the new snow glitters cheerfully over every square yard of Oslo. Like the sheet over Harry, the snow is only a covering, clinging tight like a surgical glove, hiding the stains and the rubbish, but faithfully revealing the contours of what lies below. Its purity does not go deep. In the uniform glare, there is no longer any differentiation, all meaning is gone; it makes no difference where I walk.

The twilight feels like a release. I prefer the false light of the neon advertisements, tinting the faces round me with garish reds and oranges, and the fluorescent blue I always associate with Oslo. I allow myself to slow down and feel the icy cold in my toes. My shoes are too thin for this weather. I shouldn't stay out any longer, shouldn't be here, should stop playing at being a shepherd – it's too cold to look for lost lambs. The ground's frozen deep under the snow and asphalt. It's too hard for anyone to scatter a handful of soil over an old queer and say the words, "earth to earth, ashes to ashes" . . . rest at last in the lap of mother earth.

A butterfly fluttering its wing in an imagined meteorological system. A conversation in a bar. A nose poked into other people's business. And the track has changed direction. The butterfly can do nothing about it, it can't flutter backwards with its wings. Everything has already adapted to the new signals, the co-ordinates are no longer the same. Someone has placed a sheet over his face so that I am released from seeing him or he me.

If there are good shepherds, then there must also be evil ones. Who has said you can't freeze standing up? The fact that I can feel the ice biting into my soul as well as into my toes does not alter the course of events; the system rolls on, colouring the faces in the centre of Oslo with chaos, neon and halogen never more beautiful than against the black night. It would make you want to cry, if only tear-drops didn't freeze on your cheeks.

At the stage when larvae turn into butterflies, the body dissolves into a homogeneous mass, a mush inside the pupa – not larva, not butterfly, not anything. Without functions, organs, nerves, only mush. The butterfly is never more homogeneous, it's nothing but itself. This is the stage when the larva-that-was and the butterfly-to-be become one and the same, whole, indivisible and in balance. Mush.

No one asks the larva if it wants to become mush. No one looking at a butterfly can tell that it has been mush, and no biologist in the world would consider asking whether it hurts. Transformation, Igi. Transitions. The kind a psychologist should be able to help her patients through, with well-chosen words of advice, before she is dissolved and comes into balance. Transformation, transubstantiation, transvestite. Whole and indivisible, male and female. I never remember which is yin and which yang.

I have no rites for Harry, this lamb I've taken to the slaughter. I can't drink mineral water at the Black Widow, and I can't stop anywhere else now – I have to keep walking until I can no longer feel the ice in my toes. I can't drown my memories of Harry with a funeral beer. There is no wake, and he's no closer to the grave than a slab in the morgue.

I have somehow arrived at Frogner park. I don't want to stop on the bridge with its troubling Germanic statues, celebrating a mascu-line beauty which Harry perhaps once dreamt of, when he used to go cottaging in the wood at the other end of the park, behind Vigeland's Monolith, rising up like a super phallus of indivisible human forms, carved from a single piece of granite.

I cross the bridge and make for the wood where, one spring, I and other local children ran through the trees, coming into leaf, in the hope of frightening queers. What they were I had no idea – an unknown species of insect, or butterfly, perhaps, for I understood no more about them than about the birds and bees.

I can't remember whether we disturbed anyone on our raids – trade was probably slack just after school. I pass a lonely car waiting in the dark by the cemetery with its engine running, before I reach the wood, where Harry's and my paths may once have crossed. I remember yelling to alert anyone hiding in the long grass. Perhaps my shout was not so different from his muffled whisper; perhaps we were both calling for our fathers . . .

The snow lies softly on the wooded hillside, covering the dead grass, but that is not what I shall remember of this day: it is the bare branches against the greenish-orange lights reaching up like helpless, skinny arms towards the lofty winter sky.

For a moment I think my father has come back.

From the pavement in Bernt Ankersgate I can see the desk lamp shining through the drawn curtains, and I grab a handful of snow to throw at the window so that he knows Igi's coming on up.

I don't make the snowball. The snow lies cold in my palm and my arm is robbed of strength as I remember that no one is leaning over the desk up there. No one will open the window and smile almost bashfully at me. I wonder how long I will continue to think I'm seeing my father somewhere – in the street, on a passing bus.

Did I turn that light on? Did I forget to turn it off when I left this morning? Maybe. Maybe not.

I stand in the entrance to the rear courtyard. It feels as if I've stopped breathing, but I can see my breath in the dim light that seeps out of the cracks around the door. I'm a big girl now. There's no one I can ask to see me home.

The door upstairs is locked. If anyone is inside, he'll hear me turning the key, so there's no point in standing out here in the dark hallway – except that I can't get my feet to cross the threshold. I clutch my bag: it's not much of a weapon.

"Igi?"

I've heard that soft voice a thousand times before. I allow my legs to turn to jelly under me and I slither down into a heap on the floor. It's suddenly too much to take responsibility for my legs, or for my ice-cold toes, or for making my way inside on my own.

"Carry me," I say as Benny opens the door. "I want a hot bath, and a big dinner, and a couple of bottles of red wine would be no bad thing."

"There're some tea-bags here," says Benny. "Is that any good?"

"Carry me home," I reply.

And that's more or less what he does. Sometimes his arms seem long enough to wrap round me at least a couple of times, gathering up my body that feels as if it has fallen apart.

He massages life into my toes without once suggesting that I ought to wear thicker boots, and I'm even more grateful for that than for the dinner and the wine. It's as it should be: if anyone can share a wake for Harry Skau with me, then it's Benny.

Astrid phones the next morning.

"Is that where you are? I've been ringing and ringing Bernt Ankersgate. Are you still looking for that Dikemark patient?"

"Yes, I am. Has he turned up at Gaustad after all?"

She laughs. "No, but if you came to work a little more often, you couldn't have avoided seeing his name: it's stuck up all over Blindern."

"What?"

"Well, I can't be certain it's the same man, but the name's not that common – Georg Fredmann, wasn't it?"

She's enjoying herself, so she pauses.

"Come on, Astrid, get to the point!"

"Not Gordon or Gregor, but Georg?"

"That's right."

"Double n in his surname?"

"Yes, yes, yes."

"He's giving a lecture on astro-physics tonight. There are posters about it all over the university. Half past seven at Sofus Lies. So, any more roses for me?"

"You can have the rest of the bunch."

The main university lecture theatre is no more than half full, and the atmosphere a good deal calmer than when I was last here – that night the film society's programme had featured some vintage puppet shows for children's TV, to the great jubilation of the puppets' die-hard fans.

No doubt some of the same fans are present among the audience of astro-physicists, but this evening they haven't been to the pub first, or at least not for long.

I sit in the front row, below the platform where the members of the panel are to sit, in front of the place where there's a card with the name Georg Fredmann on it.

As usual, the panel arrives over fifteen minutes late, then the sound system is checked by one of those semi-amusing student representatives always chosen for such jobs – first the audience waits for the participants, then the participants, gathered on the stage in front of me, wait for the audience. It's obvious which is Fredmann: he's the only one from abroad, and is being paid rather more attention than the others.

The sight of him makes me nervous, not because he seems impressive or authoritarian, but because he is so nervous himself – and I am prone to psychic infections.

He wears thick glasses, which he cleans too often. His forehead is already moist before he stands up in the glare of the lights, and he leafs through his papers so much that I'm sure he'll lose one of them. His suit is ill-fitting, his tie crooked and he has a round, slightly childish, cherubic face. The fact that he wishes he were anywhere else but here, preferably on his own, is written all over it. Georg Fredmann must have been a nerd before the word was ever invented.

But he's a good lecturer. He fumbles a bit at first, sorting his papers with the usual apologetic look, but once he forgets the lights and all the frightening stares from the hall, a gleam comes into his eyes, magnified behind the thick lenses, and, his face growing steadily pinker, he speaks clearly and with conviction. He doesn't once look down at the heap of papers, just turns the pages over at regular intervals as he talks. I don't know much about astro-physics, but it's clear that he doesn't have much time for Stephen Hawkings and his dream of finding the Grand Unified Theory. His audience is captivated enough to forgive him the inevitable problems with the overhead projector – quite an achievement, given that students get more fed up with upside-down tables and quotes shown backwards than with the queues in the canteen after six months at university.

I have to wait an hour or so before I can get him on my own. While the other lecturers are speaking, Fredmann sits with his hands in his lap, without making notes, nodding or smiling in a superior way; then, when they have finished, he asks precise and sometimes obviously difficult questions. He has no difficulty in answering the questions put to him from the floor and from the members of the panel. Now there is no sign of the first-time nerves he displayed when he first stood on the platform.

I wonder whether he will tackle my questions with equal equanimity.

He does not.

He appears to share in the general post-performance cheerfulness of the other speakers as the audience leaves, and doesn't welcome my interruption.

"Could I have a few words with you?" I say. "It's about . . . something private."

"Private?" He is rather taken aback, as if the word brings him back to earth with a bump, and is more confusing than the contents of a black hole.

"A death," I say.

The disapproving looks from his colleagues have an effect: he moves a little way away from them.

"It's about a young woman who was killed in Asker sixteen years ago," I explain. "I've been told you were there at the time. Is that right?"

The black hole is within, and it's expanding. He tries to blink it away, but it fills his eyes, enlarged by his thick glasses.

"Perhaps we should go somewhere else?" I suggest. He glances at his colleagues, at the platform, at the hall where the last students are on their way out. He even looks at the ceiling before he has to accept that no one in the room, nor some unknown heavenly body, is going to help him. He looks like a schoolboy who has been called in by the dentist.

We go to the student pub, as that's the nearest. Some of those who attended the lecture are there, but otherwise not many people. I find a table for us in one of the inner booths, where we are unlikely to arouse curiosity. Not that I think anyone would be interested. Fredmann cuts an awkward figure in his scarf and overcoat, and his body language is offputting. Unless you were drunk, you could not fail to notice his nervousness, and I am not the only one to find it infectious. So far the only person here who has drunk too much is a stout classics professor trying in vain to persuade some under-graduates to join in his bacchanalian revels.

Fredmann looks at the glass of beer I fetch for him as if it might transport him back to the nebulae.

"It was 1979," I say.

"I'm sorry, I don't think I can help you. I was . . . unwell at the time. I had been overworking, and . . ."

"And you were admitted to Dikemark?"

"How do you know that?"

"From another patient who remembers you – Harry Skau, his name was. He must have been in his fifties. Small and thin. He's dead now."

"I can't say I remember him."

"Do you remember the girl who disappeared, Petra Holmgren?"

"No."

"She didn't disappear, in fact. She was killed."

He puts his glass down on his left, changes his mind and moves it back again. His forehead is shiny now, with fine wrinkles almost up to his hairline.

"Really? Oh. But . . . I don't understand what this has to do with me. I was . . . in hospital. I had been overworking, as I said – I was totally exhausted. Yes. It was good to get a bit of rest. But I didn't know much about what went on outside the hospital. In the locality, I mean."

Helpful, friendly, but he keeps on moving his glass from one side to the other.

"This other patient, Harry Skau, remembered you talking about her."

"Really? And what am I supposed to have said?"

"You're supposed to have said you killed her."

I'm not a fan of shock therapy, but there are no nice circum-locutions left.

Fredmann looks as if he has fallen from Mars and is beginning to wish he were back there. He adjusts the position of my glass.

"No, but my dear . . . This is terribly . . . I don't know what to say. Did he tell you that?"

"Yes."

"I can recall very little about that time. I was sick, that I do remember. I was missing my work, although it was so exhausting. And my mother had just died, you see, and that . . . upset me."

"Is it possible you might have said such a thing?"

At this rate we're going to have problems deciding whose glass is whose.

"I don't know. I really can't imagine I did."

"But if you had said it . . . would it have been true?"

"What?"

"That you killed her?"

He swallows, although he hasn't drunk a drop of beer.

"No. No, of course not."

"But you knew who she was?"

"I may have done."

"So you did have some local contacts?"

"Now, how shall I put it . . . I did go out for walks and so on."

"And you met her?"

"What? No, I never met anyone. Like that."

"Like that?"

"Well, to talk to . . . But I might have heard the name . . ."

He looks helplessly at me.

"Who might you have heard it from?"

"From one of the patients, perhaps?"

"You don't think you talked about her to your doctor?"

"To my doctor?"

"Yes, could you have said something similar to what Skau thought he'd heard?"

"I . . . I can't believe that."

"Who was your doctor, by the way?"

"What was his name now? I'm afraid it escapes me . . ."

"Østgaard?"

"Ah, yes, that was it." He looks relieved. "That's right, Østgaard was his name. He was . . . a good man."

"He transferred you to Gaustad, didn't he?"

"To Gaustad? No, I don't believe so – I've never been there."

"That's what it says in your papers. In fact, that's all it says."

"But it's not true, I've never been to . . . Gaustad."

He shudders, as if the name has worse connotations than Dikemark.

"Do you have any idea what happened to your case notes? It's pretty unusual that they're not there."

"I'm sure it is. Are they missing?"

"I don't know."

"They're not the kind of thing one wants . . . lying around."

"No."

"Not that there was anything . . . anything unpleasant in them. Not at all. I was just . . . exhausted. I'd overworked . . . I was having problems concentrating. That was all."

"What kind of treatment were you given?"

"Mostly medication, I'd say."

"Do you remember what kind?"

"What're they called now . . . neuroleptics?"

Anti-psychotic drugs – nothing odd about that: psychosis is the most common disease in psychiatric hospitals.

"But you must have had some therapy? Did you talk to Østgaard?"

"Oh, yes. Yes, I did. I talked . . . to Østgaard, yes."

"So you were discharged from Dikemark?"

"Yes. Then I got a grant, to go to the USA to study there. That's what I did – I went there. Yes, yes."

"And you stayed there?"

"It's an exciting subject to be involved in, you know. And there were opportunities . . . There wasn't much to keep me in Norway, not after my mother died. So I stayed there, yes."

He straightens his spectacles. I dare say he is the kind of lecturer female students call sweet, and he never gets to know that's what they say.

"But you come back for an occasional visit?"

"Not very often. Very rarely, in fact. Actually, this is the first time. I didn't think I could say no to this invitation. I was a student here, although that was some time ago."

"So have you been back long?"

"Oh, a few weeks."

"Does the name Siv Underland mean anything to you?"

He has stopped fiddling with the beer glasses, but he still hasn't touched his beer. Maybe he prefers it flat.

"No, I don't think so. Who is she?"

"A young woman. She's dead, too. She was the daughter of the medical director of Dikemark hospital."

"Really? What a lot of strange things happen. I haven't helped you much, I'm afraid, have I? I think perhaps I ought to go now ... the others were going on to a restaurant in town and ... Do you think I can phone for a taxi from here?"

"Don't you want to finish your beer?"

"What? Oh, the beer. Yes. Just a sip, anyhow. Yes."

His hand is shaking slightly, and it can't be due to over-consumption of alcohol.

"A bit flat, isn't it?" he says, straightening his glasses. "Do you ask the waiter, or what?"

"About the beer?"

"About a car. You know, a taxi. Now, what's happened to my scarf? Oh, thank you, thank you."

I order a cab for him and follow him down the icy path to the street.

"Well, thanks, then," he says. "It was ... well, nice. To meet you."

The driver has to help him open the rear door. He's still trying to button up his coat as the driver slams the door. A bit of his coat gets trapped in it. I would have liked to tell the driver where to go – Fredmann looks like the type who wouldn't dare complain if he was driven to the wrong address.

What do murderers look like?

I go back up the path to the pub. The classics professor has changed tables in his search for bacchanalian revellers.

23

A T THE CORNER of Torggata and Bernt Ankersgate I realize I hadn't meant to come back to the office, but as I pass number seven I look up and see that Benny must be paying another surprise visit – I know that desk-lamp trick of his now.

Lina is sitting in a huddle outside the entrance in the courtyard and for once she looks wide awake.

"You haven't seen my cat, have you?" she says. "He's never gone off like this before."

"Tomcats do tend to now and again," I say, acting the expert. "Or has he been neutered?"

She looks at me, appalled.

"Are you crazy? Doctored! I'm not an animal torturer!"

I don't consider Bernt Ankersgate very appropriate territory for animals, so I sympathize with Oswald.

"Tell me if you see him, will you?" says Lina as I go in.

Benny is not waiting for me at the door, but it is ajar. It's dark in the hallway. I think Benny's overdoing it a bit. He doesn't answer when I call.

"Come on, Benny, it's only funny once."

I deliberately make a racket as I go in, stamping my feet and flinging the doors open. If a couple of glue-sniffing idiots are in there, I don't want to surprise them.

But it doesn't smell of glue, or meths, and no one's lit a joint. It just smells of dust and grief, and the only sound I can hear is from the street outside. Lina is on the pavement, calling for puss. She's out of luck, because I've found her cat.

It's hanging on the wall between the two windows, lit up by the desk lamp directed straight at it. Someone has driven four large nails through its body. I just hope all the blood that's run down its stomach means they cut its throat first. They must have done, otherwise Lina would have known exactly where to look for him.

My fingers search frantically for the light switch by the door, which normally I can find in an instant. I have to block out the sight of the crucifixion over there, and when at last the ceiling light answers my prayers, my legs give way and I sink down in the doorway. The sofa and the table have been overturned, the desk, too, one of its legs broken. All the drawers in the filing cabinet have been wrenched open and are gaping dark and toothless. Papers are lying about all over the floor. I have to avert my eyes for a moment when I see that some of them are stuck together, soaking up the pool of blood in the middle of the floor where the cat must have been slaughtered.

I force myself to look up at the crucified cat. Above the dangling head is an inscription, scrawled with a thick marker pen: not INRI, but, "Next time it will be you." The letters are so childish that whoever wrote it must be almost illiterate, or they have disguised the handwriting by using the wrong hand. The child-like writing makes the corpse of the cat look even more appalling: innocence juxtaposed with such brutality.

The door to my father's bedroom is also ajar. My legs feel too weak, and an icy chill is running down my spine, but I have to go in, I have to assure myself that the cat-killer isn't in there. I pick up the broken desk leg, avoiding the pool of blood, go over to the door and fling it open. I stare at this room where I have never set foot. It's empty.

I can see that at once, for there's nowhere to hide. The door of the wardrobe is open and his clothes are scattered all over the floor. And his narrow bed has been violated: someone has slashed both the quilt and the mattress, the steel springs are sticking out of it like coils of intestines, and there are feathers everywhere. The slashes in the mattress are edged with red, like bleeding wounds, and there are sticky spots on some of the pillows, too. Whoever carved up the cat then set about the bed before planting the knife in the wall above the bedhead. There it is, in the middle of the wall: my father's breadknife, which he used to sharpen so carefully. Perhaps this is what closed rooms look like, if you wait too long before going in.

A scream rips through me as I stand there clutching the desk leg

– it takes me a moment to realize it is coming from the floor above. Someone has switched on the hi-fi. If anyone was in upstairs when the cat-killer was wreaking havoc down here, the noise would have been effectively drowned out by the music.

The telephone is on the floor beneath the cat. I can neither turn my back on it nor look straight at it. Half turned away, I dial the police, my hands trembling, and I don't recognize my own voice when I speak. By the time I get out of the room, I feel as if I'd run a marathon – even my legs are shaking. I walk straight into a body on the landing. The face that stares at mine is white and narrow, feeble hands clutch at me. I tear myself free. There are two of them – young men dressed in black, looking at me with fear in their eyes.

"Are you ill?" says one. I nod. He helps me to sit down on the stairs and, while I fight off the nausea, the other runs up to the second floor and comes back with Lina's boyfriend.

"Don't go in there," I whisper, curling up as my stomach lurches. "It's your cat. Someone's killed it."

Another friend of Lina's appears as I throw up, then the front door downstairs opens with a crash. Lina's friends take one look at the police, then they try to escape. One of them pushes past, knocking my head against the banisters so hard that it feels as if my jaw's broken and there's a taste of blood in my mouth.

A policeman hauls me up off the stair and shoves me against the wall. A few steps higher up, they catch Lina's boyfriend and bring him down.

"Fascists!" he yells. The riposte is a toe of a boot in his stomach.

The door on the second floor is kicked in, drowning out the racket from the hi-fi, and the music stops in a screaming whine. I hear the thuds of their boots, a yell, then more dull thuds as someone lands on the floor.

I get to my feet and stagger upstairs to put an end to this misunderstanding. But, of course, it's too late. Lina's flat reeks of dope. Two of her friends are face down on the floor already; the third takes a lunge at a policeman as I go in. He is soon overwhelmed and hurled brutally against the wall. He carries on yelling as the handcuffs are clicked into place.

"I'm the one who phoned," I begin, but then Lina storms in and wrecks it all. She flings herself at one of the policemen and pummels him with her fists.

"Swine!" she screams. "Bloody pigs!"

They lay her out on the floor, too.

"Leave her alone," I say, rather indistinctly, but as loudly as I can. "This isn't some domestic disturbance – it's . . ."

"Have you been drinking?" one of the policemen asks.

"The cat," yells Lina's boyfriend. "Tell'em about the cat!"

"Oswald!" wails Lina. "The fascist bastards have killed him!"

The policeman bawls at them to shut up. My jaw is throbbing where it hit the banisters.

"It's about the floor below," I say, "not this floor."

"We decide things here!" barks the policeman. "And you shut up!"

They then set about searching the apartment for a stash of dope. They find some, of course, and a flourishing marijuana plant. They seem well pleased, and Lina's friends are each rewarded with a well-aimed kick.

That's when I snap. I hit out at them, but naturally they hit harder, and, by the time I come to, the whole lot of us are handcuffed and are being frog-marched down the stairs.

"Assaulting a police officer," says the policeman in the guard room at Oslo Police Station. "Disturbing the peace. Possession of illegal drugs."

"For God's sake . . ." I protest, but I can hear how thick my voice is, and I smell strongly of vomit.

"How much have you had to drink?" asks the duty officer.

Police cell, in custody. Hole in the floor. Window in the door. Blanket on folding bed. Nothing loose.

My jaw aches. The hole in the floor stinks and so does the blanket.

Two hours have passed, so they say, when the doctor comes to look at my jaw.

"It'll hurt for a few days, but there's nothing wrong with it."

"I want to report something," I say.

"How much have you had to drink?" asks the doctor.

* * *

191

When it's fairly quiet I thump on the door. A quarter of an hour later, a policeman comes.

"I want to report something," I say in my thick voice.

"Tomorrow," he says. "When you're sober."

How original.

It must be morning, for the corridor has been quiet for a long time, although quietness is a relative concept.

"Igi Heitmann?" says a policewoman.

"Yes, what's left of her."

"Hans Ivar Søreid wants to see you."

I catch a glimpse of my reflection in a window on my way to his office. I've thrown up on my sweater and look quite deranged — positively criminal, I imagine.

Søreid, in contrast, is impeccably turned out. He waits until I've sat down in front of his desk. It is as if I've been summoned to the headmaster, to a cancer specialist who knows how many cigarettes I've smoked.

"Disturbing the peace, possession of illegal drugs, assault on a police officer. However, that isn't the reason I wanted to see you."

He pushes a piece of paper across the desk to me.

"It's a copy, of course. We'll keep the original. But the letter is addressed to you, so I suppose you have a right to read it. He left it in reception at his hotel."

The letter is signed Georg Fredmann.

> I've always known that this day would come, that sooner or later someone would find her, and then find their way to me. You can't run away from your past. I've never forgotten it, and there hasn't been a single day when I haven't looked at myself in the mirror and said: murderer.
>
> Perhaps I've suffered enough, knowing who I am, and what I've done. I don't know. It's no real excuse, no consolation, that I was mentally disturbed, sick enough not to remember anything of the actual event. Perhaps I've always been too much of a coward to allow myself to remember it, to recall how I struck her down. I had

hardly seen her before, and I didn't know I'd grown fond of her. Ever since, out of fear, I've had to deny myself every form of human closeness, but that does not expiate the sin.

There was something inside me, something I didn't understand, which was capable of committing such a hideous crime.

At one point I thought I could make amends through my work, by doing something meaningful. But it's not like that. I never became anything other than what I am: a man who didn't know he was capable of killing.

I have two scarlet patches of shame on my cheeks when I look up at Søreid.

"Overdose of sleeping pills," he explains. "He was dead when the staff at the hotel found him this morning. He was due to leave today, so they were to wake him early. Why do you think he wrote that letter to you?"

"Because I talked to him last night . . . . and asked him what he knew about the Petra case."

"Oh, really?" says Søreid. "A kind of confrontation, in other words. And did he confess when you talked to him?"

"No. He said he was too ill at the time to remember anything, and he'd never heard of Petra."

"How come you went to see him?"

"He was a patient at Dikemark at the time. One of his fellow patients thought he remembered hearing Fredmann say that he'd killed Petra – at the time, long before anyone knew she hadn't run away but had been killed. Harry Skau was his name – he's dead, too. You must have a file on him somewhere."

"He's dead?"

"Yes. Slipped on the bathroom floor, according to one of your men."

"Is there anything to indicate that he was in contact with Fredmann before he died?"

I swallow.

"He phoned me. To say that he'd seen him – Fredmann – in the street."

"So it all seems fairly clear, doesn't it?"

"No," I say. "Fredmann was discharged from the hospital and apparently transferred to Gaustad. But he never went there and there are no case notes on him. And yesterday some of your thugs came to my apartment and . . ."

"You can forget the charges against you. They're not terribly important. But now I really do recommend you leave this to us. If not . . ."

My face is a real mess. I haven't cleaned my teeth. I smell bad and look worse. Søreid has his brand of aftershave stamped on his chin and the price of his shirt on the collar. The idea that opposites attract each other is nonsense. Opposites can't even talk, they can only humiliate one another.

"You don't seem to have much luck with confrontations in your family, do you? But perhaps it's some consolation that, between you, you have managed to track this criminal down, despite everything?"

He comes round his desk to open the office door for me, then stops beside me as if he had suddenly thought of something.

"By the way, we've got the driver of the car which killed your father. A sixteen-year-old high on a mixture of pills and beer. I imagine not even you can connect him with the rest of the case."

The cold air brings on a blinding headache, as if the perspiration on my forehead has frozen instantly. I do not think, I just walk, taking small, slow steps like an old-age pensioner. It isn't just my head that aches – it's my jaw, my shoulders, and my back. Stiff back, stiff legs, cautious movements on the slippery ice.

I do not think. In Søreid's opinion, I need not think any more, I can just be a frozen tin soldier among all the others who know that if you step on to the ice you must be stiff and hard too.

It's a peculiar kind of not thinking; it's different to the oblivion you achieve after you've run for long enough, or made love passionately enough. This emptiness is icy cold outside and black inside. If you sink into it too deep, you risk not noticing either the darkness or the cold, and then you freeze to death.

That insight makes me walk faster and ignore the ice on the pavement – a good way of avoiding spiritual sleepwalking. I know that that kind of emptiness is called depression. And it's not the death of Georg Fredmann, or of Harry Skau, that's brought it on: it's Søreid. Grief and shame are not intrinsically the same as depression. If you have been the victim of a good upbringing, the classic response is to feel depressed instead of angry. It's important to learn to recognize that the mind plays such tricks. Right now, it is trying to hide the fact that I am tired, by blanking out my thoughts and filling my head with cotton wool.

At last I've come into my father's true inheritance. The two little keys in my pocket which give me access to what was his refuge are still the symbol of that inheritance, but now I know what the keys represent, and what the refuge is for. The keys spell humiliation and shame, and his room is a place to hide when you can no longer manage to stay outside in the frozen city, where you can slip on the ice and your lips crack until they bleed, as if you have kissed cold metal.

I was wrong when I thought Father's room in Bernt Ankersgate was where I could lay him to rest. He's done that himself, and if I go there now, from the police station, I'll be going to a mausoleum. My father still offers me that refuge, but it's an offer from a man who is dead at last.

24

I LEARN SOMETHING about violence in the bathroom in Markveien. I've had a shower and am standing in front of the mirror
trying to camouflage what has happened to my face. The bruises
are nothing I need be ashamed of – it's not my fault they are
there – yet I am doing my best to cover them up. The make-up
is only a partial success, but that's not the point. The point is that
I'm trying. There's no way a woman can display such bruises with
pride.

I don't know whether Hans Ivar Søreid is really satisfied with the
equation which gives Fredmann as the answer, but I am not. There
are far too many other considerations for it to be that simple. The
story may almost tie up, but "almost" means it may be completely
wrong.

Harald Østgaard is one of the key factors in the equation which
points to Fredmann as the solution.

He doesn't answer the phone. The woman who does is angry –
with me.

"You've got a nerve," says Vivian Østgaard, "phoning here after
. . . No, you may not talk to Harald."

"Why not? Don't you think he ought to decide that for himself?"

"Well, he could, if he were here. But he's not."

"So would you please tell me where I can find him?"

"Why should I? What right do you have to interfere in our
lives?"

I haven't time for this. My impatience may be partly due to the
fact that I've asked myself the same question, without coming up
with a good answer.

"This is not just about Harald's addiction," I say. "I don't give a
damn about that, for I'm certainly not out to expose him."

"It may be easy for you not to give a damn, but it's not that simple for him – or for me."

"Listen. A man took his own life last night because of a crime I don't think he committed. Harald can help me prove that. He might think that is as useful as making teacups."

Silence at the other end. I don't mention the reason why he can help me prove Fredmann's innocence: the possibility that Østgaard is guilty himself.

"Are you there?"

"Yes. Yes, I am. You see . . . sometimes he needs to be alone. And I'm not supposed to know where he is."

"But you do know."

"Yes, of course. You can't live together for years without knowing things like that. All right, then, you can come here, and I'll show you the way."

Yes, I think, as I ring off, you'll show me the way. Although I don't know who slaughtered Lina's cat, I don't think it was a woman.

She's standing in the doorway when I arrive, dressed in her outdoor clothes. We're not going far. She gives me brief directions, but otherwise is silent. She doesn't look at me when she tells me to stop the car at the top of a hill sloping down towards a field that extends blue-black until it is one with the winter sky.

"I'll get out here," she says. "No point in my going down with you." She goes round to my side of the car and I wind down the window.

"There." She points to the edge of the field where a light is shining in a window. "It belongs to a friend of his, a painter, who works there in the summer. Harald sort of looks after the place for him. It has a wood stove, I think."

"Don't you want me to drive you back?"

"No, I can walk – besides, I've nothing else to do."

The snow hasn't been cleared up to the house, so I leave the car by the side of the road and trudge through the new snow towards the light. When I get close I see it isn't a house; it's even smaller than a cabin – just a hut equipped with a chimney. Harald's friend must like painting out of doors, for there can't be much room for many canvases inside.

There's a good smell of wood smoke.

When I knock, I realize why Vivian didn't want to come to the hut with me. The voice that answers is loud and shrill, as if Østgaard himself were not sure how to pitch it. Harald is drunk.

"No," he shrieks. "Go away. You've no business here!"

I wait before opening the door.

"Vivian!" the same voice yells. "Go home!"

"It's not Vivian," I say, "it's . . ."

I hear something fall over inside, a chair or a table, followed by the sound of breaking glass. I really feel like turning back, but then Østgaard wrenches open the door and stares at me, his mouth half-open, his eyes bloodshot. He doesn't look as if he has ever held a teacup in his hand.

"You! You here? What do you want of me? You can go away, too. Did Vivian send you here, the bitch?"

Suddenly, I'm tired. The glimpse of the room behind him – an overturned chair by a rickety table, empty bottles chucked in the corner by the stove – it fills me with disgust. Drunken men. Tired women.

"Georg Fredmann died last night," I say. "But perhaps I'd better come back another time."

"Who did you say?"

"Georg Fredmann. One of your patients. The one you transferred to Gaustad but who never got there."

The door, which Harald was holding on to, is blown open as he falls forward. He just manages to grab hold of the door-frame with one hand and teeters on the threshold, his arms outstretched, trying to regain his balance. He looks like a madman who has decided he wants to fly, but has second thoughts at the edge of the cliff.

"Don't go," he says, looking at me with his bloodshot eyes. "You needn't. Really."

I recognize that look: the feeling of shame mixed with defiance. He knows what I've seen, but he can't bear to admit it, so I refrain from helping him.

"Come on in," he says, straightening himself up and gesturing towards the room. "It's not very . . ."

"That doesn't matter."

I close the door behind me and let him find me a chair. The little room soon warms up. The walls are covered with plasterboard and the floor is insulated with glass fibre, bits of which are protruding. It smells of drink, of course, but most of all of birchwood.

Østgaard rinses his face in a bowl of melted snow and a pine needle or two remain stuck on his forehead after he's wiped it on the sleeve of his sweater. He fills the kettle from the same bowl and puts it on the stove. It hisses as the water touches the hot metal.

"This doesn't happen often," he says, glancing round the room. His beard doesn't quite conceal the brief grimace as his eyes settle on the empty bottles. "But occasionally everything becomes . . . a bit too much."

"Yes. Was it my visit that did it this time?"

"Partly."

"Was there something else?"

"It doesn't matter."

It may do, I think; it may matter, but I can wait to find out whatever else made him come here. For all I know, he may have quarrelled with Vivian – but I don't think so.

"Now, what was it you were saying?" he says.

"Well, it's about a young girl who died recently, Siv Underland. It looks as if her death is linked with another death several years ago, when you were working at Dikemark. Last night, Georg Fredmann, a patient there at the time, took his own life. And in a letter he maintains he killed the first girl, Petra Holmgren."

He stares at me, frowns, and leans forward. More than a splash of water is needed to enable him to follow what I'm saying.

"Last time when I came to see you, you said you couldn't recall any of your patients. Does his name mean anything to you now?"

"I remember the name. Oh, yes, I remember the name."

"Do you remember discharging him from the hospital and transferring him to Gaustad?"

"It's possible. I can't recall the details, you understand. That would be in his notes."

"But do you think what he says might be true? That he could have done such a thing?"

He draws a deep breath and glances up at the ceiling before looking at me again.

"I've no idea. He wasn't my patient."

So that's it. Østgaard gets up, fetches one of the bottles, and puts another log in the stove. He finds a cup and pours some spirits into it.

I can give him all the time he needs, because now I know he wants to tell me. But first he has to look back over years of bitterness. He swirls the contents of his cup round and round as he stares at it, as if there were something at the bottom, something apart from the gleaming spirits.

"It's so . . . bloody awful. All those years – all that time I've gone around being sort of grateful. To him."

"Yes."

"Do you understand? I thought he was doing me a favour. That I was lucky to get away with it so lightly. Lightly! But it wasn't like that at all."

"Was it the other way round – was it you who helped him?"

"Yes. But I didn't understand that. Idiotic of me. Of course, I wondered about it, about why he wanted me to sign the papers for him. It didn't seem all that important. And I couldn't very well refuse."

No, he wasn't in a position to refuse.

"You see, I always expected someone to find out . . . about that business – the fact that I prescribed drugs and used them myself. For the whole of that last year, anyhow, I was waiting for someone to discover it. I was scared stiff every single day . . . and, at the same time, in a way I wished it would happen. You know what it's like. I couldn't believe they were all so blind."

Not all of them.

"When it eventually happened, it didn't turn out as I thought it would. No report to the ethical committee, no immediate dismissal, no report to the police. Nothing. Only sick leave, and a message that I should resign. And then those papers. If I signed them, that would be that. Don't you see, I had to? It wasn't as if Fredmann wasn't going to have treatment – he was going to have private therapy."

"Really?"

"I thought that was the reason – that it had something to do with money, taxes or whatever. I didn't understand anything about the transfer to Gaustad . . . And I didn't know he was so sick . . . that it was about something quite different. But even if it's now a question of one of his patients killing that girl, why should Underland wish to conceal it?"

He hasn't touched the cup with spirits in it. A log in the stove crackles, a dry, pleasant, holiday sound.

"She was a neighbour of his."

The flame in the oil lamp between us flickers a little in the draught from the window. Harald Østgaard puts the cup down carefully. He rests his hands on the table in front of him, his fingers intertwined.

"The bastard," he mumbles.

We stay in the hut for a little while longer. He wants to tell me the story all over again. He drinks and keeps asking me whether I understand — that he had no idea what he was doing, that he had no choice. Do I understand, I wonder. And do I understand what all these years have been like?

He doesn't want to go back to Vivian and I spend a lot of time persuading him to. When he finally agrees, he gathers up his clothes and I go on ahead to start the car.

Outside the hut, I can't see the main road up on the hill, only the fields stretching out south and disappearing into the darkness. The sky is dark and studded with stars that are always invisible in the city. Far away a train hoots once on its way to Tønsberg. Then it grows quiet.

I shiver and start heading down to the car.

Suddenly I hear the kind of sound-effect they use on the radio — someone squeezing a bag of cornflour to simulate footsteps crunching in the snow. What a fool, I think — you don't need to use cornflour in midwinter. That's when the blow falls.

25

THE DARKNESS EXPLODES into red flames and I almost expect to see the glorious shining apparitions that are meant to welcome us to the other world. But something tells me that I'm not quite dead yet: the searing pain in my head – only life can hurt that much.

It feels warm lying here. A piece of Boy Scout wisdom floats into my head: when snow feels warm, that's when it's really dangerous.

Igi moves a cautious hand out from her body. I can move my fingers. I can fumble. The snow isn't just warm, it's smooth and hard, like rock or plastic – like a plastic sheet.

For a moment I'm grateful that someone has helped me in from the cold, but only for a moment. Perhaps that someone is still there, holding whatever it was that hit me on the head . . .

I listen. No movement on the plastic-covered floor. Instead there's a new radio sound-effect, but this time it's not cornflour being squeezed – it's cellophane. Cellophane crackles like a cosy open fire. Or, more to the point, like a blazing fire.

My fingers close round a small metal object lying on the floor. I grip it tightly to give myself enough courage to open my eyes and face what I know to be true: beads of sweat are breaking out on my face not because I'm warmly dressed; nor is it the pain in my head that makes it feel as if I have a flame-thrower behind my eyelids. There is a wall of fire facing me when I half-open my streaming eyes. I'm lying curled up on the floor of what must be Østgaard's hut, but it's hard to recognize now: the flames have almost consumed one wall and the smoke is thick.

I can just make out a rectangle in the midst of the flames. It must be the wall with the door. I stretch out one leg and knock over the table with the oil lamp on it. I grab the lamp and curl up blindly on my right side, facing the wall where I think the window is.

Harald Østgaard's body is lying by the wall. He doesn't react when I shake him and I don't know if he's breathing. But that's not surprising because I'm hardly breathing myself. What little oxygen is left in here is down close to the floor. I don't know for how many seconds I can stand upright. But I have to try. I can't get a hefty great man out through a window, and if I jump out first myself, enough oxygen will be sucked in to turn the room into a bomb. So I have to try the door, and I have to drag Østgaard with me. I put one arm over his chest and with the other I grab the collar of his sweater, then I start crawling on my elbows and knees.

It's a peculiar jerky motion, but I tell myself that we haven't far to go and it doesn't matter that I can't open my eyes or that it feels as if I'm gulping fire straight down into my lungs.

I can't do it. It's too slow. It hurts too much. I bury my face in his sweater and breathe in something that isn't fire, once, twice, three times. Then I put both hands under his arms, haul us both up and hold him tight, as if in a passionate embrace. I can see nothing. I just lurch into the flames using Østgaard's body as a shield, towards where I think the door is. We hit it. I can feel the door-handle against my hand, but it won't open. And I know it opens outwards.

I stagger back two steps and realize that I can't do this more than once, so I shove Østgaard at the door as hard as I can. The whole frame gives way. The door and the burning woodwork fall to the ground, with me and Østgaard on top.

Someone screams and I think I can hear sirens. My face is still pressed into Østgaard's chest. Then my coughing turns into laughter as I wonder what we look like, the two of us locked in this embrace. Someone grabs my arm, lifts me off him and drags us both away from the burning hut. I carry on laughing hysterically until I hear what the woman bending over Østgaard says:

"Is he breathing?"

The fire engine roars down the road and the wail of the sirens drowns the reply. The women turn Østgaard over on his side. One of them sticks her finger into his mouth, his body twitches and he retches.

I sit there in the snow until one of the firemen comes over.

"How are you feeling? If you can manage it, it'd be better if you stood up."

He helps me. I'm dizzy, but I can stand. It doesn't occur to me to tell him about the violent thumping in my head.

"I'm OK," I say. "There's nothing wrong with me except slight hysteria, and that's over now."

I think. I hope. The firemen confirm that there's no point in trying to put out the flames. The whole hut is on fire. An ambulance fetches Harald and the police are on their way. The place is swarming with people and all I can think of is getting away. But there are two things I must do first. The shattered door is lying in front of the hut. One of the firemen drags it away for me and I try the door-handle once again. There's no doubt about it: the door has been locked.

The firemen have a mobile phone and Vivian Østgaard answers at once.

I tell her about the fire and that Harald has been taken to hospital in Tønsberg.

"I think he's all right," I say. "They got there amazingly fast. I'm sorry if it seems rather unfeeling, but can I just ask you whether anyone else was trying to get hold of him today?"

"No. But he did phone someone . . . before he went up to the hut. I don't know who – he didn't want me to hear the conversation."

"You didn't see anyone near the hut when you left?"

"No. But . . . there was something I thought rather strange. A car came along just after you'd gone on, and it stopped up on the hill. It seemed an odd place to stop."

"Did you see what kind of car?"

"It was a dark colour. That modern kind . . . you know, an estate which is low in the front. Do you know what I mean?"

Yes. It sounds very like a Pontiac TransSport.

I lie to the firemen. I say I want to drive down to fetch Vivian Østgaard and take her to the hospital. They hesitate, but finally they agree.

I can't resist putting my foot down hard once Gorbie is on the deserted E18. My attempt to break the speed limit isn't that impress-ive, but it does make me concentrate on driving, instead of on the question which is tormenting me more than the pain at the back of my head. Has the person who struck that blow attacked someone else, as well as me? And I don't mean Harald Østgaard.

I wonder what the consequences of a blow to the head are for a pregnant woman. I suspect I look rather crazed as I sit behind the wheel. I have a feeling that I would go slightly crazy if . . .

Timing is not my strong point. I have chosen an awkward moment to realize I do not want to lose this child.

I slow down before I get to the Nesøya junction, and as I approach the house in Otto Blehrsvei I reduce Gorbie's speed to a crawl. There, outside the garage, is Øyvind Underland's Pontiac.

The house is in darkness apart from a light above the front door. A man is standing there with his arms folded. He's thin and not very tall: it's Charles the Midge.

As I drive past I see the house isn't completely dark. A couple of lights shine from the windows on the great façade facing the terrace with its swaddled rose bushes. That is the room where Ellen Underland received me – it now seems a very long time ago.

I park the car further up the road, where it can't be seen from the house. I can't decide whether the Midge's stance reminds me of a bouncer's or a bodyguard's, but he's never given me the impression that he belongs in the Underlands' social circle.

I creep under the bushes along the fences of two neighbouring gardens like a thief. The frozen crust of the snowdrifts takes my weight, and I make it to the open snowy expanse at the back of the Underlands' glasshouse. The Midge can't see me here, and this part of the house is in darkness. I have to cross the expanse of snow to reach the house. The frozen crust breaks after a few steps, with a sound like a scream, like a saw. It must be audible hundreds of yards away, as must the pounding of my heart, and my breathing. I can taste blood in my mouth. I stand dead still, with one leg sunk deep in the snow, like a lopsided garden sculpture, next to a birdbath.

No one throws open windows, lights don't blaze forth, the Midge doesn't come running round the house. Another step – the crust breaks. It's better to jump it, and in four or five clumsy long strides, I reach the glass wall.

Still no reaction from inside. The great panes of glass seem to refract the cold, just as they did with the sunlight, refusing to absorb it, repelling it. The darkness inside is dense, impenetrable. I creep along, following the angles of the wall, one hand on the frosty glass. In places the surface feels rough under my fingers: ice crystals whose beauty is invisible in the dark. Before I reach the steps to the terrace, the glass is interrupted by a timber wall.

I stop at the end of it for a moment before daring to lean forward and look in. What I see is like a Rembrandt study. A single lamp at the far end of the long room partially lights up the man standing beside it. Yngve Caspari's profile, illuminated from below, is facing the part of the room hidden from me by the timber wall. His lips are moving. He's talking to someone sitting there in the gloom.

I want to see the rest of the picture. I edge forwards, hoping that Caspari has the full attention of his invisible listeners. Øyvind and Ellen Underland are sitting in front of him, each in a corner of the sofa, together but separate, a great empty space between them.

They are both looking straight at Yngve, and I see how much they resemble each other. Their expression is a mixture of fear and rage, as if they weren't there by choice, but are sitting in their own living-room under duress. Yngve Caspari has something in his hand: a square object, a book.

I am so fascinated by the trio, I don't hear the cautious footsteps in the snow until a figure appears round the corner of the house. Now the Midge throws caution to the winds. He bangs hard on the window.

"Yngve!" he shouts. "Bloody hell, there's someone out here!"

Then he leaps at me. I don't stand a chance of getting away. Suddenly I'm drowned in a sea of light, which leaves me blinded for a moment. Yngve has switched on the terrace floodlighting.

Charles grabs my collar and jerks, but loses his footing on the slippery stones of the terrace. We fall together, head over heels. I kick him hard and am the first to get up on all fours. I grab the object he's dropped, stand up, take a few steps back and point the gun at him.

"Stay where you are," I say.

Charles moans, lying in a foetal position in front of me. I couldn't care less that I've kicked him in the crotch.

The trio inside are all staring at me. Ellen's mouth is open as if in a soundless scream, and I know what she is seeing: a young woman with a gun in her hand.

Yngve opens the door to the terrace, then turns back to the couple.

"Sit down," he says harshly. "And you can come on in," he adds, referring to me.

"What about Charles?"

"Leave him there for all I care."

The room looks different now, drenched in the light from the terrace. It's no longer a Rembrandt scene. This cold interior with the married couple huddled in each corner of the sofa reminds me more of a David Hockney: modern and distanced, full of trivial details revealed in the flat light.

"Welcome," says Yngve. "Perhaps you'd like to sit down. You look as if you need to."

I take a seat by the table with the lamp. Only now do I realize my knees are knocking.

"Have you been to Bernt Ankersgate recently?" I ask him. "Or did you send Charles?"

He looks blankly at me. My judgement may not be very reliable, but I don't believe he did in the cat.

"What's happened to your face?" he says.

"We can go into that later," I say.

"Perhaps you'd give me . . . that?" He's pointing at the gun.

"No, I don't think so."

"As you wish. It's no big deal. The problem is that Ellen and Øyvind here are not that keen to talk to me. And, unlike my father, I don't have any money to buy secrets I can blackmail people with. So Charles brought that . . . disgusting object with him. What do you think, Øyvind, has Father backed the wrong horse this time, or do you think you will still be able to pull strings on his behalf? Do you think anyone will listen to you, from now on, when you go to the Ministry of Health and try to sell my father's plans for Dikemark? Or do you think they will think you've too much shit on your fingers now, and too cheap a house?"

Øyvind Underland doesn't reply.

"Please answer. We're listening. As will the police."

Underland clamps his mouth shut, the muscle in his jaw working overtime, repressing everything he doesn't want to say.

"And if you're thinking that Igi here, with that weapon in her hand, wants to stop me from finishing what I've begun, you're mistaken. Isn't that so?" Yngve says, turning to me.

I'm thinking about what I looked like on my way here: wild-eyed, clothes reeking of smoke, a Fury with revenge in her heart. But that was when the person who hit me on the head was just a figure in the dark, not a real person like those two sitting opposite me, prisoners in their own home, imprisoned behind these glass walls. Being careful must become second nature here – there's so much that can be smashed.

"That depends on what you've begun," I say.

"What shall we call it?" Yngve replies. "A conversation, perhaps. Or . . . an interrogation. You came at an opportune moment. I need someone to read and it's much more effective if a woman reads it."

He places a hand on the book he's put on the table between us.

"Charles has had this in his possession for far too long, and, besides, I don't know whether he's even capable of reading. I bet he contented himself with looking at the illustrations. The drawings. He's stuck in some photographs – naked girls. Siv and Petra. What do you say about that, Øyvind? Siv and Petra! Attractive girls?"

Only now do I register that he's high – not on drugs or other forbidden fruit, but on knowledge. Yngve Caspari is full of holy wrath because he knows the truth. And I'm glad that I, as yet in ignorance, am the one holding the gun.

Øyvind Underland shifts uncomfortably on the sofa. His wife sits quite still, but she's gripping the arm so hard that her knuckles show white, as if they are about to burst through the taut skin.

Siv Underland has decorated the cover of the book with her own name surrounded by artistic scrolls in Indian ink. There's no warning to keep your hands off, but then it isn't a child's diary. It doesn't consist of girlish confidences, or casual remarks; it is a kind of logbook of a journey with a limited but definite aim: a journey back into childhood.

I look up at Yngve.

"So Charles took it, when he broke into her cabin with that . . ."

"With the lingam, yes. The little shit has rather fetishistic tendencies. Now, read. I've marked the sections which are of most interest, as you can see."

I'm holding Siv's diary in one hand and a gun in the other. I don't like it, but suddenly the two things are connected: the description of her journey and what became the end of it.

26

"READ!" ORDERS YNGVE.

"'To see Siri'," I begin. "That was her therapist."

Øyvind Underland leans forward.

"Therapist? A quack, a healer! She could have got the girl to believe anything. That kind of thing can't be called therapy, it . . ."

"And what you are doing can be? It turns out that one of your patients committed suicide as recently as last night. Not a great success story for your therapy, is it? Georg Fredmann, his name was. And you needn't pretend you don't remember him."

I draw a deep breath, unsettled by the streak of hysteria in my voice. My heart is a blind bird trapped in my chest, beating its wings in frustrated rage.

"Read," Yngve says again.

"'To see Siri. Feel clean in a way, but at the same time confused. Made masks of Mother's and Father's faces. Neither of them has eyes. They don't see me. And they've got pencil-thin lines for mouths. I feel like screaming when I look at them. Why don't they scream?'"

I have to clear my voice. Ellen has turned her head away, towards the darkness outside.

The gun gets in the way as I turn the pages.

"'To see Siri today. Drew a girl I thought was me at first, but which became Petra. She's about to leave. It becomes a sort of wedding picture, with a border of flowers. Should be lovely. But when I tried to put in the man, it became nothing but brown and black – shitty, all of it, around the flowers and over them. It's crazy. I think I have some memory of them leaving together. But then it's as if the memory fades, as if it's just something I've seen on a photograph, or been told. Or something I wished had happened? Even my memory isn't my own, not something I can trust.'"

There are no other sounds in the room, only my voice and Siv's words. I swallow a few times when I see what's in the next section. Then I read it.

"'To see Siri. Drew a man with nothing but a dirty red mess down below. Bastard, bastard, BASTARD.'"

New date.

"'To see Siri. Drew a man in a square. The square is the door into my room. Siri asked if I knew who the man was and I said no. But it's not true.'"

New date.

"'At the cabin for the first time. Hardly anything is as I remembered it. Apart from the smell, which I recognized the moment I went in. They're in that smell – Petra and Father. I know we've been here together. I'm very small and I feel like crying. Mother isn't here. Why isn't she?'"

Yngve raises his hand to interrupt me.

"About how old was Siv when you began to rent the cabin?"

Øyvind has lowered his head. He doesn't look up as Yngve speaks. But Ellen answers from the dark she's staring into.

"Two, three. Something like that."

Her voice is dry, sober.

"So a very small child?"

She doesn't reply.

"And Petra?"

No reply.

"Fourteen? Fifteen?"

"I must have a glass of water," I say. Yngve nods.

"The kitchen's to the right at the end of the passage," says Ellen automatically, still without looking at me.

I'm about to turn on the tap when I find I've brought that loathsome gun with me. There is a chilling clunk as I put it down on the tiles next to the sink. I splash my face with water. Having filled a jug and hunted out four glasses, I have no free hand for the gun. I lean my forehead against the cupboard above the sink for a moment, then I stick the gun inside the waistband of my trousers. Oh, my God.

None of them looks at me as I put the jug down on the table. All three shake their heads when I ask them if they want water.

"Go on," says Yngve.

A sound comes from the sofa. Øyvind is almost bent double, his powerful hands resting on his knees.

"Stop," he whispers. "For God's sake, stop."

"It's too late now," says Yngve. "Go on."

And I think I see Ellen nodding.

"'To see Laila today. It's sick. Nothing makes sense any more. Did I really see Petra get into that car? I remember her sitting on the edge of my bed, saying goodbye. She said goodbye! But she didn't give me the butterfly. I found it, I do remember that. I found it in the basement room. And I remember Mother shouting.'"

"She came home rather too early, didn't she?" I say. "From her friend's. Just as you did. Was that how it happened?"

Ellen Underland nods. I put the gun down. We don't need it any more.

"You had a staff meeting after school, didn't you? So you were going to be back late. But then you weren't late after all."

"I left before the meeting was over. I didn't feel too well, and we'd finished discussing my subject."

"But Siv wasn't home when you got there, although she should have been, because she'd missed school that day."

"No. Siv wasn't at home."

She turns towards me, but doesn't look at my face. She's staring at the diary in my lap. You have to do something with your gaze when it has no place to go.

"But there was someone in the house?"

"Yes. Oh, yes. Petra was there. She was going to look after Siv. And . . . Øyvind was there."

For a brief moment she looks at her husband's bowed back, then turns her eyes back to my lap.

"In the basement room?"

"She screamed at me, you see. Screamed so terribly – and I had a headache. It was horrible what she said. I asked her to stop, but she went on and on, screaming about what he had done to her. One of those little bronze sculptures was standing there. My parents gave it to me, do you remember, Øyvind?"

"Yes," he whispers. "Stop now, Ellen."

"Why should I? We've never talked about it. I didn't know . . . that you went to the cabin with them. Is it true? That Siv saw you there? Had it gone that far?"

Something has happened to her voice – it no longer fits her body. It takes me a moment to grasp that it's a child's voice. It's wrong, somehow, like everything else here.

"Be quiet," says Øyvind.

"Is it true?"

"I may have gone there, yes."

"And Siv?" Yngve's voice is loud and harsh.

"I never touched Siv. Never!"

Øyvind's hands are shaking and he stares at Yngve, enraged.

"But what about that drawing – of you in the doorway to her bedroom?"

"Christ knows. Of course I went into her bedroom – I was her father!"

"You fetched Petra that day, didn't you?" I say. "Before you asked Siv to go and see her friend?"

He doesn't reply, but he has no need to: the answer is written all over his face. I turn to Ellen.

"Did Siv scream at you, too?" I ask. "They both wanted to hold you responsible, didn't they? They wanted to know why you did nothing to stop it, isn't that so?"

But Ellen is far away, and I can't see her eyes behind her large glasses, which reflect the light from the lamp. A blind mask, with a pencil line for a mouth.

I take the little metal object I found in Østgaard's hut out of my pocket.

"You lost this, you know."

It's a blue enamel hair-slide. She reaches up to touch her hair in a gesture that is almost like a caress.

"What gave you the idea of the fire? Was it Charles setting fire to the church?"

She nods.

"You looked like her," she says after a while. "Out there on the terrace."

"I know. The gun."

She nods again.

212

Øyvind Underland raises his head a little. Slowly, the unbearable truth begins to dawn on him.

"Did you and Siv fight over it?" I say. "Did you fight over the gun?"

"She wanted to know what . . . Øyvind had done," says Ellen Underland, looking at me. "She was so angry about Petra. And . . . I couldn't answer her. I just couldn't. And then . . . it all happened so quickly — so terribly quickly."

There is a scream from her husband, who leaps up. She doesn't look at him. Yngve silences him and pushes him back down on to the sofa.

It's not just distance separating the couple now: between them lies their daughter. Ellen Underland knows that only too well, so she doesn't turn to her husband, but to me. She averts her eyes, but it's me she's talking to.

I have heard some confessions before, and I know it's not true that people with a sin on their conscience long to confess. Confession hurts, it means going down to hell for a while; that's why the Catholic Church made it a duty and a sacred act. Without the obligation and the absolution afterwards, all but a few of us would prefer to keep quiet. I have no absolution to give Ellen Underland, but perhaps she feels she is under an obligation — not to me, or to her husband, but to the girl I resembled, standing there in the snow with a gun in my hand. But she doesn't believe in redemption. None of us does. We who fail to confess always let those who could forgive us die first.

"I managed to forget it all at some point. Quite when, I don't know — after we moved here, perhaps. Isn't that odd? It disappeared from my consciousness, as if nothing had happened. But then when Siv . . . Siv . . . when she came . . . Then it reared its head again. Grey and shadowy, as if I were sleepwalking when it happened. I think I was a sort of sleepwalker — just going through the motions, not thinking."

Her mouth is dry and I pour her a glass of water. She holds it in both hands, as if afraid of losing it.

"But it was a kind of relief, that there was so much to do. To be arranged, I mean. I could think about all those . . . practical details, provided I didn't think about the actual . . . the fact that Petra was dead. I steered my thoughts around it, in a way. I had to. We couldn't both fall apart. And Siv was there. I remember that was almost the worst thing: we had to leave her on her own that night while we went over to the church. What if she'd woken up, and neither of us had been there?"

She's talking in euphemisms. Like Harry Skau, there are words she can't bring herself to say. Petra is "dead", not "murdered". That doesn't surprise me, but what amazes me is that she's capable of using her name at all.

"When Øyvind told me Petra was thinking of running away with that chap, Johansson, the idea of the chapel came to me. We had to get her out of the house. We couldn't leave her lying there in the basement room – Siv might have found her. Once she'd gone, it was almost as if she had run away. I got Øyvind to put that note in the Holmgrens' mail box. She'd sent it to him at the office – afraid I'd see it, I suppose. He gave me that photograph, too. It was the only thing he had of hers. I thought I would burn it . . . But then I went to Copenhagen for a weekend. After that I suppose I stopped thinking about her. It was as if it was over."

"What about Fredmann?" I ask.

"Oh, him. The problem was he'd seen Johansson's car – he'd seen she wasn't in it. Øyvind didn't know what to do about it. But I knew, straight away. It was as if I was on autopilot or something. I came up with all the answers."

She's still addressing my lap. She falls silent for a moment and her voice is reduced to a whisper when she goes on.

"But when Siv . . . I had no answers then. There was nothing I could say. Something just happened – something . . . dreadful."

There is no more. The glass she's holding is almost empty. She puts it down carefully on the table and turns her head away again. The room is quite still, as if we weren't even breathing.

Later, after I've rung the police, Øyvind Underland joins me in the kitchen. I'm making coffee and it gurgles in the percolator.

He sits with those empty hands on the table. He looks old.

Some say that everyone longs to be opened up, like a tin can. Whether or not Øyvind Underland has longed for that, he's cut himself on the jagged edges.

"I didn't know . . . about Siv," he says.

I don't answer. If he's practising what he's going to say under interrogation, it's not up to me to help him. But because there's more than one possible solution to complex equations, I have to ask him one more thing.

"What about Fredmann? Did he blackmail you?"

He doesn't like me reminding him that he's not exactly blameless.

"What? No. It wasn't my idea, really."

"But you made him believe he'd killed her. Ellen couldn't have done that."

"No, that's true."

"And what about the chapel? She didn't go there alone."

He puts his head in his hands now.

"I suppose we did do it together."

He doesn't have to say any more. He doesn't have to tell me what that kind of togetherness must feel like. His wrestler's hands are shaking, his armour shattered for good.

Ellen Underland is standing by the window looking out on the terrace when Samuel Hansson arrives. There is no sign of Charles, who presumably sneaked off ages ago.

Outside the snow-covered garden is a dead white sea. When I switch off the floodlighting, there's only the reflection of her own face to fix her gaze on, but she waits for a while before turning to Samuel.

27

B ENNY HAS LEFT a note on his pillow before leaving.
"Burnt children smell bad," it says. "Try a shower before
you meet Samuel. The Polo at twelve o'clock. I recommend Elizabeth Arden's foundation."

I gave him a confused résumé when I got home last night and
now he's pretending he isn't worried.

I've got half an hour, so it's a quick shower. By the time I get
to the café, Samuel is halfway through his open shrimp sandwich.
Not that he's necessarily waited for long – the rest disappears in two
gulps. The smears of mayonnaise on his plate give me my first
experience of morning sickness. Afternoon sickness, to be precise.

"How's your head?" he says when he sees my expression.

"I only feel it when I cry. And if you say anything about my face,
I'll tell them you did it."

But Samuel is too tired to laugh at girlish jokes. He's been up
with the Underlands all night, at separate interrogations. That sounds
very lonely: separate interrogations.

"Surely the gun wasn't your idea, was it?" Samuel asks, after my
cup of tea arrives.

"No. You must talk to Yngve about that. Or rather, to Charles.
He's got several other things to answer for as well. I imagine he was
trying to impress Yngve by setting fire to the church. Or else he
has a tendency to be more rebellious than Yngve thinks – quite
apart from his fetishistic tendencies, I mean."

"You mean Yngve didn't know he started the fire?"

"No. But he probably guessed both he and Charles would be
under suspicion. Yngve thought some crazy defectors from his order
were plotting against him."

"And Charles? He hung on to that diary ever since he stole
it?"

"Yes. God knows what he wanted it for. Maybe he felt it made him one up on his boss – a part of Siv Yngve hadn't had."

"And how did Yngve discover he had it?"

"I bet he likes to think it was revealed in a trance or something, but of course he had seen her with it. They were living together while she was going to see Siri Ekelund. And Yngve knew perfectly well that Charles had broken into her cabin, so it wasn't difficult to figure out the rest. The diary identifies Øyvind Underland pretty clearly as the man who'd abused Petra, doesn't it? When Siv came home that day, Petra was already dead, but what she remembered, according to the diary, was that her father fetched Petra from her room and told Siv to get lost. So then she made up this fairy-story of everything turning out as Petra had wanted, with her going off in Johansson's car. Siv didn't realize it was actually Ellen who killed Petra until it was too late. Is Ellen talking, by the way?"

"Not much. But she's quite coherent. It's Øyvind who's at a loss."

"That's not so strange. And he must have been in quite a state the day Ellen came home and caught him with Petra. He certainly was afterwards. It was Ellen who took the initiative. She knew about the work on the chapel and realized how they could use the farewell note Petra had sent Øyvind at his office. Enterprising lady, in a way. She got the photograph out of him, too. Sent it from Copenhagen when she went there for the weekend."

"And when did you realize it was Ellen?"

"Not until I found the hair-slide. No one except Underland or Østgaard could have got Fredmann to think he'd killed Petra. And when it turned out that Fredmann wasn't Østgaard's patient . . ."

"Østgaard contacted Underland after you paid him that first visit. When Ellen heard about it, she realized there was a danger you might see the connection."

"So did she follow me there?"

"Not to Åsgårdstrand. She went there after Underland had told her what Østgaard had said. And then she saw you and Vivian on the way to the hut."

"Yes, Vivian noticed her car – after she'd shown me where her husband was."

"So it wasn't that car which ran down your father. Ellen knew nothing about him until you produced the butterfly pendant that day."

"Chance. Just like Harry Skau's death. Old men do die, at some point. And my father's death was a coincidence – it's up to us to discover whether or not there is any meaning in it. What do you think, shall we toss for it? Heads for meaningful, tails for meaningless?"

He slips a coin on to the table, but my hand is quicker than his and covers the coin.

"If we leave it there and don't look at it, then there's a fifty-fifty chance that it's tails and fifty-fifty that it's heads. So in a way it's both – until I take my hand away. Should we leave it there, do you think?"

"That's up to you, isn't it? It's your hand and . . ."

"And my father."

I put the coin in my pocket.

"Theft," says Samuel.

"Reward," I say. "There's one bastard I want you to make Søreid find. Someone who cuts up cats to frighten off inquisitive people. Caspari senior's hangers-on should be a good place to start. He wasn't exactly thrilled that I'd found out about the information he'd bought from Holmgren. Naturally Caspari expected something in return for paying off Holmgren's gambling debts; what he got was information about the backhanders being exchanged by Underland and Holmgren: a cheap house for Underland, contracts at Dikemark for Holmgren. That made it terribly easy for Caspari to get Underland to lobby for his plans for Dikemark. Caspari will presumably have to give up trying to buy the property now. And, while you're at it, you can make sure Søreid drops those drug charges against my neighbours, or else I'll insist on having the charges against me taken up again."

"I'd better go," says Samuel. "Now I've got so much to do."

"Don't you want to go home and get some sleep first?"

"We-ell, I don't know." He hesitates. "She's come back, you see."

I ought to have known. That's why he hasn't got Lola with him.

* * *

I have one more visit to make before going home.

The house seems as quiet and deserted as last time I was here, but now I know what the single lighted lamp means: Laila Holmgren is at home alone.

She peers at me through the crack in the door, then smiles and opens it quickly.

"I knew you'd come back," she says, letting me into the soft shadows of the living-room. "Your father did, too."

"Why didn't you tell me you knew him last time I was here?" I ask.

"Maybe I thought you wouldn't want to know. After all, you're his daughter – or you were."

"Leonard didn't know that he came here, did he?"

"No. Leonard wanted to surprise me, if Andreas found her. But he came all the same. He thought I ought to know. He was so nice – so gentle . . ."

"Yes."

"Sometimes we just sat here, without saying much. He knew I couldn't leave Leonard. Because of Petra. I didn't want him to lose both of us. Do you understand?"

"Yes."

Her hands are lying calmly in her lap this time. There's nothing they need smooth out, no muscles they need to soften. They lie together, relaxed.

"He was proud of you," she says.

"Was he?"

"Yes. He often talked about you. But you were much younger then. I told Siv about him, when she came here and saw that photograph."

Of course. That fits. It was here that Siv first came in contact with Father, and hence with me.

"Will you come again?" she says as she lets me out on to the small, carefully swept steps.

"Yes," I say, knowing I won't look for him in the shadows of Bernt Ankersgate any more. There's more of him here.

As I drive back into town, light snowflakes, like stars or angels, have begun to fall.

* * *

Benny is sitting at the kitchen table when I get back. He's cutting a green pepper into thin slices and he smiles wryly when he sees me, as if he's just thought of a good joke.

"So was it Elizabeth Arden?"

"You'd used it all up – it had to be Revlon."

Another smile. He doesn't intend to go over old jokes. He must have thought up a brand-new one.

"You didn't buy any fags on the way?" he asks.

I know I'm blushing under my make-up.

"No. I . . . I forgot."

"It doesn't matter, really. I've given it up, too."

I sit down.

"You mean, you know?"

"I knew before you did. Something was missing."

I know perfectly well what he's going to say, but I don't want to spoil his punch-line.

"And what was that, Mrs Heitmann?" I ask.

"PMT, of course. I haven't had pre-menstrual tension for at least two months. What do you think we should call her?"

He'll make a much better mother than I will.